Auberon Waug

The Foxglove Saga

Penguin Books

Penguin Books Ltd, Harmondsworth,
Middlesex, England
Penguin Books Pty Ltd, Ringwood,
Victoria, Australia

First published by Chapman & Hall 1960
Published in Penguin Books 1966
Copyright © Auberon Waugh, 1960

Made and printed in Great Britain by
C. Nicholls & Company Ltd
Set in Linotype Granjon

For Bobby, Grizelda and Toad

Part One

I

In the calefactory Brother Thomas's illness was discussed with a certain restraint since nobody seemed quite sure how far one could go in anticipating his death with good taste. Only Brother Theobald did not attempt to disguise his relish at the prospect of the ancient and complicated procedure which accompanies the death of a monk. As the oldest sane member of the Community (nobody counted old Brother Alfred) it would be his duty to lead the prayers for the dying round the bed, and the pleasure which the good old man derived from the practice was not only attributable to the satisfaction which any pious monk might feel at witnessing such a good Christian death.

'Mere slip of a boy, too' – the elaborate regret with which he shook his head was not intended to be taken seriously. Besides, Brother Thomas was nearly seventy. 'They're not making them like they used to, Brother. Can't stay the course, can they? I hope you've recovered from your little attack of billiomyelitis, or whatever it was you were telling me about. It made one quite uncomfortable seeing you looking so miserable, and running out of Compline every minute.'

Nobody ever paid any attention to the old man and Brother Timothy, to whom his remarks were addressed, pretended that he had not heard, although his curious plasticine ears were crimson, and some nervous reaction made his eyes water so that he had to blink. Brother Theobald's savagery was as unfathomable as it was indiscriminate, and the lonely delight he took in tormenting the more sensitive Brothers seemed to their minds a little callow. The years of religious contemplation had not broadened his outlook, nor made him more tolerant of what he regarded as his fellows' shortcomings. It was not as if they were lacking in a sense of humour. Brother Jeremy, especially, had a great sense of fun, and as a novice had once climbed out of the lavatory, leaving it locked behind him, and nobody found out for weeks. Luckily the Abbot had heard nothing about it, but then Brother Theobald had spoiled it by saying that he had known about it all along, but he supposed that old Brother Alfred had died there, and *he* wasn't going to get him out.

No, there was no doubt about it, thought Brother Timothy unhappily, that the old man had not developed intellectually since his school-days. Of course, he was a terrific character, he added, determined not to be uncharitable, but jejune, definitely jejune. It was surprising what words came into one's head; he must remember to try that one out on Brother Augustine when next they had a heart to heart talk. It would be wasted, he feared, on Brother Jeremy. It was to him that he now turned.

'Tell me,' he said, choosing his words carefully, 'I don't suppose there's much really the matter, but should anything happen to Brother Thomas . . .'

'Which Heaven forfend,' exclaimed Brother Theobald unnecessarily, crossing himself.

'. . . and I am sure we all pray that it won't,' Brother Timothy continued, blinking hard, 'although we must, of course, be realistic, and they say that Dr Norton has been consulted, which means that it must be a bit more than a little tummy upset.'

It was no good. One could not be humorous, or anything for that matter, if Jeremy would not listen, and there was that odious old man delighting in his discomfiture. Dr Norton had never been consulted when *he* was ill, he regretted dismally, although if they could have seen what he had seen, but then it hadn't been exactly the kind of thing one could show people, although they were meant to be medical, after all, and he might have shown them, but then he hadn't had the courage so there it was, and they all believed to this day that he was making a lot of fuss about nothing. Bright green, it had been; but it was too late now.

'What are you thinking of?' asked Brother Augustine suddenly. Before there was time for an answer he continued earnestly:

'It is a mistake, you know, and I am sure if you think about it you do know, unconsciously at least, to suppose that any awareness or understanding or, how shall I put it? Being is found in the mind in its own reflection. The oriental likes to find himself in perennial introspection. For him the contemplation, as it were, of his navel is sufficient. But it is at once the blessing and the agony of the Christian religion, as I think you agree, as indeed you must agree if you see what I'm getting at at all, that we must look outwards to find what you and I like to call the Thingness of Things. Can you see what I'm getting at or am I putting it badly? Shall I put it this way?' He drew a deep breath, which gave Brother Theobald time to utter one of his significant grunts. He considered it an old man's privilege to grunt occasionally, and he saved them up for moments such as these.

'Well actually,' interposed Brother Timothy, who felt that this was not the time for one of his chats with Brother Augustine although he enjoyed them so much and they really did help to clarify everything, 'I was wondering what would happen to Brother Thomas's things.'

'And why should anything happen to them, Brother?' asked the theologian with a touch of coldness.

'I wondered if anybody might want his typewriter, or the ormolu crucifix in his room, or the Dunlopillo mattress the Bursar let him have for his arthritis,' said Brother Timothy desperately.

'One can only suppose they will be divided with the usual

regard for seniority and need. I remember remarking some months ago to the Abbot that if one has important work to do a typewriter is essential nowadays and he seemed to be in agreement. But of course if he thought that your comparative analysis of Shelley and Hopkins were more important than the search for truth he might prefer your claim were it not that you were received into the monastery two months and four days after myself. As for the mattress, I am not yet crippled by arthritis, and will gladly surrender it to anyone who is.'

At that moment a bell was rung outside the calefactory, and without unseemly bustle the monks gathered together their books and left to take their various classes in Religious Instruction.

High above them Abbot Hill was playing a solitary game of chess when Dr Norton was announced. He sat in the pool of light around the marble chess-board, his long white fingers with the massive topaz ring of his abbacy stroking the White Queen, the heavy pectoral cross shining on his black habit, his watery blue eyes staring from a thin ageless face. Specially for the occasion he had donned a black velvet skull-cap. Dr Norton was not at his ease. He was the school specialist, though the field in which he specialized had never been clearly defined. In effect, whenever anybody was thought not to be responding to the school doctor's treatment, he was called in. Today he had a difficult job to perform, and the Abbot was determined not to make it any easier.

'Well, Father Abbot, the picture is quite clear now, and I'm afraid I must tell you that it is not too pretty. The carcinoma which I suspected was there has its primary growth in the lower lobe of the left lung, but there is a secondary outbreak which threatens the colon and lower intestine. I don't need to tell you, I suppose, what that means.'

'It means, perhaps, that he has not long to live?'

'Oh I don't think we can make a final prognosis just yet, but it means that unless something is done fairly soon things won't get much better.'

'What do you propose to do?'

'We must get him into a hospital and see what they make of him.'

'You think they will cure him?'

'Oh come, now,' said the doctor as bluffly as he could in the face of those humourless, scaly eyes, 'cure is a comparative term, you know. We can't work miracles I'm afraid, that's more your line than mine. But what we can do is to stop it getting any worse, for a time, at any rate; that is, supposing that it has not gone too far already.'

'I think I understand,' said the Abbot slowly. 'Doctor, does it seem to you entirely necessary, under those circumstances, that he should be taken away from here, where he has spent all his life preparing for death, and where he can die fortified by the last rites of the church, which would be of considerable solace to him?'

'I would not be doing my duty if I let him stay here,' said Dr Norton.

'Your duty to whom?' asked the Abbot.

'To my conscience,' said Dr Norton stiffly. He was a little uneasy, although determined not to show it. Had the old fool never heard of the B.M.A., of the N.H.S., of a P.M.?

'I do not know, doctor, what God you worship, or what moulded your conscience, but remember the saying "Thou shalt not kill; but need'st not strive officiously to keep alive." The doctor was getting more and more uneasy, but a wave of obstinacy kept him on. The determination not to be browbeaten strengthened his genuine horror of Abbot Hill's callousness. His training had taught him that if he were to lay any claim at all to professional integrity, the claim must be judged in terms of his regard for the sacrosanctity of human life.

'I am sorry, Abbot, I cannot allow him to stay here in his present condition.'

'I believe that I am his legal guardian; what would you say if I did not allow him to be moved?'

Now Dr Norton was on home ground, and something of his former confidence returned.

'You know, Abbot, that I could not be responsible for the consequences.' He cleared his throat ominously. 'There would have to be an inquest, and naturally I would be asked why I did not move him to a place where he could receive proper medical attention.'

'I see,' said the lonely black figure by the chess-board and stared at the White Queen. The doctor fidgeted in his tall oak chair with its spiky Gothic ornaments. He fingered the Angel Gabriel with his chubby wet hands, and delicately adjusted his position to remove his coccyx from the uncomfortable pressure of the patriarch Abraham's nose. If this is Christianity, he thought defiantly, you can keep it. He calls it Christian to let people die by the wayside, does he? Might never have heard of the Good Samaritan the way he acts. It was a High Priest who left the poor fellow naked and dying and walked by on the other side of the road. It just shows how history repeats itself, he added smugly. I don't suppose he's ever done anything for anybody in his life; just lived here thinking how holy he is. We Rotarians may not be terrifically hot on Religion, but at least we believe in giving people a helping hand as well as having a good time.

The Abbot reached out for the White Queen and seemed about to move it, then changed his mind and turned to the doctor.

'Very well, doctor. One must accept it as a sign of the times. The Brethren have died here as they have lived since the establishment of the Community. This is the first time the modern world has interrupted us, to drag one of our number away from us in time of illness.'

The inscrutable old eyes flickered for a moment. Nobody counted Brother Alfred, although it was true that he had spent a few weeks in a Rest Home for Elderly Clergymen after he declared that he had seen the Devil talking to the Bursar in the Gregory cloister after dark. Such truths are relative, thought the Abbot in justification; after all Brother Alfred had not been ill so much as mischievous.

After the doctor had gone he removed his skull-cap and resumed the game of chess.

In St Bartholomew's Library Brother Augustine looked round the circle of desks with a slight frown. He liked to think that his religious instruction classes represented the cream of the intellectual set of the college; yet somehow he was never quite sure that his ideas made quite the impression he would have liked. There was Kelly fidgeting with his desk, and Stoat would never stop picking his nose no matter how hard one stared at him. They seemed a trifle impatient of subtlety in any form, which was only to be expected at their age, but what was worse they seemed to be unwilling to recognize it, let alone respect it. Who was it who said *"Qui non intelligit aut discat aut taceat"*? he wondered. No good asking them, of course.

'It is all summed up,' he said, 'in the what one might call the catch-phrase of the Last Gospel.' That was daring. That should make them sit up. 'In the beginning was the Word, and the Word was with God, and the Word was God.' He paused and stared at the ceiling with an intent look on his face, allowing his tongue to creep out, pointed and glistening, until it almost touched the tip of his nose. To allow it to do so would have been a self-indulgence, and Brother Augustine for all his broad-mindedness was an ascetic.

'Can you see now what I am trying to get over to you?' he asked, when he thought that sufficient time had elapsed for his words to sink in. 'You see it is not so much the Existence as the Inherence, the essential Isness which transcends existence as we can comprehend it. Words! words! words!' he cried dramatically, beating his forehead. 'It is no good pretending that there are, or ever can be, words to describe what I am trying to put over to you, but if you can just get a glimpse of this terrific idea, I think I shall have achieved something this afternoon. Well, Kelly, do you think you have?'

Kelly looked up from his handiwork, which so far constituted the name SLIGGER TWO neatly carved eleven times on the surface of his desk. Once for every time he had had to sit through all this Isness piss, he reflected, as he tried to imagine what Augustine had been talking about.

'I think so, Sir,' he said slowly.

'What about you, Stoat?'

Stoat gave a little jump of fright and removed his finger, which produced a titter of laughter. Stoat looked frightened; one could be as idle or as stupid as one liked, so long as other people did not laugh, and Augustine's temper was very uncertain.

'Well, no, Sir,' he said argumentatively, going crimson. His only hope was to show an intelligent critical interest. 'I didn't quite follow you about this Isness business. It was quite unintentional, but it produced hoots of laughter as soon as it was out of his mouth. Augustine smiled sarcastically. Stoat held his breath. If Augustine could think of a good enough snub before the laughter died down he would be safe, but if he could not it would mean the long walk to the study of the Prefect of Discipline, and the ignominious return through rows of eyes anxious to see the smallest trace of a tear.

Augustine continued to smile sarcastically, his mighty intellect searching for something that would put the revolting little boy in his place, and demonstrate to all the victory of brains over brawn. The smile sickened and died. It was no good, nothing would come.

'Pea brain,' he said, but he felt it lacked dignity. 'Take your impertinence out of here and explain yourself to Brother Jeremy.'

'Who? Me, Sir?' asked Stoat, playing for time. Augustine ignored it. 'Get out and don't show your silly weasel face in here!' he shouted, getting angrier and less controlled. 'Fool, oh my Heavens, you fool! When I try to explain something important, something that really matters this is all that I get. What's the use in Heaven's name?' His voice soared higher and higher in the unnatural stillness of the classroom. Everybody stared at his desk. Kelly hid his penknife under his ruler. 'I exhaust my brain power night and day trying to let a ray of light into your cretinous lives and here's your answer. Get out.'

So loud had his voice become that Brother Aloysius in the next classroom had to titter into his hand to stop himself laughing outright. His class were all his friends, especially Martin Foxglove who so resembled his mother, surely the kindest and most beautiful woman in the world. Lady Foxglove had led him aside three years ago and said that she knew he would look after her boy, and stop him from coming to any harm, *serious* harm she meant, and so Brother Aloysius had kept a parental eye on the little fellow for her, until now, he flattered himself, they were the *greatest* of friends. Out of the corner of his eye he saw Stoat crawl past the classroom door. He would never be able to understand Martin's liking for the boy. Of course, they were the same age so there was nothing he could really object to. It wasn't just that he was so horrible to look at, but he was so dirty, and one would have thought that with his father a dentist he should have been taught at least the rudiments of hygiene; and there were so many nice people like young Frank Pratt-Bingham who always took such an intelligent interest in his religion. Perhaps he should talk to him about it one day. On the other hand he didn't want Martin to think he was prying into his affairs; and he could be so wilful when he wanted.

Stoat tried to hold his head high as he marched down the long corridor to the dark little room which the Prefect of Discipline ruled. He was acutely conscious of hundreds of eyes following him down, and he felt the blood rushing to his cheeks, and his hands got in the way, and suddenly he wondered if he was wiggling his behind, and in his efforts not to he marched in a grotesque zigzag over the slippery parquet flooring.

'Good old Stoat,' whispered Sligger Two to his best friend Frazer-Robinson. 'I wonder what he's done this time?' If Brother Timothy saw him, he did not say anything. Sligger Two could get away with a good deal.

To his enormous relief, Stoat found a notice on the Prefect's door to say that Brother Jeremy had gone to take Brother Thomas's R.I. class for him. It was only a respite, of course, but now the final settlement seemed infinitely remote. He hoped that there was nothing seriously wrong with Brother Thomas, who was the only monk for whom he felt any affection at all. He was the school confessor, and although a bit old-fashioned at times, was kindly enough taken by and large. Besides he had been a junior teacher when Stoat's father was at the school and showed an interest in him which nobody else ever had. No fond hand had ever carved the name of Kenneth Stoat on a desk-top, nor had any monk taken him under his wing. The small share of the world's esteem which was his he had earned. By clowning, breaking laws, being discovered and beaten he had worked hard for the occasional murmur of 'Good old Stoat'.

He walked slowly along the Old Scriptorium where he knew he would find Brother Jeremy in charge.

'Come in. Oh, it's Stoat, I should have known it. What is it, Stoat?'

'Brother Augustine sent me to you, Sir.'

'Oh he did, did he? And why, may I ask? He can't have thought I'd enjoy your company much.'

'He said it was for gross impertinence, Sir.' The class squirmed with pleasure.

'And what did you say to him, may I ask?'

'I wouldn't like to say, Sir.'

'Come now, you had better tell us, or we shall all think it was much worse, won't we?'

He winked familiarly at the class. Two pasty little boys in the front row laughed obediently, until something they saw in Stoat's eyes made them reach for their handkerchiefs and pretend to be coughing.

'I've forgotten, Sir.'

It was too much to expect him to go into the long explanation of that Isness business, and it would probably only make it worse by raising a laugh from those drips in the front row. He knew for a fact that Fitzgerald Two used to wet his bed at his prep. school, and he rather fancied that the other's Christian name was Gabriel, and so one more squeak out of them . . .

'Very well then, Stoat, I shall have to ask Brother Augustine after the lesson. In the meantime sit down. No, not right at the back, down here where I can keep my eyes on you. I think next to Fitzgerald Two will do nicely. Now,' he said, addressing the class at large, 'what was Brother Thomas teaching you about last week?'

Absolute silence. People looked awkwardly at the ceiling, at their shoes, at the clock.

'Something about sex, I expect,' said Brother Jeremy indulgently. Fitzgerald Two went very red in the face, but his hand shot up eagerly. Stoat wrote carefully in Biro on his wrist *filthy-minded pig*. It was a habit of his.

'Please, Sir,' shouted Fitzgerald Two, 'I think it was something about school-life being a preparation for death or something.' A vague murmur of assent was heard from the rest.

'Well, I'm glad someone was paying attention,' said Brother Jeremy, a little nettled at having been caught out so easily, especially with Stoat in the room. What was the boy up to now?

'Why, Stoat, are you holding your nose?'

'It was itching, Sir.'

'If that is the case, let it itch. But if you are intending to convey to others that you find your next-door neighbour's smell disagreeable remember that those who live in glass houses should not throw stones.'

The gusts of laughter which followed compensated for his earlier mistake. Kenneth clenched his fists under the desk and swore, as he had sworn so often before, to revenge himself one day somehow. It was so unfair that the man should be allowed to get away with anything he chose to say. Brother Jeremy was an old enemy of his since their first meeting, when, like a cat and a dog, they had each recognized in the other an antipathy which was so fundamental as not to need any rationalization. Brother Jeremy, in addition to his other duties, was the rugger coach, and every afternoon he trotted up to the playing fields wearing a colourless muddy shirt which had not been washed for thirty years. He cultivated the odours on that shirt just as a scientist cultivates growths on a broth. They were at once the proof of his virility and his humility. The world might know, as he went past, that there was nothing effeminate about him, that he was a plain down-to-earth fellow with no pretensions. He shunned any contact with the boys except on a jocular, ragging level, and was always slightly embarrassed when cornered alone. He could not look into anybody's face, for fear the person think he should be seeking to make friends with him. So conscious was he of his own potency that whenever he accidentally touched someone, he would withdraw his hand as if it had been burned. In short, thought the nasty little Stoat, he is as queer as a grass-snake. (He and Foxglove had kept a pet grass-snake called Grill on which they had lavished all the love of which an adolescent soul is capable; but then they had one of their quarrels and, being unable to settle ownership, had cut it in two. For a delirious twenty minutes there had been two grass-snakes, but when they had tried in a moment of over-excitement to make more, the experiment had failed, and the pieces were still scattered around in the junior changing-room. But their quarrel was forgotten in the thrill of it.)

'Well,' said Brother Jeremy, becoming serious again, and pulling out an enormous brown pipe, 'of course there are two sides to any given question.' He began sucking and blowing into the pipe, which, being empty, magnified the noises like an Alpine horn.

'Brother Thomas has been telling you that this school is a preparation for death. And so, in a sense it is.' He frowned thoughtfully. He wasn't an intellectual type but when it came to something important, he could give as much concentration to it as the next man. 'But I prefer to regard it as a preparation for life. You chaps must go out of here prepared to do something for your faith. Show people that you're not ashamed of it. You've got nothing to be ashamed of. I suppose ninety per cent of the people who leave here go to church once a week or so, and the rest of the week they just sit on their bottoms and do nothing. You don't want to be one of those. Of course Brother Thomas was right, in his way; but you don't want to just worry about yourself all the time; think of the rest of the world first, and you'll find you're all right yourself. That's how I like to look at it.' He stared belligerently round the room, as if expecting someone to rise, and slam his desk and shout 'You liar!' He was ready for it. But the class had relapsed into the comatose state which always accompanied religious instruction just before the tea-bell. Stoat was holding his nose again, and staring significantly at Fitzgerald Two. He would have to give the boy a good thrashing after the class. It wasn't that he enjoyed it, of course; personally it just bored him. But there was no doubt that some people needed it more than others.

The tea-bell rang. Instantly the class came to life. Desks slammed, rulers were dropped, somebody began to whistle piercingly. 'You may go now,' said Brother Jeremy magnanimously. Fitzgerald Two dropped all his books with a little moan and clutched his leg staring reproachfully at Stoat, who slouched off to meet his doom with a slightly lighter heart.

2

Lady Foxglove was coming down to make arrangements for Brother Thomas's move. 'He was such a great friend of Derek's,' she explained to everybody, although the truth was she had never quite shared her husband's blind devotion to his former house-master. Sir Derek was an unemotional man, but when his loyalty was once given it was unshakeable and nothing his wife could say or do would make him regard the old monk as anything but the epitome of goodness, the rock on which all his own notions of behaviour, taste and ethics were built. It was too silly, really, that he should not have out-grown his childish trust, because anybody could see that the old man was far from perfect. He was testy, and on occasions downright rude, and seemed impatient with some of the finer points of conscience, when she discussed them with him in the confessional.

The rest of the world could not understand why they were not greater friends. They were both so good, so saintly, each in his own way. Perhaps there were spiteful voices muttering far beneath anyone's level of consciousness. Perhaps enemies put it into words, for even Lady Foxglove had a few enemies, people whose feeble pretensions to goodness she surpassed with that effortless ease which characterized everything she did. If these people had said that she was jealous of her husband's affection, they would surely have been treated with the contempt they deserved. Julia Foxglove, at the age of forty-five, still possessed the extraordinary, sublime beauty of a quattrocento madonna. Her smile, so kind, so understanding, seemed to emanate from a soul in repose. Her obvious chastity added lustre to her grace. Her only child, Martin, had had to be delivered by Caesarean section, and it was feared that another might endanger her life. Sir Derek had accepted the situation humbly. He was a good, simple man, and if he seemed at times to be a trifle brusque with his wife, it must be remembered that beside her St Simon Stylites would have appeared impatient, St Aloysius lecherous, St Francis Xavier brutal.

How sweet of her to think of coming down herself to look after the old man! In the evening, she was to take Martin out to dinner, and Martin has asked Stoat out, too. They presented themselves, scrubbed and shining, to Brother Jeremy before being allowed down to wait by the main gate.

'Amazing what a little soap and water will do, isn't it, Stoat?' he asked nastily. 'I see your new resolution doesn't extend to your teeth. Go and scrub them now; we don't want Lady Foxglove to think we're all gutter-snipes here. I would have thought you'd have been brought up to look after them at least.'

When Stoat rejoined his friend at the main gate they were both a little uneasy. Foxglove was wondering how Stoat would appear to his mother, and above all whether he would quite do. Their curious friendship had started during their first term at Cleeve. Stoat, ugly, unloved and as prickly as a hedgehog, had been adopted by Foxglove as a buffer between himself and the rest of the world. The young Foxglove was the cynosure of all eyes, and the conqueror of many hearts, but anyone wanting to know him had to run the gauntlet of Stoat's nasty sharp little mind. And so, although everyone agreed that Foxglove was a first-rate fellow, nobody could really claim him as a friend. In the course of time they had grown indispensable to each other. Far too many confidences had been exchanged, and a kind of mutual blackmail held them together as much as mutual understanding.

Stoat was wondering what on earth he should call Lady Foxglove. His father, although a bore, and a man in whose company he had never been comfortable, was one of the best dentists in Nottingham, although these snobbish fools didn't know it. Nevertheless, while his practice took him among the privileged and great of Nottingham, his social life did not, for some reason, include anybody with a title, or 'handle' as he liked to put it. 'Your Ladyship' sounded a bit pompous, and 'My Lady' a bit familiar.

'What time did her Ladyship say she'd be arriving, Foxy?' he asked to try it out.

'For Heaven's sake, don't call her that,' answered the other, alarmed.

'What should I call her then?'

'Oh, don't call her anything. And you'd better call me Martin, I suppose,' he added, a shade too carelessly. 'Though goodness knows what I'm going to call you. Kenneth would not go down at all, I'm afraid.'

'My father calls me Ken,' said Kenneth miserably. Martin was a kind boy at heart, and he did not pounce on this as he might have. Instead he stored it up for their next quarrel.

'I think I'd better say you're called Henry,' he said. This did not appear at all incongruous to either of them at the time, and so it was arranged.

Lady Foxglove arrived in an aura of ethereal scent. To Stoat, thinking about it later, it seemed that this must indeed be the odour of sanctity, in which so many people one knew about died.

'Martin, darling, how lovely. I know I mustn't kiss you in front of your friend.' She turned to Stoat with a smile of such dazzling purity that he immediately began to feel clumsy again.

'This is Henry,' said Martin.

'Henry, of course,' she said. 'I have heard so much about you from Martin, but we never seem to have had the opportunity of meeting before. Well this is nice. Now, Martin, come in and sit beside me and tell me what you've been up to.'

Really, she thought, what an extraordinary friend for Martin to choose. I must talk to Brother Aloysius about him; I should think he could find somebody more suitable.

Later on in the meal she said:

'Tell me, are you always called Henry, or do your friends sometimes call you Harry, or anything?'

'His father sometimes calls him Hen,' said Martin, a little under the influence of the cider, and throwing a malicious glance at his friend. Kenneth felt himself blushing, and there was nothing he could do about it. Lady Foxglove saved the situation with one of her laughs.

'Now that was very unkind of you, Martin, to let the cat out of the bag like that.'

Later still, when Kenneth stumbled to his feet, and knocked over his glass as he went out to the lavatory, Martin asked:

'Well, do you like him?'

And his mother replied: 'Yes, dear, I think he's very nice.'

Had he been more sober, he would have noticed the restraint of his mother's comment. As it was he was satisfied, and felt a great relief.

After the taxi had deposited them, Lady Foxglove went off to read to Brother Thomas. She had several good works to do before she could settle down to a cosy chat with Brother Aloysius about Martin.

On the way up to the dormitory in the dark, Kenneth felt a warm glow all over him. He had been very quiet all evening, but now he reached for his friend's elbow in the dark, and whispered earnestly:

'Martin, I think your mother is the most perfect woman I've ever met.'

Next morning was Sunday and throughout morning church Stoat wondered whether he had made a fool of himself the night before. So great was his preoccupation that he lost eight cigarettes running to O'Connor who knelt beside him and who owned the poker dice which helped to while away the long hours of worship. Eventually one of the dice rolled away and bounced irretrievably down the aisle. There seemed nothing left to do but pray, and as he lifted his little black heart and mind in the direction he had been taught he prayed that he might be made nicer. It was his only prayer, and it had never yet been answered. He was sharp enough to see how mean, how intolerant, how incredibly nasty he was, but somehow lacked the technical ability to do anything about it. The only thoughts that ever came into his mind were uncharitable, spiteful ones, often quite shrewd in their way, but he knew that they only showed one side of the picture. There was probably some good in Brother Aloysius, even in Brother Augustine he reflected dismally. This was his lowest hour, just before breakfast, and the slight hangover from the dinner on the evening before made him begin to speculate as to whether there might even be some good in Brother Jeremy, but he dismissed the thought. Make me, he prayed, be more like Lady Foxglove.

In the school sanatorium, where he had been moved from his cell in the monastery so that Lady Foxglove could visit him, Brother Thomas heard the rise and fall of voices as the

26

school sang the final hymn before breakfast, and tried to shut his mind to the voice which went on and on from the chair in the corner.

'Oh, all right,' said the good-natured Rat, 'rest away. It's pretty nearly pitch dark now, anyhow, and there ought to be a bit of moon later.'

So the Mole got well into the dry leaves and stretched himself out, and presently dropped off into sleep, though of a broken and troubled sort, while the Rat, covering himself up too, as best he might, for warmth, lay patiently waiting, with a pistol in his paw.

When at last the Mole woke up, much refreshed, and in his usual spirits, the Rat said, 'Now then I'll take a look outside, and see if everything's quiet, and then we really must be off.'

On the wall outside his window the magnolia was beginning to open, but its scent was drowned by Lady Foxglove's expensive odour of sanctity. 'I wish Julia would not come to torment me, but I suppose I must put up with it for Derek's sake. I wonder,' he mused 'what Heaven can really be like? When all is said and done, I think it must be very much like Cleeve.'

Lady Foxglove looked up from the book and smiled bravely. There were black circles round her eyes and she looked desperately tired and fragile. Brother Thomas was asleep, and she tiptoed carefully to the door, but the noise she made closing it woke him up again. Really, she thought, he does not look very attractive lying asleep with his mouth open, but still one must do one's best. She took out her little notebook in which she wrote her day's good works. On each page was printed a little list: Bury the Dead, Visit the Imprisoned, Clothe the Naked – goodness she must remember about Martin's new uniform – give Food to the Hungry – well, that's myself, she thought humorously. She put two little ticks, once each against Visit the Sick and Comfort the Afflicted. The book was her little secret from the world, and nobody must know about it until after her death, or she might become spiritually proud which would spoil it all. But first of all she must have a frank talk with Brother Aloysius about this young Stoat and see if he could do anything about it. It wasn't that she was snobbish, but he didn't even seem a very nice boy and she was sure Brother Aloysius would understand, he was so kind; he always sent her a copy of his new books with such sweet inscriptions on the fly-leaf. The last one, she remembered, had been about St Paul's pet Pekinese called Chooty which had started life as a tiny puppy and had then grown into a big dog, wise in the ways of the world. A little bit sentimental, she supposed, but the illustrations really were good, and the story made quite a few good points underneath all the banter.

There was always a slight air of disaffection about the school on Sunday mornings. Boys lounged around the day-room wireless with their hands deep in their pockets, or played ping-pong with a ferocious look of concentration, or slipped away to secret places for a hasty, shared cigarette.

'Well, are you coming for a bine?' called Stoat. He had not dared call his friend Martin again, but Foxy seemed somehow outgrown.

'I can't, said Martin. 'I've got to wait for my mother. She's gone into a huddle with the Pimp.'

Kenneth felt left out again; Foxglove seemed to be coming out less and less these days; although it couldn't be that he was scared; besides it was safe as houses behind the swimming pool during the morning, since nobody ever went there. He believed that Foxglove felt almost shy to be alone with him after their confidences of the evening before.

'Kelly and O'Connor will be there,' he said, 'and Pyke said he might come out later.'

'I can't risk it. The Pimp's got such a crush on her that

you never know how long it will be before she can get away.'

'He certainly has one on you,' said Stoat nastily.

'Oh, shut up.'

'Well, you know he has.'

'It isn't my fault if he has, is it? You're just so unpleasant you like to see something nasty in everything. He just happens to like me and not you, and I can't do anything about it. I think you would rather like it if someone did take a fancy to you, only it's so bloody unlikely it'd be impossible.'

Kenneth felt the sudden fury coming over him which he had experienced with Brother Jeremy the day before. The feeling of his own impotence brought him nearer to tears than any pain ever could. It wasn't what Martin said that hurt him, because the idea was too pathetic for words, but the depth of malice he showed, and the sudden knowledge of the extent to which he was prepared to go in order to wound him as much as possible. And if he showed any of the resentment he felt, he knew that Foxglove would think that he had hit the target pretty hard, that he had found an Achilles heel in Stoat's elaborate armour. There were some things he was not prepared to admit even to himself.

'Oh, bugger off,' he said; 'just because you're such a filthy tart you think everyone else is. You mustn't judge the whole world by your own standards.'

He thrust his hands deep into his pockets and strode off, to hide his red face and the tears which came prickling to his eyes. My God, I can do with a bine, he thought, as he walked to join O'Connor and Kelly behind the swimming bath.

'I quite understand,' Brother Aloysius was saying comfortably. 'I had wondered if they were a really suitable pair, but there never seemed anything I could really do about it,

29

if you see what I mean, but now I have talked to you I will see what can be done.'

Julia Foxglove looked up from the little cup of coffee she was balancing on her knee, and gazed yearningly at the shiny pink face of the monk, who was busying himself, in order to tide over an emotional moment, with the sugar-tongs.

'Oh, will you really, then?' she asked, much moved. 'It is so kind of you. I don't know how I would feel if you were not here to look after Martin, but now I know I can feel safe about it all.'

After she had left the room something seemed to have gone with her. Perhaps it was just the delicate fragrance of a lady of taste, but to the infatuated Brother Aloysius it seemed as if the guest-room had lost its soul.

3

In the Annie Zunz (Chest) Ward of the Royal Bermondsey Hospital the new house-surgeon gathered together a sheaf of admittance forms, and wandered over to the desk of the orderly staff nurse who was writing out the day reports before taking them to Sister.

'Know anything about this new intake, Herring?' he asked casually, but with a touch of sternness. It had been all right in the old days, when he was plain Ron Dooney, the medical student who was always game for a rag, but now he was Mr Dooney, the houseman of St Matthew, St Mark, St Luke and Annie Zunz, he had to be careful not to be too familiar with the nurses, or nothing would ever get done.

Nurse Herring put down her pen and looked at him. Automatically her fingers started adjusting her frilly lace cap which signified to the trained eye three years' seniority with a diploma in midwifery and mental diseases (physical).

Goodness, she thought, I've come across some raw eggs in my time, but this little earthworm just about takes the biscuit.

'No, Ron,' she said, and felt very nearly like adding Sir just to put him in his place. 'I think he's a patient of F.G.'s though.'

'Well, we'd better keep on the ball then, if we're not going to catch a rocket,' said the Olympian Dooney, unbending a little and stroking his hairless chin. He cleared his throat with a curious bleating noise, adjusted his stethoscope round his neck, and strode importantly to the end cubicle where the new patient had been put.

'Hullo, good evening,' he said breezily to the old man in the bed, rubbing his hands together in a way which was at once friendly and showed that he was a busy man with quite a lot to do, 'I'm Ron Dooney, Mr Dooney the house-surgeon, and you might as well get to know me as I'll be looking after you from now on.'

'Oh, really,' said the old man, puzzled. 'I thought I was to be under the care of Sir Derek Foxglove.'

Dooney frowned. So he was going to be one of those barrack-room lawyers, was he?

'Old F.G. will probably visit you once a day before your operation, if he has time,' he said a little sharply. 'He is, of course, the consultant surgeon on the case, but for all practical purposes I'll be in charge here, and if there's anything the matter, better not trouble the big white chief about it, see, but just give me a line and I'll see what we can do.' He cleared his throat again, and then made another of his swoops into friendliness which only really tactful young men could manage while still preserving the element of respect which was so essential in patient-doctor relations. 'Now we've got a lot of bumf to get through and frankly, as far as I'm concerned, the sooner the better, as I want to be off and get my tea.'

'Toy?' asked the patient, slightly alarmed.

'Tea,' said Mr Dooney, as if speaking to a child. 'You know, what you drink.'

'Oh, *tea*,' said the patient. Why couldn't the young man speak more clearly?

'Now first of all we'll want your name, if you don't mind.'

'I'm Brother Thomas, of Cleeve.'

'Thomas what?' said Mr Rooney, patiently.

'Aquinas,' said Brother Thomas. Abbot Broom had not specified which Thomas when he chose the novice's name in the Order, and Abbot Hill had said he was quite at liberty to choose whichever he liked.

'You're not a foreigner, are you?' asked Mr Rooney suspiciously. They made more trouble, these foreigners, than all the rest put together. There had been a terrible Italian woman in St Luke's a week ago who had kept the whole ward up, yelling that she was dying and going to go to hell and wanted to see a priest, and nothing the night nurse could say would quieten her, so in the end they had had to give her an injection just to shut her up. She had died in the night, too, of a delayed post-operative embolism. There was no doubt about it, the foreigners were more trouble than they were worth.

'Oh no,' said Brother Thomas, 'at least my mother was half-Irish, you know, but she lived in England all her life.'

'How do you spell it then?' he demanded, only partially convinced. It didn't sound very British to him, but you never knew.

After Dooney had left to get his cup of tea, Brother Thomas heard a cackle from the next bed, and a large toothless face appeared round the curtain.

'That was good! Thomas A-bloody-Quinas, and he swallowed it. Some people are just so ignorant you just wouldn't believe it. Old Bill over there in the corner said he was called Jack Ketch, but he wouldn't buy that one, not even 'im wouldn't. I don't know how you did it, mister. Look 'ere, you call me Fred, see, and I'll just call you Tommy. What are you in for, then?'

By the time Sir Derek came on his rounds, Tommy had made several fast friends among the patients in the ward, and listened sympathetically to a series of complicated and morbid case-histories.

Sir Derek Foxglove was more than the most eminent chest-surgeon of his day, he was a great one, and his name would undoubtedly be considered in years to come as of equal stature to Lord Lister, Pasteur, even to Mr Dickson Wright. The Foxglove Aspirator for Abdomino-Thoracic Drainage would probably remain the only treatment for cases where a chronic empyema was complicated by paradoxical breathing, and there were many people alive to that day who owed their existence to a Foxglove-Hennessy Tube gently bubbling its way through a damaged bronchial tree.

Lady Foxglove was usually a little reticent about her husband's professional life, but when she heard of the nature of Brother Thomas's illness she had insisted that he be put under his care although Sir Derek had protested with all the scientist's dislike of being emotionally involved in his cases. He was also a little bit embarrassed, as he marched down the ward accompanied by the registrar, Mr Hunt, the junior registrar called Larry, Ron the houseman and Nurse Herring. It was a bit awkward, he felt, to confront in this way the man who had beaten him into a jelly for smoking in the main lavatories, into whose ear he had, at an early age, poured his religious doubts, his sexual problems, his romantic affection for – what was his name? – Tackaberry? Huckleberry? He had quite forgotten. The man who had officiated at his wedding to the beautiful Julia Stearne, and who had christened his only son.

'A Mr T. Aquinas, sir,' said the thin voice of Mr Dooney importantly from the back of the queue, 'For left lower

33

lobectomy query colectomy query colostomy admitted seventeen hundred hours today care of Sir D. Foxglove.'

'Hullo, Derek,' said old Brother Thomas, a little bit pleased at all the fuss that was being made. There was a certain air of competitiveness in the ward which had already communicated itself to him. For all these people to be coming to him must mean that he was quite a lot iller than old Bill in the corner, even though everybody agreed it was a miracle Bill was still alive; and as for Fred they had just cut him down from two injections and four tablets a day, so there couldn't be much wrong with him.

'Hullo, Sir,' said Sir Derek, a habit he had never been able to get out of. 'I've just come to see that you're comfortably settled. Is there anything I can do for you? You will let me know, won't you? Have Julia's flowers arrived?'

'No,' said Brother Thomas with a certain satisfaction, 'they have not.'

'There are some flowers just arrived, F.G., for someone called Brother Thomas Plunkett,' said Sister, smiling benignly at the doctor.

'That's right, Sister,' said Sir Derek.

'Here we are,' said Sister, producing from nowhere an enormous bunch of pink carnations. The label, which smelt slightly of the sender, read:

> With all my Prayers
> from
>
> JULIA (FOXGLOVE)

Sister handed them to Mr Hunt who sniffed them and handed them to Larry, who removed one for his button-hole and handed the rest to Mr Dooney, who gave them to Nurse Herring who went away to put them in water, where they remained in the room called The Sluice beside the morning specimens until the night sister noticed them a week later and threw them away.

By the time Sir Derek had gone it was time for cocoa and before cocoa was over it was time for visitors. Brother Thomas was haunted by the fear that Lady Foxglove would arrive, but in fact she never came during the period of the day which was reserved for visitors, preferring to drop in at any odd hour between more pressing Good Works, always a little wan and exhausted but always lovely. After her first visit Fred had said: 'Blimey, look what old Tommy's got over there. He's a fly one if you like; who's the Jane, Tommy?'

But after a time even his exuberant spirit was a trifle quelled by her overpowering sanctity, although he still waved enthusiastically to her whenever she arrived, and was often rewarded by a sweet, sad smile.

After visitors little Nurse Pickles brought round the medicine tray with aperients for anyone who asked for them.

'No, Mr Coggins, we haven't any of the chocolate stuff left, I'm afraid, and I'm not sure you need it any more, either, you wicked old man. If you like I'll make you a little senna tea, or you can have some Casco-Lax which is meant to be quite nice. Yes, we'll have some chocolate for you tomorrow if you behave yourself in the meantime.'

To Brother Thomas, Nurse Pickles became identified as The Lavatory Lady, which was really not very fair as she was a pretty little thing and all the old men loved her. She was walking out with Dick Fellowes, the houseman of King George V (Orthopaedic) and Queen Alexandra (Women), but her parents said she'd have to wait until she'd got her S.R.N. but what they really meant was that she'd have to wait until Dick got his F.R.C.S. which might be a long time because Dick was the most popular of the house surgeons and had many calls on his time. But she never let her private worries interfere with her work, and her cheerful smile and anxiety to please made her the favourite of them all; she was always called Nursie as a mark of their adoration, while

Nurse Herring was just Nurse, or, behind her back, That Perishing Kipper.

Brother Thomas was soon accepted by the rest of the ward, and his kindliness and gentle humour endeared him to the nurses who were used to the nervous Cockney wit which quite ordinary people seem to affect when in hospital.

It was arranged that a preliminary operation should be performed on the Monday after his admittance to hospital, in order to ascertain the extent and exact nature of the malignancy, and so on Sunday evening the preparations were made. It was not normal for the older patients to be given too powerful a sedative before the operation, but Mr Dooney, with his knowledge of the way foreigners are liable to behave, generously wrote him up for a little morphia, adding his signature with a little flourish which he was just beginning to perfect.

He sat down in front of the typewriter, and stroked his chin before beginning to type with one finger:

Patient for Bronchoscopy 1030 hrs Monday 25th,

AQUINAS T.

Surgeon Sir D. Foxglove. Dr Plum, Anaesthetist.
Suspected Ca. lung.
Premed. 0945 hrs Monday 25th, Omnopon grs. 2/3

Scopolamine grs. 1/150.

Post-Op Pethidine xl only S.O.E.

Signed

On second thoughts he crossed out Omnopon and Scopolamine and substituted Om., and Scop. It looked more business-like, and in his job you had no time to waste being long-winded. That ought to keep him quiet, he thought, before going off for his cup of tea with Nurse Herring.

At eight o'clock they brought him a white gown and some heavy white stockings, and at half past eight little Nurse

36

Pickles came into his cubicle, wheeling a trolley which contained a great deal of apparatus to do with jugs and tubes. She drew the curtain after her.

'I'm afraid I've got to give you an enema, Mr Aquinas,' she said nervously. 'Do you know what that is?'

Brother Thomas knew all right; he had been hearing varied accounts from Cogginsy and Fred all the previous day, and had summoned all his bravery for this moment. Nurse Pickles hated to see the old man looking so distressed but she had to get it over with as kindly and quickly as she could.

A great silence fell upon the ward. When all is said and done there is nothing funny about an enema, and they had all suffered the indignity and wretchedness of it in their time, and poor old Tommy wasn't really made for that sort of thing.

'Now you must try and relax,' said Nurse Pickles sympathetically. At that moment the euphonious voice of Lady Foxglove was heard at the other end of the ward:

'But I'm afraid I really *must* see him; I could never forgive myself if anything happened to him under the anaesthetic and I had not been to see him. You don't realize how much this means to me, Nurse, or I wouldn't dream of interrupting your work now. I'll just go over to him and say a few words and come away immediately, you see, and I'll be no trouble at all to anybody, so you can't refuse, it would be too unkind, and I know you nurses are all terribly kind really.'

By then she was outside the cubicle. Nurse Pickles covered him up and vanished like a shot rabbit through the curtain. Lady Foxglove smiled triumphantly at Nurse Herring who was trying to bar the way, and walked through the curtain.

'Poor Brother Thomas, you must be going through purgatory,' she said, rather more loudly than was necessary. 'They really are too difficult and unpleasant here, and I don't believe they try to make things any easier for you. Never mind, I shall see that you are moved to somewhere more comfortable as soon as we can possibly get you there. I really don't know where I have met more disagreeable people.'

'I don't want to move,' said Brother Thomas, 'and I think they're all very kind.'

Really, thought Lady Foxglove, it is no good trying that holier-than-thou stuff on me, my man. But she said:

'That's just your goodness. But never mind, I know some charming nuns who will look after you much better, and who will at least understand about you. Now I mustn't stay a minute longer or Nurse will never forgive me; but remember you have all my prayers from now,' and with a delicate flutter of her slender white fingers she was gone.

When Nurse Herring came in with his injection she said: 'I wish you'd tell your girl-friend to keep her nose out of other people's business.'

But Brother Thomas was too nervous to reply as he watched her adjust the syringe so that a tiny bead of liquid appeared on the end of the needle.

'Now then, which part of you shall we take?' she said jocularly, but she chose his arm.

At first, as the morphia began to take effect, he felt a slight nausea and dryness of the mouth, but soon his bed was soaring and dipping, and the world was a dark shadowy place of no substance, and all that really mattered was a kind of dull content which lived in the pit of his stomach. A fly crawled over his face, but he did not bother to brush it off and Death seemed as unimportant as the fly, and his only uneasiness was in case someone should come and disturb him so that he would have to make the effort to talk and be polite. This, he thought, is Limbo.

When they came to collect him for the theatre he was practically asleep, although he heard and understood all that was happening.

'He's well away,' said the First Theatre Attendant, who was round and Irish and jolly.

'We've got ten minutes,' said the Second, who was tall and Irish and miserable, 'shall us have a quick woody?'

'Youse can,' said the first. 'I've got my job to think of.'

'These are the angels,' thought Brother Thomas stupidly, as the lift carried them up to the top floor, 'and they've come to take me up to Heaven. Should I tip them now or would they go away if I did? I do so desperately need them, because I'm sure I wouldn't manage to get there alone in this trolley.'

When he woke up he had a sore throat and felt dreadfully unhappy, and for the first time in nearly sixty years he cried and cried, and Nurse Pickles tried to comfort him, holding his hand like a little child and saying:

'There, there, it's all right now. You're back in bed and it's all over.' But she couldn't give him anything to drink just yet, and then he felt a little prick in his leg and he went to sleep again.

'Really it wasn't much worse than having his tonsils out, and you should have seen the way he carried on,' said Nurse Herring later that evening to Mr Dooney in the staff nurse's office. 'Goodness knows how he'll behave when they start work on him properly.'

Mr Dooney agreed and said all foreigners were like that, and yes perhaps he did just have time for another cup of tea, if it was all the same to Nurse Herring.

Lady Foxglove had rung up Mother Alice, and it was perfectly all right, they had a room for the old man, not that they could ever have refused Lady Foxglove anything, and he could be moved round as soon as he had recovered from the effects of the anaesthetic. She rang up Sir Derek, who said he supposed it was all right, if the old man really was as unhappy as she said, but it seemed a pity when the Royal

Bermondsey was so well equipped for chest cases. Lady Foxglove felt that really she had done her best.

'Good-bye, Tommy, best of luck,' shouted Bill and Mr Coggins and Fred as he was wheeled out of Annie Zunz, 'Come back soon.'

'And give my love to the girl-friend,' yelled Fred as he disappeared.

'Good-bye, Mr Aquinas,' said Nurse Pickles demurely with a shy little smile as he was lifted into the ambulance, and she stood and waved as he was driven away until he was out of sight, and then she turned back to prepare the evening tray of aperients.

4

Mother Alice's home, as it was popularly known, was situated in a quiet mews off the Paddington Canal; Lady Foxglove was well known and loved at Mother Alice's, as she had sent her old nanny there to spend her last days, when it became necessary to convert the old nursery into a compact and highly remunerative little flat. Nanny Bill was notoriously grumpy and ungrateful, but Lady Foxglove had not hesitated to recommend the home to all her friends, and had quite rightly, she considered, stopped visiting Nanny when her ingratitude and complaints became so loud as to be embarrassing. Every Christmas she had sent Martin round with a jar of the gooseberry jam from Bidcombe, and a pound note, and a little card on which she sent all their love. Martin usually kept the pound note. The nuns all thought how charming it was of the beautiful young Lady Foxglove to remember such a horrid old woman, and every year they made Nanny write in her uncertain spidery hand a suitable letter of thanks, saying how grateful she was to her Ladyship (although she had always called her Julia at Bidcombe; but those days were over now and the old cat's teeth were drawn) and how clever it was of her to remember her partiality for the gooseberry jam, and she hoped that they had all had a merry Xmas. When the old woman died she had brought Martin down from Cleeve for the funeral, because he had always been so devoted to her and the only other person there had been Mother Alice herself, but they had had a memorial service at Bidcombe to which Lady Foxglove had gone, looking very lovely in a black veil.

Brother Thomas just caught a glimpse of the notice outside the main door as he was wheeled in:

ST BRIDGET'S HOME FOR THE DYING, PADDINGTON
INQUIRIES TO MOTHER ALICE O'CALLAGHAN, PRINCIPAL
SILENCE PLEASE

There was something pleasantly unequivocal about that, thought the monk as he was wheeled down a long dark corridor with rows of doors on each side. The rubber wheels on his chair made no noise at all on the invisible parquet flooring, which smelt strongly of beeswax and turpentine.

'Here we are,' said the nun, who was called Sister Alfreda. She averted her eyes as she helped him into bed, and then sat down herself on a rickety chair in the corner, and stared out of the small, grimy window while she fingered her beads, and her lips moved soundlessly. They were the first words that had been uttered, the first sound to break the quiet since his noisy exit from the ambulance. Sister Bridget, the Day Portress, had made a slight obeisance in deference to his clerical standing, but otherwise the silence lay like layers of dust on a forgotten tomb. In each tiny box-like bedroom the patient was watched over by the unmoving, marble figure of a nun who fingered her beads and awaited the Hour.

After a time, Brother Thomas said:

'Nice and quiet it is here, after Bermondsey.'

Sister Alfreda gave a tiny nod, but kept her eyes on the

window, and continued to say her beads, with only the rapid fluttering of her lips to show that she was alive at all.

'I must say, I expect the change will do me good,' said Brother Thomas, as a preliminary to a discussion. This time Sister Alfreda made no acknowledgement but the knuckles showed white on the hand that held her Rosary as she concentrated on her prayers in order to avoid distraction.

After a time he began bouncing up and down in his bed in order to listen to the squeaks, and imagining maps and narrative pictures, and portraits of people he knew in the stains on the ceiling and walls. He played Up Jenkins with himself, using a pyjama button which was about to fall off anyway, and tried to think of all the words he knew beginning with B. At the hour which would have been cocoatime in Annie Zunz, he dropped into a dreamless sleep.

When Lady Foxglove telephoned later that evening, Mother Alice said: 'I think he is more composed now, but he was very restless when he first arrived.'

At Cleeve, Stoat began to realize that he had gone too far. It had happened several times in his career before, when, without warning, his entire world had seemed to collapse about his ears, leaving him just a shade more lonely and spiteful, and not a jot wiser than before. When his first Nanny, called Freda, to whom he was passionately attached, had suddenly been teased too much about her boy-friends, and had turned and thrashed him savagely, and given her notice the same evening; when his spaniel puppy, Rollo, had been pushed once too often into the gold-fish pond, and had caught cold and died, and his father had sworn that he would never have another dog: when, at his first prep school, a game of Cops and Robbers had got out of hand, and a boy had nearly lost a finger, and Stoat had been asked to leave.

So now, he realized, his clumsiness had made an indefinable and irreparable difference in his relation with Martin.

There had been a formal reconciliation after the quarrel, but he detected a certain evasive wariness in Martin's eye whenever they were together, and an odd politeness which held them apart more than anything else.

Once, after Martin had refused for the third day running to come out for an evening cigarette, Kenneth asked him:

'You're not still angry about what I said, are you?' and he answered:

'Why on earth should I be? I'd forgotten about it years ago, as a matter of fact.'

And the subject was never again mentioned, although Stoat brooded about it in bed and during the day. Once, during an R.I. class, he wrote on his cuff *You are an unnecessary pig*, and after that he seemed to have the disaster in perspective. More frequently, now, Martin was seen to be going about with Pratt-Bingham, and apart from one sharp pang of jealousy when he saw Martin, radiant and good-looking as never before, laughing at one of Pratt-Bingham's jokes, Kenneth resigned himself with a fairly good heart, and became more and more intimate with O'Connor, Pyke and Kelly.

At the end of the term, they shook hands solemnly, and Martin said: 'Don't do anything I wouldn't do,' and Stoat said: 'Not bloody likely.' But somehow the exchange lacked spontaneity, especially as Kenneth had just heard that Pratt-Bingham had been invited down to spend a week of the holiday at Bidcombe.

On the way up to Nottingham in the train, he wondered what it was that prevented him ever from asking a friend home, or even out to dinner on the rare occasions that his father had been able to get away from his surgery for a week-end. It wasn't that he was ashamed of anything, but perhaps neither O'Connor nor Pyke would understand that the Stoats weren't quite the same as everybody else. It wasn't his mother's fault that she suffered from nerves, but with his father coming in a little irritable and cross in the evenings, and his mother having had a trying day shopping or arranging about meals with the cook, it was no good pretending the three of them hit it off as other families did. If only, he thought in his ungrateful way, I had a mother like Lady Foxglove, a father like old Brother Thomas, and I was a little bit more like Martin.

After Sir Derek had visited Brother Thomas for the first time in Mother Alice's Home, he determined to take a firm line with his wife. The old man was developing some nasty bed-sores as a result of the nuns' reluctance to give his pressure-points a daily massage, and they were obviously hopelessly ill-equipped to deal with any complication which might occur between then and his next operation.

'But Derek, aren't you being a little hard-hearted on poor Brother Thomas?' she pleaded. 'It is much more suitable for him at Mother Alice's and they are so much more friendly and nice. I know he was quite miserable at the Bermondsey Hospital, and the people were so dreadful there, and I shan't be able to look Mother Alice in the face again if we just take him away, and she was so sweet to Nanny Bill, it really is no way to show our gratitude for all she's done.'

But Sir Derek paid no attention at all. Men were so unreasonable, thought poor Lady Foxglove, as she watched him write a note for his secretary to give to Hunt. Mr Hunt dropped a line to Larry, and Larry asked Sister if she could tell Mr Dooney, and Mr Dooney told Herring to get the bed made which had unexpectedly become free the evening before, and Herring told Pickles to get cracking as she was just off to her tea.

When they came to fetch him, Brother Thomas said: 'Goodness are you moving me again?' And Sister Alfreda gave a tiny inclination of her head before pushing him back down the long silent corridor, with her beads clicking very slightly as she walked.

Sister Bridget looked up in surprise. It was very seldom a patient left by that door.

'Hullo, Tommy,' shouted Fred as he was wheeled back into the ward. 'Blimey I thought we'd got rid of you last time. Still, it's all right to have him back, isn't it, Cogginsy?'

'Hullo, Tommy,' shouted Mr Coggins waving the stump of his leg excitedly in the air.

'Hullo, Mr Aquinas,' said Nurse Pickles with a little smile as she helped him between the sheets. He was in the opposite corner to his old bed.

'Where's Bill?' he asked. Nobody answered, and Nurse Pickles busied herself tidying his counterpane. 'Oh, I'm sorry,' he said, and to himself added, 'May his Soul of all the Souls departed rest in Peace, Amen.'

'Yes, we were all sorry about that,' said Fred, and Mr Coggins leant over as soon as Nurse Pickles was gone and said in a stage whisper: 'It was that Perishing Kipper done 'im in. 'E couldn't stand her, I'll tell you.'

'Where've you bin, then?' asked Fred.

'Oh, I had to be kept under observation,' said Brother Thomas over his cup of cocoa. 'Sir Derek wanted to see if I would produce any interesting new symptoms.'

'And did you?' asked Fred breathlessly.

'I'm not sure,' said Brother Thomas mysteriously, and happily dipped his bread into the sugar.

'You oughter of been here the night old Bill bought it,' said Mr Coggins, to keep his end up. 'The noise 'e made was something fantastic, weren't it, Fred?'

'It may of been and it may not of been,' said Fred severely. Clearly there were some things one did not discuss.

In the infinitesimally small world of Mr Dooney things

45

were not going well. If the P.M. report on the patient who had died the evening before was unsatisfactory, there might have to be an inquest, and Mr Dooney was too new on the job to have built up the network of friendship and loyalties and interdependence which normally sustains the medical profession at such moments. It was Nurse Herring's job to keep an eye on the patient during the transfusion and she should have noticed the signs of rigor as soon as they appeared, and she, of course, should have noticed if the drip gadget had speeded up to a hundred and twenty a minute, as she told him in confidence afterwards. In short, she had let him down. He would get all the blame, of course, and it wouldn't help things if they discovered that he had needed three attempts to get the blasted thing into the old man's vein in the first place; it had been as slippery as an eel, and at times he had wondered if there was a vein there at all. And it had been his job to adjust the drip-regulator, and he was almost sure he had got it right before going for his cup of tea, which, God knows, he had earned. And the next thing he knew as he was chatting about this and that to Herring was that Mr Coggins had come hopping into the staff nurse's room saying he thought there was something wrong with his mate. No, there was no doubt about it, Nurse Herring had let him down, wasting her time chatting there with no one on the ward. Well, he wasn't going to lift a finger to stop her getting into trouble after that. It just showed, he thought, that you couldn't be too careful with these nurses.

Nurse Herring had had rather a sticky interview with Sister after Day Report in the morning, but she had ended by saying it was going to be all right. Nurse Herring had been going to check the D.D.A. cupboard in the office, when she was waylaid by the houseman who wished to tell her of a re-admittance next day. He had not mentioned the time of the patient's transfusion, and she had assumed that it was not until later on. If any questions were asked, Sister had said it was all right to leave the ward for ten minutes to check the D.D.A. cupboard, so long as nothing was happening which needed her attention. She sighed with relief, although it looked pretty black for poor Ron, who was rather sweet in spite of all his airs. If only he wasn't so small, she thought impertinently.

However it all blew over; it turned out that the clot which killed Bill could have been caused by an accumulative embolism, and that was what went down on the post-mortem report.

In his bedroom at 12, Park View Drive, Stoat stood in front of his mirror, and rubbed a pungent green after-shave lotion into his face until it hurt. He adjusted his tie, and applied a large globule of hair cream to his coarse mousy hair with the same vigour, until its crinkles shone and glittered like a prize-fighter's. He parted it with great care, leaving a broad grey scar running in a straight line over his head. Then he put on the coat of his new brown suit, and stood back to assess the result.

His bedroom was completely his own, and nobody was allowed in there at all except Elsie in the mornings. His mother sometimes called it his Den, and really, felt Stoat, that was just about what it was. There was the framed Titian print, which was Art, as he had explained to Elsie, who wasn't sure, and the partially stuffed frog which he had done himself, which was Nature. There was a coin collection kept in an old cigarette tin and a collection of birds' eggs in cotton wool which he had bought from O'Connor at prep. school. There was his trunk, partially unpacked, which he kept in one corner, and a copy of *The Golden Ass* under the bed, and a dutiful photograph of his mother in her fox-fur on the chimney-piece. It was his only home, and whenever he felt especially miserable, his thoughts returned to the warmth and security of this little hole between the kitchen and the attic, although when he was actually there he never seemed to have anything to do.

He climbed down the stairs noisily and slammed the front door of the house after him, which made his poor mother, who was spending the day in bed, nearly die of fright.

The cook looked up from her colander in which she was draining the cabbage for tomorrow's Bubble and Squeak, and thought: 'Well now, our Ken's gone courting. Best thing in the world for him, too, if you ask me.' She was very fond of her Ken, and enjoyed heaping his plate with the mountains of food which he was able to consume without difficulty, potatoes and gravy, mostly, of course, or they would all be in the poor house by now. She wondered benignly who the lucky girl was, as she rattled the plates in the sink so that Mrs Stoat should know she was hard at work.

In fact Kenneth, now in his seventeenth year, had begun to feel strange stirrings inside him which manifested themselves in this new activity. Hitherto his sex life had been solitary and unholy, but now a yearning for companionship sent him out every evening, fragrant and gleaming, to pace the sedate streets around Park View Drive in the quest for His Girl. Many a housewife returning home after dark had been startled to see a lonely figure with its hands deep in its pockets break into a horrible leer as she passed. Every evening he returned from his prowls frustrated and footsore and lonelier than before.

This evening he was surprised to find the light on in the drawing-room when he returned, and his father waiting for him in his favourite armchair.

'Come in, Ken my boy,' he called when he heard the front door close softly behind the sinister figure of his son. 'Where have you been then, eh?' he asked with a knowing wink. 'Well I mustn't enquire too closely, I don't suppose.'

Kenneth thought: 'How pathetically pleased with himself he looks tonight. Of course, all we've got in common is the fact that we're both male, so I mustn't grudge him his little joke.'

'A one for the girls, is he?' thought Dr Stoat. 'Well, like father, like son, they say. I could tell him a few things which would surprise him.' From that day he began to regard his son with a new interest and respect.

'What I really wanted to tell you,' said the dentist, 'is that I have heard some news today which is going to make a lot of difference to all our lives. It has been a long time coming, and at times I don't mind telling you I nearly despaired of ever leaving Nottingham, but now I have been offered the Dental Department at the Royal Bermondsey Hospital in London.' He paused, to allow the full import of the momentous news to reach his son. He did not seem as much moved as one would have expected. 'I shall be taking over as Chief Consultant in Dental Surgery from Dr Deekin, who is going to London University as the MacIntyre Professor of Dental Sciences,' he added, mentioning reverently the ultimate laureate of the dental profession.

'Tomorrow I must go to London to interview the Board of Governors. It seems to me you could do with a holiday, and I wondered if you'd care to come.'

'Yes, please,' said Stoat awkwardly, perched on the edge of his armchair, although he felt immensely grateful to his father for his kindliness; he could quite well have gone to London alone, and it was sheer goodness which made him invite Kenneth, because they were always uncomfortable in each other's company, and it would only be a bore to him. However, Stoat was quite unable to signify his gratitude and sudden burst of affection for his father; his years of loneliness had left him well equipped to deal with malice and obstruction, but kindness left him embarrassed and speechless. Suddenly a thought occurred to him:

'The Bermondsey Hospital is where they took Brother Thomas to,' he said.

'Old Thomas Plunkett?' asked his father, a little uneasily. In his hot youth he had been a great friend of the old monk, and had confided all sorts of things which it would be rather embarrassing to have brought up again. Now he was old and sour it was impossible to recapture the days of hope and despair, of love and religious enthusiasm, of sin, of idealism and wickedness which he had lived when he was young, before he had met his wife or gone to the war.

All his friends of those days were dead or scattered and, like him, respectable professional men. Their one or two attempts at reunions had been dismal failures, and in most of them the memory of those mad summer months had been allowed to die, or firmly put aside as something out of their past which did not belong to the present.

'Well you can go and visit him while I'm being interviewed,' he said, and there the matter ended.

At Bidcombe, Martin and his new friend Frank Pratt-Bingham splashed in the swimming pool, or wrestled on the springy turf of the Manor House lawn under the fond eye of his mother. During the holidays, out of consideration for Martin she usually gave herself a respite from the Good Works which would normally be carrying her all over the country, from death-bed to funeral, from newly-widowed wife to newly-orphaned children, spreading comfort and solace by her example and her own simple goodness.

She had every reason to be a happy and proud mother as she watched her son darting like a dragon fly in his bright blue bathing pants from summer house to swimming pool and back again, his enormous almond eyes laughing out from a golden olive face, his lithe sprint carrying him noiselessly over the warm tiles. But she was unhappy about Stoat. It was all right now, of course, but had it been all right before? she wondered. Martin in his obvious innocence was such an open target for all that was most evil in the world, and one did read such terrible things of what went on in the public schools, although Brother Aloysius had assured her that there was none of that sort of thing at Cleeve; but when she saw Stoat that evening with his terrible hair oiled down she had begun to wonder. If only, she thought, I could find someone who would be really frank with me, who could tell me all that really does go on; not that I should want to be inquisitive, but I do think it is the sort of thing one should know. Anyway, thank Heavens, he's found Frank, and seems to have forgotten about Stoat.

That evening was the last of Pratt-Bingham's visit, and as they were changing Martin thought he heard him make a suggestion which left him dumb with horror and fright. He ran out of the room and locked himself in the bathroom in tears. It was the first time he had come up against the real thing, and the disgust and shock left him shivering, and he longed for the days when he had Stoat on whom he could rely to protect him. But he was alone now and too ashamed to confide in anyone.

At breakfast Lady Foxglove noticed that the two boys were very silent, and thought in her grown-up way that they had had a quarrel, but that they'd soon get over it.

In the course of the morning she remembered that she had a bottle of Lourdes water which she had intended to give to Brother Thomas in his last illness, but she felt that she really could not go back to that dreadful place where everyone had been so rude to her. She had done the best she could for the old man, and her husband had spoilt it all just when he had been most prepared for the good death which she had arranged. It will be Derek's fault, she thought, if the old monk goes to hell. She had done her best, and nobody could expect more of her than that, could they? she asked with a whimsical smile, lifting her beautiful face to God. She would give the Lourdes water to Martin to take up that afternoon, and anyway she would have to visit old Mrs Hathaway in the village and see how her blindness was getting on.

Kenneth always enjoyed his occasional visits to London with his father. Dr Stoat was quite a prosperous man, and his journeys to the metropolis were rare enough to allow him to do them in style. Besides, he rather liked to show his son the way things should be done; it was part of the boy's education, he felt. Kenneth felt very grand as he was bowed into the Dorchester by enormous brown-coated lackeys, although some of his old awkwardness returned when he met the cheeky, critical gaze of one of the page boys who was swinging his legs from the hall porter's desk. If only, he thought, those snobbish fools at Cleeve could see me now, they'd soon change their tune.

'Oh, Stoat, we wanted a new secretary for the Thomas More Society,' they would say, and, 'Oh, Stoat, there will be a vacancy for a new monitor next term, and we wondered if you'd care to take it on.' They could keep their bloody laurels, he would say savagely; but he made a mental reservation that perhaps he would relent about the monitorship after a lot of persuasion.

Kenneth and his father always drank champagne when they were in London, although at home it was orange juice for luncheon and beer at dinner if Dr Stoat had remembered to buy some on the way back from the surgery. Mrs Stoat always refused to go into a pub and Kenneth was under age.

Over a glass of port at the end of luncheon, Dr Stoat said:
'Give my regards to old Thomas à Plunkett, won't you? I don't know if he'll remember me, but tell him I'm sorry I couldn't visit him but it just wasn't possible.' It was inconceivable, he thought, that the old man should have forgotten those days, when the world was young and carefree

and irresponsible and incredibly beautiful, and while there might have been tragedy, there was no drabness, while there was sorrow there was no boredom.

Stoat wondered why his father was so anxious to avoid Brother Thomas, and thought he could guess.

In Annie Zunz the patients were settling down to their afternoon snooze when Nurse Proudfoot, the new staff nurse, came bustling in to tell Mr Aquinas that he had a visitor. 'Are you respectable?' she asked doubtfully, and brushed his hair for him and tidied his bed, and scolded him as she removed an old orange skin from his pillow case and a little nest of grape pips from his tooth glass.

'Now don't you dare untidy yourself while I go and fetch him in,' she said threateningly, and ran precipitously to the door. She was a great improvement on old Herring, thought Brother Thomas, as he wondered where to put an orange pip he had just discovered in his woollen bed-jacket. Eventually it joined a secret clutch he had been building up for some time in one of his slippers.

Kenneth felt very lonely and afraid amid all the scurrying and the smells of the hospital, and far too intimidated by the gleaming white starched figures of the nurses as they flew past on their various errands to try one of his leers, although there could be no doubt that the uniforms were most becoming.

When Nurse Proudfoot came to fetch him, and he followed her busy figure down the long silent length of the ward he thought what fun it would be to give her prim little behind a good hard pinch. That would make her jump, he thought savagely, and she was a buxom little piece under all that starch.

Brother Thomas was touched and pleased that Kenneth should have come to see him; he was not at all as his father had been, he reflected, as he watched him shuffle his feet and fidget with his temperature chart, unable to think of anything to say. He remembered the day Michael Stoat had come to him and announced he was going to commit suicide, although he could not remember the reason now. He had had to pretend to take him seriously, and they had discussed it quietly together for a whole evening, at the end of which he had given him a cigarette and Michael had said that perhaps he wouldn't after all. After that day Michael had always seemed a little shy of him; perhaps he thought he had made a fool of himself. Well, so he had, but they all made mistakes at that age, and in many cases he thought the magnitude of their mistakes was the measure of their later grace.

'Hullo, Kenneth,' he said. 'How nice of you to think of coming to see me. What's become of your father, these days? I hardly ever seem to hear from him.'

'He said he was very sorry but he couldn't make it, and he sent his regards,' said Kenneth, a speech he had carefully rehearsed.

'How typical of Michael to be ashamed to look one in the face after so many years,' he thought. 'Still, I would have liked to see him again, if only to see what has become of him.'

In the entrance hall of the hospital Martin looked with distaste at the bottle in his hand. It was large and blue and plastic, and slightly sticky to the touch. It had formerly contained a deodorant and the remains of a label on which the letters ODORONO were just legible survived. Lady Foxglove had failed to see why she should pay the exorbitant price demanded by the street hawkers at Lourdes for their bottles of water; it would have been practically encouraging the sin of simony to have paid them such an outrageous sum, and so she had saved both her conscience and her purse by this little economy.

Before he had noticed the label, Martin had tasted the

water surreptitiously, and a little fearfully, on the train, and had been amazed to find a faint cloying fragrance on his palate. It seemed obviously to be an attribute of the water's sanctity that it should taste like roses; but then he noticed the label and realized that it wasn't a miracle after all.

Back in Annie Zunz, Nurse Proudfoot came running into the cubicle in a great state of excitement.

'Quite a social afternoon we're having, aren't we, Mr Aquinas?' she said. 'Another visitor, and here we are with you half out of bed and looking as if you'd been in a wrestling match.' She winked at Kenneth as her busy fingers started dexterously to rearrange the old man's bed. 'And *what* have we got here!' she cried delightedly, staring into his slipper. 'Pickles, come here at once and see what I've found. Why, you old villain, I've got half a mind to show it to Sister, and then you'ld be for it. You don't deserve to have visitors the way you behave.'

Stoat's eyes followed her wistfully out of the ward. He wondered just what she had meant by that wink. He prided himself that he really was looking his best that afternoon and perhaps she had taken a fancy to him, and had meant, 'You follow me.' Or perhaps it had been an hallucination and she hadn't winked at all, in which case he would look awfully silly padding after her with his tongue hanging out like a dog. Or perhaps she hadn't meant anything by it, and had some affliction in her eye so that she couldn't help winking at everyone. Stoat decided he would play hard to get, and stuck his hands nonchalantly into his pockets.

Old Brother Thomas, watching him, thought, 'Poor creature, he is in a bad way, perhaps he has a little of his father in him after all.'

When Martin arrived he came empty-handed. He had deposited Lady Foxglove's present in a tin box he had found outside the ward, which was reserved for out-patients' two morning buns, and he felt as if he had shed a great burden. He stopped in surprise when he saw Stoat.

'Oh, hullo, Martin,' said Kenneth, equally alarmed.

'How surprising,' thought Brother Thomas, 'that they should be friends; what an extraordinarily handsome boy he's grown into; the danger for him will always be that everything comes too easily, and it is easy enough to lose your head at that age. I wonder what it feels like to be as beautiful as that, and to know that everybody will always love you. I think it is just as dangerous as having to fight as Kenneth does and Michael did before him.'

'Hullo, Martin,' said Brother Thomas, and affectionately pinched his cheek, which he felt was an old man's privilege. In anyone else it would have set nasty little Stoat thinking.

'Where've you come from?' Martin asked, speaking to Kenneth.

'He just popped in to pass the time of day,' said the monk, 'and it's very nice to see the pair of you.'

'Well, actually,' said Stoat, 'I just came across from the Dorchester where I'm staying. My father's got to go up and see the Board of Governors or something.' His first instinct on being cornered alone was always to show off, although, whenever he thought about it afterwards he realized that everybody knew he was showing off, and kicked his bed in anger at his own inability to do anything about it.

'Oh, really,' said Martin. 'I believe Daddy's on the Board so they will probably be meeting each other. It will be interesting to hear what they think of each other.'

'It may interest you to know,' interposed Brother Thomas mildly, 'that Sir Derek was Michael Stoat's fag at Cleeve in the days when there were fags, so they will hardly be strangers to each other.'

That made honours about even, but Foxglove realized that he could never now confide to Stoat about what Pratt-Bingham had said to him; their hostility had become something too fundamental, and any future confidence would simply be supplying ammunition to the enemy.

'Why didn't you tell me before?' he asked Stoat angrily.

'I didn't know,' said Stoat quite truthfully. He never discussed his school-life with his father, except occasionally to mention cricket scores or football matches against other schools, in which neither was faintly interested. To Dr Stoat Cleeve and everything connected with it was a sacred memory, and he wanted no ripple to disturb the tranquil lake of his sentiment. Perhaps, too, he unconsciously realized that any discussion of the place with his son would churn it up, so that all the mud which had lain dormant under its surface for thirty years would again appear, ugly and stinking, and the occasional fragrant lilies which the dentist liked to savour would be lost on the bottom for good.

Nurse Proudfoot came in carrying something wrapped in a sterile towel, and handed it to Martin. 'I think this is yours,' she said, but there was an infinity of rebuke in the way she said it.

Martin glared at the bundle in his hands and tried to tuck it into his trousers pocket. 'I will keep the towel,' said Nurse Proudfoot sternly and walked out, leaving Martin holding something obscene and blue and covered in crumbs and currants, the relics of the morning buns.

'What is that?' asked Brother Thomas, interested.

'It is some Lourdes water Mummy told me to give you,' he said in a small voice. 'I must have stupidly forgotten it outside.'

'How sweet of her,' said Brother Thomas, without a touch of rancour. 'What does one do with it, drink it or rub oneself all over, do you know? I've often wondered. I must give it to Nurse Pickles and she can bring it round on the medicine tray every morning, or I'm afraid I should hog it all at once, which would never do.'

It was the first time Kenneth had seen Foxglove at a disadvantage in the company of a third person, and it **was** not an opportunity to be missed.

'It says "The safe way to dispel Body Odours",' he said, reading from the label. 'I didn't know Lourdes water was meant to be good for that too.'

'It's wonderful what it can do,' said Brother Thomas tactfully, although truth to tell he was rather enjoying the situation.

'I don't know why she supposed Brother Thomas should need it,' said nasty little Stoat relentlessly, but as soon as the words were out of his mouth he wondered if he had not gone too far.

'Tell your mother that it was immensely kind of her to think of me, and thank you very much for bringing it, Martin,' said the monk, and added, as a concession to Stoat, 'and I'm sure it will do me a lot of good.'

Nurse Proudfoot made another of her alarming entrances. 'Now then you boys,' she said bossily but genially, 'out you go, or you'll get the old man all excited and we'll none of us get a wink of sleep tonight for trying to keep him quiet. He's bad enough as it is, and you don't want to encourage the Old Wickedness.'

As the boys left, Brother Thomas tied a knot in the corner of his sheet so as to remember the two of them in his prayers that evening, and after a time he began to feel sleepy, and soon his eyelids drooped and closed, not to reopen until third cocoa sounded through the ward.

Dr Stoat was surprised to find Sir Derek waiting for him in the lobby outside the hospital's board room. They had not met since the war, when Derek, as surgeon-major of the Halberdiers, had arranged for Dr Stoat to be attached to the same regiment as Dental Officer. Sir Derek had not enjoyed the war, nor the rough surgery and unnecessary pain and inadequate equipment but to Dr Stoat they seemed to have been Elysian days, with the easy comradeship, and getting slightly tight in the evenings among friends, when it didn't matter what you said or did, and the simple pleasures of being an officer and having anybody you spoke to freeze into a statue of respect and saluting, and the opportunities for kindness and magnanimity which such an Olympian position commanded. He always referred to the Halberdiers as his regiment, although, of course, he had worn the insignia of the Royal Army Dental Corps. Tactfully, during the war, they had both avoided any mention of Cleeve, except occasionally – to discuss cricket scores or the results of football matches.

'Hullo, Michael,' said Sir Derek, warmly shaking his hand. 'I am glad you've decided to join the staff here. You'll find it's a very pleasant, friendly place here when you get used to it, and I'm sure you'll like your colleagues in the other departments. I always used to hope you'd come down here to get on with some good research work when you got bored of your lush practice in Nottingham.'

He did not mention that it was largely through his influence that Dr Stoat's name had appeared as a candidate before the Board, nor that it was his support and that of his claque which had pushed the nomination through, but Dr Stoat thought he detected something faintly proprietorial in the surgeon's attitude towards him which he rather resented. It had been bad enough, during the war, when he had had to call his former fag 'Sir' until his majority came through, but he was blowed if he could see why he should let himself be patronized by someone who was practically his equal now; after all they were both Senior Consultants, even if Sir Derek did have a few years start.

'If you will come through,' said Sir Derek, 'I shall introduce you to the chairman and other governors. I shouldn't take them too seriously, they are just one of those things that people in our profession have to put up with.'

It was very difficult to handle Michael properly, thought the surgeon, because he really was stickier than a tar-baby these days. But unknown to the other, he felt an immense debt of gratitude to the older man for his kindness so many years ago at Cleeve. Michael had always been immensely kind to people who were smaller or less powerful, but he had never been able to get on with his superiors for some reason; however good or tolerant they were, there had always been a tendency on his part to twist and bite any hand which patted him on the head.

'Lord Robinson, this is Dr Stoat; Lord Robinson is our chairman.' Lord Robinson stood up from his enormous desk and shook hands formally.

'Stoat,' he said, trying to sound interested, and rustling some papers. 'Ah, yes, Stoat. You're the new Catering Officer, aren't you?' A secretary whispered something in his ear, and put some more papers in front of him. 'Oh, of course, how stupid of me; you've come to take over our dental department. Well, we place a lot of importance in our dental department,' he said looking round the room for support; 'as you probably know it has some of the newest and most expensive equipment of any hospital in England. Under Dr Deekin it got quite a name for some excellent pioneer research work in dental implants. In fact, last year we were so pleased with the name it was making for the hospital that we increased its annual grant by five per cent. We rely on you, Dr Stoat, to keep it up to that standard. What field is it that you specialize in, let me see.'

Again he rustled the papers on his desk.

Sir Derek Foxglove saved the situation by saying: 'Before the war Dr Stoat was following a very interesting line on masculatory anaesthesia, although, of course, at Nottingham he hardly had the facilities for serious research work. We were hoping that if he could pursue that line with the

equipment we've got here we might get some fairly revealing results.'

'Oh yes, to be sure. Good of you to remind me, Foxglove.'

Lord Robinson was not a medical man ; he had built an
enormous fortune slowly by scrupulous attention to details,
and by a considerable shrewdness which was not at first easy
to detect. His chairmanship of the hospital was as much a
calculated step in the seemingly endless ladder of his self-
elevation as any business merger had been. It had lent his
name a respectability which had justified his barony and
which lent greater weight to further business mergers. He
had no social ambitions, no desire for power or fame, no
wish to make his influence felt for better or worse. His life
was just a solitary, instinctive climb, up and up.

He paused, pen poised, over the agenda sheet. He ap-
proved of course, in principle, the Royal Bermondsey being
a progressive, go-ahead hospital, and had even seriously considered sanctioning, at one moment, the appointment of a
black Dean of the medical school. But there must be no
breath of scandal or all his work would be undone, and what
Sir Derek had said sounded suspiciously like euthanasia,
which was far too controversial a subject for his hospital to
handle.

'What did you say he specialized in ? '

'Masculatory anaesthesia, sir.'

'I know, I heard you, but what's that ? '

'Putting to sleep by an oral intra-muscular injection the
effect of which would be regulated by a voluntary movement of the neck muscles,' explained Dr Stoat, who had in
fact abandoned the project twenty years ago.

Just what he thought. Putting to sleep.

'Well, we'd be delighted to have you on the staff, but
we'll want a broader field of research than that. In fact I'd
be tempted to say drop the whole thing, and concentrate on

61

these dental implants,' said Lord Robinson, and signed the agenda.

On the way down in the lift, Martin said:

'He didn't look too bad to me, old Plops. I thought he was in rather good form.' and Stoat said: 'No, I thought he looked all right. Perhaps it's all a lot of fuss about nothing.' There was an awkward silence as they each tried to think of something to say. Foxglove longed to throw his arms round Kenneth's verminous neck and say: 'Oh, Stoat, I love you, so sympathize with me, I've no one to tell about that bugger Pratt-Bingham and I'm fed up with pretending to be a nice little boy and I'm fed up with my bloody mother, and I do so want someone to talk to.'

And Stoat longed to say: 'Oh, Foxglove, forgive me, I didn't mean to hurt you, but I am such a spiteful little pig I can't help it, and I think your mother is the most wonderful woman in the world and I wish mine was a quarter so lovely or kind or good.'

But the moment passed. 'Well, I'll be going back to the hotel, I suppose.'

'Well, see you next term.'

'I suppose so. No need to rub it in, though.'

'Don't do anything I wouldn't do.'

In the lobby outside the board room, Sir Derek shook hands with Dr Stoat and said: 'Congratulations, I knew you would pull it off. It was an uneasy moment, though, when Lord Robinson started off about whether anaesthesia was really a desirable thing to have in a State Hospital. I thought you showed a lot of restraint.'

'I don't know why you had to start him off on it,' said Dr Stoat ungraciously. 'I could see that there was nothing in my idea of masculatory anaesthesia twenty years ago.' It had been the brain-child of his first and last enthusiasm in dentistry, and when a colleague had shown him its impracticability he had put it primly behind him, like Cleeve and all his memories of the army.

Watching his pudgy form with its nasty little moustache disappear through the glass swing door, Sir Derek wished he could have done more for the dentist, done something to make him smile and feel happy and feel that he was important.

When they came round later that evening to give blanket baths and make up the beds, Nurse Proudfoot noticed the knot in the corner of Brother Thomas's sheet.

'What have you been up to now?' she asked stridently, showing it to Nurse Pickles.

'I put it there to remind me of something,' said Brother Thomas, feeling that for once he had got the better of the staff nurse. He thought it showed great business efficiency to contrive such a device, and was rather proud of his handiwork.

'And what, may I ask, was it to remind you of?'

'You know, Nurse, now you ask, it has completely slipped my memory. But do leave it there, and perhaps I shall remember later.'

'Well really, Mr Aquinas, sometimes we begin to wonder about you, don't we, Pickles? Well, out you get, you old idleness, and let Pickles and me do something about your bed.'

Suddenly Brother Thomas felt very tired and useless. It had been something quite important, he felt sure, which he had wanted to remember. Was it to ask Nurse Pickles for a bed-pan? he wondered; or to send a birthday letter to someone, or to tell Cogginsy some story he had just remembered? But it never came back to him.

Later on in the same day, Brother Thomas took a turn for the worse, and that night Stoat found His Girl in a back street off Piccadilly Circus. It cost him thirty-five shillings, and he came away disillusioned and rather sore. It had not been at all what he was led to expect. There had been no sudden coming together, no dipping, soaring, gliding meeting of two bodies and souls in harmony, no novelist present to draw a discreet curtain over the more revolting biological aspects of the whole business. Sex, he decided, was definitely over-rated.

But thinking about it afterwards he wondered perhaps whether it had not been a bit better than he had first supposed, and the account of the incident he eventually presented to O'Connor and Pyke was definitely rosy. But as they refused to believe him, it had really been thirty-five shillings wasted.

Martin had no such opportunities to sow his wild oats. His mother was determined that, when the day came, he should be offered up, spotless and unsoiled, on the altar of marriage, just as she had been, and his beautiful young bride (they said that Sarah Pratt-Bingham was turning into a charming young girl, and it would be so nice for Martin to marry the sister of his best friend) would come in for a tender kiss on the forehead from her beautiful mother-in-law, and the radiant young couple would come and live with her at Bidcombe, and the young bride would conquer all hearts as she went her way about the village doing good, and she would relieve some of the burden of work from Lady Foxglove's shoulders, who as she got older, would be seen about less and less, but would sit by the fire in the great drawing-room doing *petit-point* with her slender white fingers, and enchanting the new bride with tales of Martin's childhood, and his wild ways with Nanny Bill.

Martin was always very shy with the girls his mother allowed him to meet; or, when he overcame his shyness, tended to be too rough and boisterous, and not to make allowance for their gentler up-bringing. The truth was that the knowledge that his mother's fond eye was upon him the whole time, and that she was drawing her own cosy grown-up conclusions from everything he said or did, put him off to such an extent that he resolved to be as recalcitrant as possible, and would often in the middle of such parties, talk of the gay times he had had with his friend Henry Stoat of Cleeve, and would enjoy watching his mother, so pure and perfect, start in alarm. But he did resolve to marry as soon as he possibly could, if only to get away from his mother.

At the Royal Bermondsey, Sir Derek discussed the new development in Brother Thomas's illness with Mr Hunt, the registrar. The small specimen of tissue which had been removed from his bronchus at the time of the bronchoscopy had shown a complicated histology, and they had decided to wait a few weeks until the general picture became clearer, and they could make the decision whether to operate or turn him over to the radiotherapy department. Now they decided to take him up to the theatre the next day and perform an exploratory thoracotomy, or in Mr Hunt's phrase, 'Open him up and see what we find.'

Brother Thomas knew he was much iller, because he now found difficulty in moving his left arm, and there was a slight burning feeling whenever he breathed too deeply. Nurse Proudfoot, too, had become much less brusque, and had only called him an 'old muggins' when he spilt his cocoa all over his nice new sheets, and from then on little Nurse Pickles had been detailed to feed him, sitting on his bed and coaxing him with little teaspoonfuls of meat jelly, which would have been very nice, only he somehow did not feel like food. His physiotherapist, who used to come in the mornings for a good chat, and to swap gossip about what was going on in the other wards, and what nurse was walking out with whom, suddenly started making him do exercises which were as painful as they were fatuous. He had to run his fingers up and down his counterpane as if he were playing 'Creepy Crawlies' in 'Up Jenkins', and then the physiotherapist would take his left hand and start twisting the fingers backwards and forwards, like a rough child playing 'This Little Pig went to Market'. Then he would have to breathe in and out and she would batter him on the chest and tell him to cough. There seemed no more kindness left in her than there was milk in a male tiger, thought Brother Thomas, who would not understand that it was all for his own good, although everybody kept assuring him that it was so.

Every four hours Nurse Proudfoot would bring him an injection in a small kidney-bowl covered with a sterile towel, and the curtains of his cubicle were kept drawn as he dozed or fitfully woke and stared uncomprehendingly round about him. In the ward, the wildest speculation was rife, and Mr Coggins was alone in stoutly maintaining that old Tommy would pull through; it would need a lot more than young Mr Dooney to finish off anyone as tough as his mate Tommy, he said, but the others weren't so sure.

When the surrealist, white-robed figures of the two theatre attendants arrived with their trolley, Sister said that she would be accompanying the patient up to the theatre, and the Second Theatre Attendant removed a partially smoked Woodbine from behind his ear and swore that it was just like the fat bitch to come poking her nose into other people's business.

In the anaesthetist's room they told Brother Thomas to clench his right hand and count, but instead, as he felt the needle sliding into his vein, he prayed 'Into Thy hands, O Lord, I commend my spirit,' and then a horrid taste came into his mouth and his eyes closed.

Before they even got him on to the table it was obvious that something was wrong, and the anaesthetist prepared to give him a fairly substantial injection immediately over the heart of a drug called Digitalin, and when that had failed,

Mr Hunt performed an emergency heart massage, but all the magic of modern science could not revive Brother Thomas now and he died in the odour of Pentothal and Fluothame and Ether Gas.

Lady Foxglove went down to Cleeve for the obsequies, looking very lovely in a black lace veil; after the service, she went round for a chat with Brother Aloysius, who thought she was looking very pale and tired.

'Oh, I'm quite well, thank you,' she said with a grateful smile, 'although, of course, the worry for the past few days has been terrific. Poor Brother Thomas, it seems such a pity, although, of course, for the last years he has not been quite the same, and it is no use pretending he has. Who knows, perhaps it is a blessing in disguise after all?' With her sweet little smile she included Brother Aloysius into the body of the few who were equipped to pass judgement on such an intimate matter, and he nodded understandingly, and said, 'Who knows?'

In the Gregory Cloister the Bursar passed Brother Augustine carrying an odd bundle surreptitiously in the folds of his habit.

'Good evening Brother,' said the Bursar, 'I hope you are feeling well?'

'Why, yes, thank you,' said the theologian, surprised.

'I just wondered, Brother, when I saw you slipping out of church early before we had even taken the coffin out.'

'Oh, it was just some business I had to attend to,' said Brother Augustine carelessly.

'Talking of business,' said the Bursar, 'I see there is an application from you on my desk for a typewriter, which you say is essential for your work, and I wondered if now that Brother Thomas would no longer need his, you might not have it ...'

'Well, yes, I was wondering whether it would do,' said Brother Augustine, revealing his bundle, 'and I thought I would just take it and try it out.'

'But apparently the Abbot had promised it to Brother Timothy some time ago for his English school,' continued the Bursar, 'and he said that you would have to wait until Brother Theobald's becomes vacant.'

Finally Lady Foxglove got the ormolu crucifix, which nobody could possibly grudge her, thought Brother Aloysius as he unfixed it from the wall; it was such a very small memento of such a very great friend, and it really was very sweet of her to think of asking for it, and so typical of her not to want him to worry the Bursar or the Abbot. But still, he would be glad when the job was finished, he added, as he guiltily hid the object in his cassock.

Possession of the sorbo mattress was hotly disputed for some weeks, but finally it was settled by negotiation, and Brother Timothy got the mattress, Brother Augustine the typewriter.

Part Two

5

On the first day of the next term it was learned that both
Kelly and Foxglove had been made monitors. This involved
the privileges of carrying an umbrella to church on Sundays,
of wearing a butterfly collar, of smoking after seven o'clock
in the evening, and of reading the *Daily Mirror*. These
privileges were enforced with a ferocity which the enforce-
ment of the other school rules seldom excited; Kelly was
delighted with his new dignity.

'He'll bloody well have to speak to me now if I speak to
him,' he said to O'Connor, Pyke, and Stoat who were
assembled for an evening cigarette in his study, 'or I'll give
him a hundred lines for cheek, and that'll teach him.'

'He probably would have spoken to you before, only you
never dared to speak to him,' said Stoat.

'I think Frazer-Robinson is infinitely the nicer of the two,
anyway,' said Pyke unnecessarily.

Kelly sighed, and looked at the back of his wrist. Carved
neatly into the living flesh were the initials S II, the ineradic-
able testimony of the purity, selflessness and depth of his
romantic devotion to Sligger Two.

'No, but you must admit, Rigid, that he's got something
Frazer-Robinson hasn't. I don't know, perhaps it's the way
his eyes seem to roll out of his head whenever he laughs. I
wonder what he thinks of me? If only I could do something
to show him – I don't know – die or something. Somehow
I never seem to get an opportunity.'

'He probably thinks you're an epileptic from the way you
always go scarlet and look at your shoes whenever he passes.
Either that or just plain loony,' Pyke added consolingly. He

had always been called Rigid, although the reason for the nick-name was lost in the passing of the years.

Stoat was far too nasty to understand or sympathize with the finer shades of platonic affection which held Kelly and Pyke so tightly enmeshed. He was as unloving as he was unloved, and his nearest approach to that self-consuming fire which is the purgatory of the adolescent heart was in his adoration of the beautiful Lady Foxglove. He felt that he would gladly lay down his lonely ill-favoured life, if it would illuminate her serene countenance with a passing smile. But this passion he felt was too deep and too holy to be bandied about in the way that Kelly and Pyke discussed their fancies. As was his nature, he kept it locked in his chest, along with many less noble secrets.

Martin had said to him on the first day of term: 'Now look, Stoat, I want us to remain just as great friends as we were, but there's no need for you to think that you can take advantage of it. I don't want to catch you smoking or anything, and so you'd better give up using behind the swimming pool, or it will be my duty to send you to Brother Jeremy. And don't think I can show you any special leniency if I do catch you, because that's just what they're on the lookout for. Brother Jeremy has told me that no matter what I've done in the past, I start with a clean sheet now, so it's no use thinking you can blackmail me into keeping your cigarettes for you. In fact, if I were you, I would try and go straight for a bit now. I found it was fighting a losing battle, if you keep on flouting the authorities the whole time, and that's how I got where I am now.'

Stoat had accepted it as his lot that the person with whom he had shared so many adventures and so many secrets should now turn and treat him like an erring child. He remembered carrying Martin drunk back from the White Hart, he remembered the nightly poker games in the Bartholomew Library, Martin tearful after a beating, Martin with a cigarette drooping from the corner of his mouth, throwing darts at a cow in a field near the abbey, the headlong flight from an irate farmer who had been watching the sport from behind a hedge, Martin joyfully cutting Grill, their grass-snake, into tiny pieces with a refectory carving knife. Now Martin was a person of consequence with a sense of responsibility, and Stoat had to treat him with proper respect, and remove his hands from his pockets when he passed. It did not seem at all incongruous to either that the temporary difference of wearing a butterfly collar and carrying an umbrella to church on Sunday should create a distinction as great as the crown had between Falstaff and King Henry V.

Stoat now spent his time exclusively in the company of O'Connor, Pyke and Kelly. Kelly, although a monitor, was what was known as a rotten one, and did not take it quite so seriously as most people, who looked upon it quite rightly as an opportunity to develop their powers of leadership and as an important part of the public-school system. Stoat, watching nearly everybody he knew sprout wing-collars and self-importance, often congratulated himself on escaping such a fate; but he knew, in his heart of hearts, that he would rather like to be able to throw his weight around a bit and give people lines to write out.

To Kelly, however, it was just an opportunity of pursuing his courtship of Sligger Two. He did not know, and never learned, what was the purpose or ultimate end of all his pains; he never summoned courage to speak to him in two years; a vague desire to be liked and understood by that round smiling face with its rolling eyes drove him from extravagance to extravagance. And Sligger Two went his own charmed way in the company of his best friend Frazer-Robinson, and never once dreamed of the deep passions he stirred in the breast of others, nor the sonnets penned nightly in his honour by infatuated hands, nor of his initials carved amid excruciating agony on the wrist of Kelly One.

Every evening Stoat would creep over the high college walls, and with three muffled figures in black would pad noiselessly through the quiet streets of the village of Cleeve to the warmth and comfort of the back parlour of the White Hart. Their elaborate precautions were really quite unnecessary, but the element of danger added an enjoyment which was far over and above the pleasure of a glass of beer; simply to have walked out of the school gates would have been to rob the pastime of the thrill of being hunted, of comradeship in arms, of everything that made it worthwhile.

When they returned they would become a trifle maudlin, and sing songs at the top of their voices, and stop occasionally to piddle in the hedge. These were the days that Dr Stoat remembered as the happiest of his life, when all inhibitions were forgotten and in the joyful communion of their young souls unmarred by the sense of responsibility that age and cares would bring, they used to stop occasionally to piddle in the hedge.

But this happy state of affairs could not last long. A particularly virulent type of 'flu visited the school, and among those most seriously affected was young Sligger Two, so that some anxiety was entertained for his life. Kelly, in a frenzy, spent the days carving himself all over, like an African tribeswoman, and a sudden burst of religious fervour kept him in the abbey church for long hours on end. Stoat said:

'Whom the Gods love all die young,' and considered it a beautiful poetic thought, but the others thought it was in rather bad taste.

Brother Aloysius led the school in prayers for his recovery, nor was their solicitousness unrewarded, because within a week young Sligger was out of the sanatorium, leaving everybody feeling a little bit embarrassed at the anti-climax. Kelly went to the infirmary two days later with a swollen arm, and was removed to Cleeve General Hospital, where he died of gas gangrene after an unsuccessful amputation the same afternoon.

There was always something very moving about the death of a child, thought Brother Aloysius, during the long funeral service which was attended by both the school and community, although, of course, it would have been still more so if it was the innocent little body of Jamey Sligger lying white and cold inside the coffin. He piously thanked the Lord that that dear little chap had at least been spared, and wondered about Kelly, whom he had scarcely known at all.

When they told Sligger Two, he said: 'Oh I knew him. He once gave me some lines on the changing-room list, but he never asked for them. I think he must have been quite decent.'

Frazer-Robinson, who knelt beside him, kept glancing at the coffin and wondering if they had put his amputated arm in too, although he did not say anything.

O'Connor and Pyke and Stoat were more shocked than they cared to admit, and although they defiantly played poker dice through the long service, they avoided each other's eyes afterwards, and did not discuss the matter for some time.

Stoat wondered, when he heard of his friend's death, whether he would experience a Moment of Truth, but found that he did not.

Slowly, almost imperceptibly, the three began to drift apart from that date. O'Connor started reading Kafka, and was seen increasingly in Brother Augustine's set worrying about the position of the Artist in the modern world, and whether Artistic Integrity was a means to an end, or an end to a means. Sometimes he tried to discuss his new problems with his old friends, but found their answers somehow very shallow beside the deeper probings of Brother Augustine's circle. Soon he was writing poetry and reading aloud to the Delphians, Brother Augustine's new Poetry Group, but

Pyke and Stoat both thought it lacked the guts of the stuff they used to hear about Sligger Two.

Pyke began in a half-hearted way to aspire to a monitorship, and found in Pratt-Bingham a fellow admirer of Frazer-Robinson, although Pratt-Bingham's admiration seemed a little farmyard, as he and Kelly had used to refer to it. He did not much like Pratt-Bingham, but at least he was respectable, and life with O'Connor and Stoat seemed a little self-conscious nowadays, as if they were trying to re-create the atmosphere there had been before Kelly's death.

Stoat had his own, more intimate problems at that moment, and hardly noticed the trend towards separation. During a religious instruction class, he heard Brother Gregory vigorously propound on the dangers of venereal diseases, and it came to him suddenly that this was an explanation of a certain local discomfort he had been suffering for the last few days. The wages of sin, he thought miserably, and spent the next week in an agony of indecision, whether to confess, and suffer the ignominy of public exposure, or whether to keep it locked in his chest, alongside his platonic devotion to Lady Foxglove in which case he believed he would reap the harvest of degeneration, his nose would fall off and he would die paralytic and insane in a State institution. During that week Stoat was alone with his soul. Eventually he confided his dilemma to O'Connor, under the most sacred oaths of secrecy known to the Christian religion.

When conversation was flagging during an important discussion on the attitude of contemporary genius towards social problems, especially in the Arts, O'Connor mentioned it to his new friend Fitzgerald One. Fitzgerald used it rather neatly to illustrate a point he was making with Brother Augustine on heredity and environment, as influences on artistic development. Brother Augustine mentioned it to Brother Aloysius, because he thought a touch of realism was needed to shake him out of his effete, escapist complacency. Brother Aloysius was too shocked and horrified to tell anyone except the Prefect of Discipline, which it was plainly his duty to do.

When Dr Norton had been summoned, he reassured them that it was merely a rash, rather akin to impetigo, to which all adolescent males were prone if they paid insufficient attention to personal hygiene.

But the story of Stoat's great romance was out, and once again it was apparent that he had gone too far. When Dr Stoat received a carefully worded letter from the Prefects of Discipline and Studies, to say that in their opinion Kenneth was no longer profiting by his stay at Cleeve, he supposed that they meant that there was nothing further they could teach him, and felt vaguely proud to have such a brainy child. Kenneth left Cleeve for good at the end of that term, under a cloud which was at first no bigger than a man's hand, but which grew to immense proportions as it followed him through every stage in his career, and became his Familiar.

The departure from Cleeve was too unexpected and sudden for Kenneth to adjust himself at once to life outside. He had vaguely supposed that outside Cleeve was a world in which one smoked openly at all hours, and drank in bars and pubs without the precautions which had been necessary at the White Hart. One had romances and one got a job, and eventually married. But the day-to-day problems at Cleeve had been too immediate to allow of any prolonged speculation on what it would be like when life was no longer divided into term and holiday, but was just one long stretch of uninterrupted holiday.

For some months he lived a life in which his mind was still at Cleeve, and Cleeve standards still ruled his daily conduct. He lived on the top floor of his father's new flat in Wimbledon, smoking and smoking in a dressing-gown, reading comics and T. S. Eliot, and listening to the wireless. He seldom went out, and he found few opportunities for romance in the quiet residential area in which he lived. His mother had decided he was too sensitive to be put to work, although his father had not been too sure, but his mother's confidence in her son's genius was unbroken. He would become a poet, she thought, or an artist.

Occasionally he received formal, rather stilted letters from Foxglove, who had been made Head of the School, in which he mentioned cricket scores and the results of football matches. More informative letters came from O'Connor and Pyke. A subversive splinter-group from Brother Augustine's Poetry Circle had formed themselves into a secret society devoted to black magic, and had crucified a frog in the name of Brother Jeremy Price, although without any apparent ill-effect to him. The Cabala, as the society called itself, had tried to get in touch with Kelly's spirit, but the medium had been unsatisfactory, and the bell for evening school had rung just as he was beginning to get going.

Pratt-Bingham had been made captain of cricket, and had put Frazer-Robinson in the team, which had made many people rather indignant.

Did Stoat know anywhere in the outside world where one could buy mescalin on the black market?

They were all getting pretty fed up with school, and envied him no end. They betted that he was having a whale of a time alone and on the loose in London.

Stoat was given two pounds a week pocket money by his father, and a further clandestine ten shillings a week by his mother from her housekeeping funds. He made friends with another public schoolboy called Joseba dà Farratoga who had left Bloxham a little younger than was customary for reasons which Stoat was never quite able to discover. They did not like each other much, but loneliness kept them together, and in the afternoons they would go to the cinema, and in the evenings get slightly drunk and boast of the exploits each had experienced before they met. One day Kenneth called him a dago, and he drew a knife and started waving it over his head shouting in some strange tongue, after which even Stoat had to admit that he was completely British. It was an uneasy relationship, and each had constantly to bear in mind the other's vanity, but they both agreed that there was no place in the modern world for Genius, and resigned themselves to the Bohemian life of the penniless misunderstood intelligentsia with whom they identified themselves.

Farratoga was one of those mysterious phenomena which abound in London more than anywhere else in the world. He lived in lodgings in the Elephant and Castle, and had no apparent source of income, nor any prospects of receiving money for some time but always somehow managing to subsist. Sometimes he was the son of a mysterious tin millionaire who lived in St Tropez and with whom he could not communicate for reasons of international security. Sometimes his father was a smuggler of arms between Algiers and the Vatican, sometimes he was the natural son of a South American dictator. None of these alarming metamorphoses was ever expressed in so many words, but always by a series of sly hints, so that it often took Stoat some time to ascertain with which of the many Farratogas he was drinking his glass of beer. Unlikely as all these roles were, there remained the mystery of what in fact Farratoga was. Sometimes Stoat imagined that he must be a pick-pocket, or have found out the secret, possessed by so very few, of how to open telephone-box coin-machines without a key. But there was still the problem of his Bloxham education; the more fantastical became Joseba's account of his background, the more Stoat liked to imagine a cosy orange merchant in Tangier who had saved up for years to give his son a good English education; but somehow the picture did not fit.

One evening after they had been drinking more heavily

than usual, Joseba tapped Kenneth on the shoulder importantly, and said:

'Now look here, old boy, I've got something to say to you which you may find rather embarrassing. I'll take you to my digs and show you everything, and everything's above-board with me, O.K.? How come you never take me and show me to the old people in your home? You're not ashamed of me or anything, are you?'

'No,' said Kenneth. 'I'm not ashamed of you, Joe, I just thought probably you wouldn't be interested.'

'Are you ashamed of me? That's all I want to know, old boy. Tell me that and I'll go away and never trouble you again.'

'No, I'm not ashamed of you, Joe,' said Kenneth.

'All right then, why don't you let me meet your parents? Can you tell me that? I've never objected to your meeting mine, have I? You've never even asked, which shows how much you care. You may not know it, but I'm just as high-class as you are, you know; I'm not out of my depth in high society, if that's what you think. In my business you have to be able to mix with all classes on terms of absolute equality, as you should know by now.'

'What is your business, Joe?'

'Oh, wouldn't you like to know,' said Farratoga triumphantly. 'That's just you all over, always wanting, never giving. I suppose you think I'm not good enough to meet your parents, is that it?'

Kenneth had avoided introducing Farratoga to his parents, partly because, as he said, he did not look the sort of friend they would like him to have, and partly because in the course of his conversation he had perhaps tended to exaggerate a little the opulence and importance of a Senior Consultant Dentist. Besides, he had never introduced any outsider into the close circle of his family, and Joseba, with his squat, swarthy body, spotted face and enormous sideburns would look most incongruous in the dentist's waiting-room atmosphere of their drawing-room.

Joseba was looking particularly criminal and strange that night, as they got off the bus at Wimbledon Common and Kenneth led him to the large modern block of flats where he now lived. He was wearing a heavy navy blue jersey with a polo neck which his brown hands with their dirty, bitten fingernails constantly touched and adjusted. His tight black jeans suddenly sprouted at the bottom into enormous black rubber-soled suède shoes. They were both slightly drunk, and curiously elated at the thought of a possible row.

'Hullo, Ken, is that you?' called his mother as she heard the door of the hall open and shut. She was always slightly nervous of burglars.

'Yes, Mum,' called out Kenneth, 'and I've brought a visitor to see you.'

Poor Mrs Stoat started pulling hair curlers out of her hair at a tremendous speed, and tidying up the newspapers on the table, and searching for her slippers. When they came in she was on all fours, peering, short-sightedly, at the carpet, with one slipper held firmly in her mouth.

'Oh dear, oh dear,' she said, getting to her feet and nervously pulling at her blouse. 'You should have warned me, Ken, that we were going to be entertaining people. How do you do?' she peered hard at Joseba, who stared back aggressively.

'This is Joseba dà Farratoga,' said Kenneth.

'Pleased to meet you,' said Mrs Stoat formally, although she was plainly uneasy. 'You'ld be a foreigner, I expect.'

'No,' said Joseba vehemently. 'Actually I'm not.'

'Oh well,' said Mrs Stoat unhappily, 'you can never tell nowadays, can you?'

'Joseba was at Bloxham, Mummy,' said Kenneth tactfully.

'Where's that?' asked his mother, trying hard to appear interested.

'Oh, for Christ's sake,' said Joseba, and sat down, yawning elaborately, in Mrs Stoat's own armchair.

After that conversation rather dwindled. Kenneth had a feeling that his friend had not made an entirely favourable impression, and wondered what on earth they were going to do to entertain him. Dr Stoat, with all the massive obstinacy of the middle class, had refused even to consider buying a television set, although Mrs Stoat had often begged for one to while away the long hours when she was alone in the house.

'Would you like to listen to the wireless?' asked Kenneth.

'No, thank you,' said Joseba politely.

'I expect you boys would like something to drink,' said Mrs Stoat eventually, with a significant glance at her son. 'I believe there's a little beer in the fridge if you go and look, Kenneth.'

'Actually, if it's all the same to you, I think I would rather have a little drop of whisky,' said Joseba.

Mrs Stoat felt very much alarmed. Normally she would not think of giving Kenneth whisky, but she supposed that now he was seventeen she was just being old-fashioned, and she wouldn't like to show him up in front of his new friend, and there was a bottle of whisky in the house which Dr Stoat kept for any of his friends from the hospital who might drop in, although none of them ever did.

'Of course, if that's what you prefer,' she said, and Kenneth felt that it had been worthwhile bringing his friend home after all. He had unwittingly won a major battle for Kenneth, simply by his casual *savoir-faire* which Stoat would have given his soul to have possessed.

Mrs Stoat removed the bottle from its secret hiding-place where it was kept to spare the charwoman any temptation, and put it on the table, rather as if she were handling an unexploded bomb which had started to feel warm.

'Well, I'll be going to bed now, and leave you two boys

to enjoy yourselves. When your father comes in remember to tell him to leave the keys on the hall table. Good night, Ken. Remember to turn the lights off if you're last up. Good night, Mr Perritogo, it was so nice to have met you.'

She clutched her shawl tightly around her shoulders, and walked in her slow, bent way to the door.

'Farratoga,' shouted Joseba after her, just before the door closed.

'Well this is a bit better,' said Joseba when they were alone together; 'I don't mind telling you I thought it a bit of a crummy joint at first, but your mother certainly believes in giving her guests enough to drink.'

Kenneth did not dare to say that he did not think she had meant them to drink all the whisky; instead he accepted the brimming sherry glass which Farratoga handed him with a flourish. He did not much like whisky, but he felt that the occasion demanded a little celebration.

When Dr Stoat returned from a hard day at the hospital, he was surprised to find the light still on in the drawing-room. To an outsider there is always something unpleasant about the sight of hopelessly drunk boys of seventeen. Drink never seems to bring out what is best in them at that age, and there is no doubt that by eleven o'clock both Kenneth and Joseba were feeling a little above themselves.

'Hullo, Dad,' called Kenneth excitedly, 'come in and meet Joe. Joseba dà Farratoga, this is my father.'

'So this is the old man, is it, Kenny?' said Joseba, surveying him critically. 'Well, I'm pleased to meet you, old boy, if only for Kenny's sake. Kenny's my best friend and I don't want to hear anything against him from anybody, see? That's the way I feel about Kenny.'

'Thanks, Joe,' said Stoat, but a tiny grain of common sense still active in his fuddled brain made him wonder if Joe had struck the right note.

'How do you do?' said Dr Stoat coldly; 'I don't think we've ever met before, Mr. . . .'

'Farratoga,' said Joe.

'Oh yes. Are you in this country for long?' The dentist's expression seemed to convey a definite hope that he was not, and that, as Joe explained later, got him narked.

'I live here and I'm not a foreigner,' he said rudely.

'Joseba was at Bloxham, Dad,' explained Kenneth patiently.

'Oh really,' said Dr Stoat. 'Of course, that makes a lot of difference.'

'Now look here, old boy,' said Joseba, getting nasty. 'You think I'm a foreigner, don't you? Well, you might like to know that my mother was English and my father was English and if I have any kids they will be just as English as you are, only not half so crummy, and they won't go round being sarcastic to people they've invited into their houses for a drink. I know when I'm not wanted, Mr Dentist, which is more than some people round here seem to, and I wouldn't stay in this lousy joint another minute if I was paid. Good-night, Mr Dentist, I hope the bugs don't bite.'

And with that insidious Parthian shot he picked up the whisky bottle, tucked it under his arm, and strode purposefully for the door.

When he was gone Dr Stoat turned angrily to his son. It was the first time Kenneth had seen him really angry. Normally the two managed to keep a veneer of politeness over the boredom they felt in each other's company, had they been fonder of each other they would no doubt have had more rows.

'Who the bloody hell was that?' he asked.

'He is a friend of mine, called Joseba dà Farratoga,' said Kenneth steadily, determined, in his drunkenness, not to be browbeaten nor to lose face over what he regarded as a matter of principle.

84

'And who said you could ask him in here?' said the dentist, spitting in his rage.

'Nobody said I couldn't. Most people are allowed to ask their friends home occasionally, and this is the first time I have inflicted one on you. I don't see what you've got to complain about.'

'Who said you could drink the whisky?'

'Mummy did.'

'I don't believe you.'

'I don't care whether you believe me or not. You can ask her if you really want to.'

Kenneth's self-confidence was returning fast. After all it was not his fault Joseba had been a bit rude to his father, and he had rather asked for it anyway.

'Go to your bedroom. I will speak to you in the morning.' Dr Stoat thought he had handled the situation fairly well, as he watched Kenneth slouch off after a grudging 'Oh, all right.' It was obviously time he gave some thought to his son's future. He thought that a few years in the army would do him the world of good.

Kenneth thought how pathetically unsure of himself his father looked standing alone in the drawing-room trying to appear Victorian and strict. It was not as if his father had any sanction he could apply. It was not like Cleeve where they could beat you into a jelly, and Kenneth reckoned he was slightly stronger than his father. Of course, he could stop his pocket money, but then, thought Kenneth, I'ld just clear out and go and live with Joe in his lodgings, and we'd both get by for money somehow.

As he lay in bed he prepared speeches to make to his father in the morning; jewels of sarcasm and wit came into his mind, and every possible point his father could make was anticipated, and a devastating reply contrived. Eventually a witticism so bold and yet so exactly on the target came into

85

his head that he switched on his bedside light and wrote it down in Biro on the back of his hand. Then he switched off the light and composed himself to sleep. But sleep would not come so easily that night, and it was nearly three o-clock before his grey, froglike eyelids closed, and he dreamed that he was back at Cleeve and Foxglove was his friend again, and everybody bowed deeply as they passed and Sligger Two knelt in front of him and asked for his blessing, and Lady Foxglove smiled and said: 'Oh, Stoat, how lovely you're looking.'

When he woke up he had a nasty taste in his mouth, and his stomach felt slightly queasy. As he washed he found that he had written indelibly on the back on his hand the words *Buggers don't bite*. He could not think what it meant, although he remembered that it had seemed frightfully important at the time.

After breakfast his father said in a forgiving tone: 'Well, Ken, my boy, I don't expect you're feeling too good this morning, are you? I expect you feel thoroughly ashamed of yourself and wish you'd never been born.'

'Who, me? Why?' said Kenneth.

'Come off it, old lad. After all, I was a boy once myself, although you'ld never believe it. I don't mind admitting that perhaps I haven't paid as much attention to you as I should have done, and not all boys find it as easy as all that to get on with their fathers, so let's make a little pact, shall we?'

'Oh hell,' said Kenneth in disgust. 'You think I hate you just to give yourself an excuse to justify the boredom you feel in my company.'

'Shut up, Kenneth,' said his father with quiet dignity, while his mind tried to sort out what Kenneth had been trying to say. 'Nobody used the word "hate".'

'Well I do,' shouted Kenneth, furious at being treated with quiet dignity, and shouting to prevent himself bursting into tears. 'I don't expect you've ever hated anybody in your life. You are incapable of love or hate or anger or joy. I may not be able to love, but at least I can hate, I may not know joy, but by God I know misery, and I'ld sooner be myself than you any day. I may be nasty but I'm bloody well right, and you're as wrong as sin and as stupid as your own boredom.'

He was not quite sure what he was saying, but it sounded good, and the important thing was to keep talking.

Dr Stoat had rallied his forces:

'I think you borrowed that from somewhere,' he said, but the contempt in his eyes was something that Kenneth tried for a long time to forget. 'So we have an angry young man in the house, have we? Just because he picked up some shit from the streets and made a fool of himself. You make me sick, sometimes, Kenneth. I shall see you this evening.'

Kenneth had made another of his mistakes. His father was not a vindictive man, and was always immensely kind to people who were at his mercy, but he very much objected to being ranted at like a character in one of the new proletarian plays which were so fashionable at the moment. It showed the infringement of the new brutalist world on his own private life, and he minded the thought that his own household should be judged and criticized by the standards of the new world culture of the common man. He was not violent in his political opinions, but he liked to keep his privacy, with its fond memories of better days and its gentle despair for the future, and at that moment he came nearer to hating his son than ever before.

But when he reached the hospital there were two new cases needing attention, and his junior registrar announced that he wanted to get married, and the smaller problems of his home life dwindled to insignificance as his deft fingers moved over the trays of shining, sterile instruments, and his cosmos was once more contained in the scarlet cavernous interior of a mouth with the powerful lights of his equipment shining on rows of teeth, each one of which was known to him by a nick-name.

Kenneth, left to himself in Wimbledon, felt miserable and ashamed, and knowledge of his own shame and impotence only made him angrier than before. He was angry with himself for having been worsted in a fight for which he had unconsciously been preparing all his life, angry that he had not been able to say all the things he could have said, and furious that he had unconsciously copied a speech he had heard somewhere else, and had been discovered. But the target for his rage was his father, and Kenneth was unable to think of any way in which to hurt him. He could always commit suicide and leave a note denouncing him, but even as Stoat thought of it he realized instinctively that there were some limits even to his wrath. Eventually he telephoned Farratoga at his Elephant and Castle lodging house. A woman's voice answered the telephone.

'No, I'm afraid there's nobody here of that name. What was it, Furrotogo? No, I am sorry. We don't take foreigners in here, anyway.'

Farratoga's voice broke in :

'Hullo, who is it?'

'It's me, Kenneth Stoat.'

'What do you want? You should not have telephoned me here.'

'Look, Joe, there's been a bit of a bust-up, here.'

'You don't say, old boy?'

'Look, Joe, you must take me seriously. I've got to get out of here, and I wondered if I could come down to your lodgings, and we could talk about it there. I could move in with you, and we'd manage somehow.'

'I'm sorry, old boy, but that's quite impossible. I wish you could, but it's out of the question, I'm afraid, so there it is. I wish I could do something for you. If I were you I'd make it up again.'

'Look, Joe, you must help me. It's all because of you I'm in this mess.'

'Now don't let's start casting aspersions,' said Farratoga threateningly. 'I didn't order you to get yourself in a mix-up, did I? You've only got yourself to blame.'

The woman's voice broke in again.

'You shut up, Joe. Yes, Mr Stoat, I think we can fix you up with a bed, if you don't mind sharing. It will cost you, mind, but I don't expect that means much to you, does it? I expect you've got tons of money to throw around, haven't you?'

Kenneth heard a violent altercation going on at the other end, and then the voice spoke again, this time more formally and with a note of reserve.

'We've got one bed you can have for thirteen and six a night, breakfast included, money to be paid in advance. You can take it or leave it.'

'But I haven't got that much money, I'm afraid,' said Kenneth desperately.

'How much have you got then?' inquired the voice, interested.

'I've only got two pounds ten a week, and even then I would have no money to eat.'

'Well, seeing as you're a friend of Joe's, we'll let you have the bed for that, only of course you won't want any breakfast in the mornings, and I don't expect you're over-fussy about sheets.'

'Oh no,' said Stoat gratefully. 'I'm not over-fussy about sheets.'

He went up to his bedroom, and started collecting the few pitiful objects he treasured as souvenirs of some earlier enthusiasms of his ill-favoured career. The collection of birds' eggs; an embryo collection of foreign coins which he had started many years ago, and retained under the vague theory that they would get more valuable as they got older; his stuffed frog; a sword; a gall-stone which had once been his most precious possession, and which Pyke claimed had been removed from the bladder of his Uncle Matthew, a famous explorer; a Penguin edition of the poems of Gerard Manley Hopkins; a silver hip-flask which he had appropriated from the attic, and which he now considered his own; a glass eye which he had removed from one of the stuffed rhinoceros at Cleeve (Martin had the other); a Victorian silver pen-holder and a pair of dental forceps which his father had once given him.

All these he packed into the battered cardboard suitcase on which he had so often sat on the platform at Cleeve station. He had a hundred pounds in war savings, and as an advance on that he collected the fifteen pounds in his mother's writing desk, meticulously leaving a note to that effect.

Then he sat down and wrote a letter.

Dear Mum and Dad
I have decided no longer to embarass you with my unwelcome presence in your house, which I had formerly thought to have been my home, but I now discover is not. If you have any communications, send them c/o William O'Connor Esqre, Abbey School of St Alexander the Lesser, Cleeve, Nr Washford.
Your dutiful son,
KENNETH STOAT.

It was not until two days later that he realized that he had misspelled the word 'embarrass', but at the time he thought that the letter was a monument of quiet dignity and unspoken rebuke. Then he wrote to O'Connor explaining the position, and giving his new Elephant and Castle address. Finally he put on his mackintosh and suitcase in hand, walked slowly to the bus stop, a solitary, unlovely figure, or so he felt, but with the future before him and the past behind.

When the letter reached O'Connor it found him distracted by his own problems. There had been a mass desertion from Brother Augustine's Poetry Circle a week before, when in answer to a fairly sensible question from O'Connor on *Can Satire ever be High Art?* Brother Augustine had launched himself into a long lecture on his own special subject, the Isness business. The members had become rather uneasy, suspecting that some sort of religious propaganda was being sold to them on the sly, and O'Connor had shrewdly asked: 'But, Sir, aren't you being rather partisan?'

Brother Augustine's answer had been so violent that it could only be interpreted as an intentional insult to O'Connor's intellect, and he had been left no choice but to resign from the Circle and join the Cabala at once, and most of the Circle had followed.

A week later, after various revolting initiation ceremonies had been devised by those who were already members to welcome the great rush of neophytes, it was planned that their first Black Mass should be held in the Classics Library at midnight.

There were about twelve people present in all, acolytes, neophytes, and the two ipsimi, Pyke and Pratt-Bingham. Pratt-Bingham, as Primus Magister Ordinis wore a pillow-case over his head in addition to the sheet which marked the fully-fledged Magus Sinister. It had been impossible to procure a baby for the ceremony, and O'Connor's attempts to secure the ginger kitchen cat which normally belonged to Brother Aloysius had resulted in some nasty scratches to his left arm. Eventually a white rat had been stolen from the biology laboratories, but just when they were settling down to discuss the details of the ceremony, Fitzgerald One said he was not going to be a party to any cruelty to animals, and that it would have to be humanely killed, but when they were trying to do this it escaped, and so it was eventually decided that perhaps after all a sacrifice was not really necessary. Such petty impediments are always to be found in the path of seekers after Truth; and anyway Pyke had read somewhere that Dr John Dee had been able to conjure up the devil just by shutting his eyes and saying the Lord's Prayer backwards.

Ipsimus Pratt-Bingham had arranged the programme, and after a Diabolical Dance of which he was the choreographer and in which a library chair was accidentally broken, they all sat down in a ring and joined hands and started to recite the Lord's Prayer backwards, but all they were able to conjure up was Brother Jeremy Price who marched in looking rather old-fashioned and took all their names and said they would hear more of the matter in the morning.

As six of the twelve present were monitors, O'Connor should have felt protected from the worst consequences of this development, but somehow he felt uneasy as he lay in bed that night, not knowing for sure how serious an offence it was likely to be considered at Cleeve to have been found worshipping the Devil.

The authorities decided to be lenient. It was obvious that the whole thing was the work of one of them who had corrupted the others; as Brother Jeremy said, when they were assembled in his study after breakfast:

'If you put one rotten apple in a tray of good ones, quite soon all the apples around it will become rotten, and if you are not careful in time the entire tray is a mass of putrefaction.'

Brother Jeremy did not have far to look for the initial rotten apple. At that moment there was a slip on his desk from Brother Augustine in which he mentioned that O'Connor had seriously contested the doctrine of Prime Existence in public and had even tried to bring the rest of the Poetry Circle round to his view. This Brother Augustine followed up vindictively with an account of how O'Connor had always been a corrupting influence, and that it was only in the hope of making him sensible to the error of his ways that he had been admitted to the Poetry Circle at all, but that his ingratitude had been such that he had even tried to corrupt that, although even Brother Augustine had not been able to guess the extent of corruption which he had achieved.

'It is not that most of you are fundamentally evil. You are just weak,' he continued, staring hard at O'Connor. 'You allow yourselves to be led by somebody just because he had the loudest voice and throws his weight around most. I am often amazed that sensible people like you, Pratt-Bingham, or you, Pyke, allow yourselves to be bossed around so easily. Can't you see how utterly rotten and good for nothing your so-called leader really is? Can't you pluck up courage to stand up to him and say "You keep your filth to yourself and don't try contaminating others or you'll find you get a bloody nose pretty quick"? That is the way to treat that sort of thing. Wash his mouth out with soap and water, if necessary. I'll back you up. Well, Pratt-Bingham, what have you got to say?'

Pratt-Bingham stared at Brother Jeremy with sorrow and eager repentance all over his honest, simple face.

'Yes, Sir, I can see now that we have been very weak and very foolish,' he said frankly, 'and I'm very sorry to have let you down so badly, Sir. But I'm sure I speak for us all when I say that we won't let ourselves be led astray again so easily, and we'll jolly well stand up for ourselves next time.'

Insofar as anybody could ever be said to be a friend of Brother Jeremy, Pratt-Bingham was a friend. It was a position he had inherited with his captaincy of games, and although Brother Jeremy never exactly let his hair down, it was his custom to treat each captain of games with a certain rough familiarity which nobody else in the school ever enjoyed. He was noticeably moved by the captain's reaffirmation of loyalty.

'Very well then, we'll say no more about it. I don't want

93

any of you to mention what has occurred to anybody, and I would rather you did not even discuss it among yourselves. For my part I can promise you the whole thing is forgotten from this moment. The rest of you can go, I want O'Connor to stay behind.'

The others shuffled out, avoiding O'Connor's eye as they passed.

'I wonder what will happen to O'Connor?' said Pyke. 'One can't help feeling sorry for him, although he did rather ask for it.'

'Well, Brother Jeremy's quite right, really,' said Pratt-Bingham sanctimoniously, 'I think we were all a bit silly to be taken in by him, don't you, Rigid?'

'As one makes one's bed, so must one lie in it,' said Pyke sententiously. 'I wonder what happened to the white rat?'

'You know what Brother Jeremy said,' warned Pratt-Bingham, and the matter was dropped.

'Have you heard that O'Connor's been sacked?' asked Frazer-Robinson speaking to his best friend Sligger Two later that afternoon.

'No, what had he done?'

'Oh, the usual thing I expect,' said Frazer-Robinson in a grown-up sort of way.

'Oh, how boring,' said Sligger Two, although he had always rather admired O'Connor for his long hair and general air of dissipation.

'Why has O'Connor decided to leave so suddenly?' asked Brother Aloysius during Religious Instruction class that afternoon.

'I forget now,' said Fitzgerald One tactfully from his seat on the front bench.

'Oh I see,' said Brother Aloysius, and his little pig eyes gleamed with prurience. 'I thought something of the sort would happen to him sooner or later.'

'And now that the agnostic element has been removed to spheres in which no doubt its talents will find a more remunerative employment, I shall endeavour to explain what I was saying last time about what I like to call the Essence of Isness,' said Brother Augustine to his Poetry Circle when they were reassembled in the Classics Library that evening. 'What it is that makes a chair a chair and not a table? Obviously it is the chairness of the chair, just as it is the Pykeness of Pyke which makes him Pyke and not me.' There was an obedient titter during the pause which followed this daring sally, but it was obvious that the attention of the Circle was not quite so concentrated as usual on what was being said.

O'Connor felt no grievance as he sat on his suitcase on the platform at Cleeve station, waiting for the train to take him into a new world. After all, he supposed, he had been the leader of the Cabala, on the intellectual level at least, and Brother Jeremy had been right to say that he was like a giant octopus of evil, with poisonous tentacles ever seeking to enmesh some new victim and then digest it into his own rotten body. That was his point of view, anyway, and everybody should be entitled to their own opinion. Personally, he looked upon himself as a rebel, but one to whom at least one should allow a measure of intellectual integrity. Wherever there was an Establishment he would fight it, he vowed, and he must not be too bitter if it occasionally got the better of him.

6

When Dr Stoat had read his son's quiet, dignified letter, he put it in a drawer and said:
    'I thought there was something on the boy's mind last

time I saw him. Oh well, I hope he enjoys himself on the loose for a bit, it should make him a bit more independent, anyway. He'll come back when he gets bored with it all, don't worry.'

But Mrs Stoat was inclined to be tearful about it all.

'You drove him to this, Michael. You should have tried to understand him more, and been kinder to him about his odd ways. Can't you see that he's not like us, he's more sensitive and cleverer, no disrespect to you I'm sure. He might do anything alone by himself. Do write and ask him to come back.'

'He'll come back,' said Dr Stoat, patting his wife's hand paternally, 'you see if he doesn't.'

He addressed an envelope to Kenneth Stoat, c/o William O'Connor Esqre at Cleeve, and enclosed fifteen pound notes without any letter.

When it arrived, it was clearly Brother Jeremy's duty to open it and see what it was all about, and when he found the money his worst fears were realized; clearly it was something very sinister indeed, and he thought the wisest course was to give the money to charity and leave it at that. Never apologize, never explain; Brother Jeremy never heard anything more about the matter, so clearly his course of action had been the right one.

But Mrs Stoat, whose nerves were never very good, went into a decline and took to her bed and after a time her husband could not go into her bedroom without being met by a stream of abuse, and so he stayed away.

When Kenneth arrived at the Elephant and Castle, he was met by Farratoga in his shirt sleeves, looking rather unfriendly.

'Why did you want to come here? I didn't ask you.'

'I told you, Joe, there was a bust-up, and I had to get away,' said Kenneth.

'What've you got in that bag?' he asked suspiciously, but when the contents were spread out he unbent a little and said: 'Not a bad sword, Kenny boy. Should be able to get a couple of quid for that with a bit of luck. What's this?' he asked, holding up Pyke's Uncle Matthew's gall-stone. 'Interesting biological specimen, five shillings,' he said when he was told. He expressed some doubt about the Victorian silver penholder.

'Depends on the mug, see? You'll get some old tart goes all gooey over an article like this, and then you can ask a fiver and she'll think she's got a bargain. But I wouldn't ask more than three and six if I were you, old boy, not until you get the feel of things.'

Kenneth was set to work to get the feel of things next morning. Joseba put him in charge of a barrow in Petticoat Lane on which were laid out all the accumulated treasures of his life, with some oddments which Farratoga mysteriously produced and put beside them.

'Where did you get those things from, Joe?' Kenneth asked, but Joseba winked and said: 'Ask no questions and you'll be told no lies.' One of the oddments was a heavy silver table lighter, and Kenneth felt slightly homesick when he recognized it as one of a pattern which they had always kept in the drawing-room at Wimbledon. But when he mentioned this to his friend, Joseba just said: 'Now look here, old boy, I said ask no questions, didn't I? If you ask me, you're a bit too nosey to be much good at this job.' And after that severe rebuke Kenneth kept rather quieter and concentrated on the new arts of salesmanship which he was learning under the tutorship of Farratoga. Quite soon he settled into the pattern of life of street-vendors. Most of his business was conducted with fellow-dealers, who would always be unshaven, and would always have an unlighted cigarette drooping from the corner of a yellow mouth.

97

'How much are you asking for this fancy cigarette lighter, mate?'

'Fifty bob. It's pure silver, you can look.'

'Blimey, you got a nerve. Fifty bloody bob for this. Pretty good shit, isn't it? I could sell you ten models like this for half that price.'

'Go on then.'

'Funny guy, ain't you? Look, I'll give you ten bob and we'll call it a deal, right?'

'No, I couldn't sell it for less than fifty bob, I'm afraid, or I'd be making a loss.'

'Coo, lah di dah, ain't you? All right, seeing as I've taken rather a fancy to you, I'll make it twelve and six. There's friendship for you; you'd better snap it up quick before I change my mind, because I don't often feel generous like this. Twelve and a tanner, is it done?'

'Look, mister, I told you this article goes for fifty shillings; two pounds ten bob, see? You're wasting your time if you think you can get it for under two quid, because you can't. It's a very nice piece, this, and would pass for new practically anywhere. Now what about trying something sensible like thirty-five bob?'

Eventually the lighter fetched sixteen shillings which was a shilling up on the price Joseba had fixed, and Kenneth felt he had done very well.

One day a rather prim little voice asked from the other side of the barrow:

'Can you tell me, please, have you got any Roman coins, ancient Egyptian scarabs, but they must be genuine and I can tell, old English pewter mugs with glass bottoms or nineteenth-century mourning rings, not too expensive?'

'No,' said Kenneth without looking up. 'Interesting biological specimen five shillings; curious example of the taxidermists' art, seven and six. Rare birds' eggs, a bob each.'

'Oh, hullo, Stoat,' said the voice. It was Fitzgerald Two,

looking very public-school in a new brown sports jacket and neatly pressed grey flannel trousers.

'Hullo,' said Stoat. Fitzgerald felt extremely embarrassed, and did not know at all how to extricate himself from the situation.

'I was looking for Roman coins and things for my collection,' he mumbled, avoiding Stoat's eye and fidgeting with the wares on the barrow.

'So I guessed,' said Stoat, unhelpfully.

Fitzgerald thought he saw a way out of his difficulty.

'These eggs look rather interesting,' he said brightly, clinking silver coins in his pocket, 'how much did you say they were?'

'That one's three and six. An exceptionally rare specimen.'

'Oh dear, I thought it looked just like an ordinary blackbird's egg.'

'That's what most people think who don't know,' said Stoat contemptuously.

'What about this one?' asked Fitzgerald, fingering an egg which could surely be nothing but a wood pigeon's, and cracked at that.

'Only one of its kind in private ownership, fifteen shillings,' said Stoat glibly, determined not to let him get away so easily.

'Well, which are the ones which are going for a shilling each?' asked Fitzgerald in despair.

'Well now I come to look I see they've all been sold,' said Stoat condescendingly; he pointed to one which seemed slightly larger than the rest. 'There's a real bargain at seven pounds ten; last time one of those came on the market it fetched forty pounds at Sotheby's and that was eleven years ago.'

'But I haven't got seven pounds, and it looks to me just like a jackdaw's egg.'

'Ah,' said Stoat, 'but a white jackdaw, you see.'

'Give me the one for three and six,' said Fitzgerald, and Stoat said:

'Thanks a lot, old boy,' as he collected the money. He was picking up the Farratoga manner quite fast. As soon as the coins were in his pocket, he shouted: 'I hope you've stopped wetting your bed by now,' and felt very jubilant.

Joseba would appear from time to time with mysterious bundles; a bunch of keys, an old leather notecase, a length of copper piping, two ash-trays with the stamp of the Hyde Park Hotel, a collection of magazines with the stamp of the House of Commons Reading Room, a wedding ring, a broken toy wristwatch, and on one memorable occasion a suitcase in which were packed two pairs of pyjamas, a sponge bag, an electrical shaving machine, a rather moth-eaten woollen dressing-gown, a worn hairbrush and half a bottle of Vaseline Hair Tonic. Kenneth dishonestly retained the hair oil for his own use. Always Joseba would fix the price of each article and Kenneth was allowed to keep a quarter of the fixed price, and anything above that he could get. The explanation of each bundle was always the same: 'Ask no questions, and you'll be told no lies.' After a time he ceased to worry.

During the summer months he spent so pleasantly at his new employment, he had no contact with Cleeve at all. He read in the newspapers of the death of Martin's father, Sir Derek Foxglove, whom he had never met, and wrote an awkward, self-conscious letter of condolence to Martin, but putting no address on the top of the writing paper. O'Connor tried to get in touch with him just after his expulsion by telephoning to his Elephant and Castle address, but a woman's voice told him that there was nobody there called Stoat, and never had been, and she thought that he must have got the wrong number and what did he want to talk to

Mr Stoat for anyway? So O'Connor gave it up, and it did not occur to him to write.

O'Connor's parents lived separately, but Mrs O'Connor's former housekeeper, Miss Fanny Wrote, was the go-between, and in face of the crisis precipitated by their son's expulsion they presented a united front. O'Connor, to purge his soul, must join the Army, and Major O'Connor had interviewed the Colonel of the Pigs to see if he could get his son a place in the Officer Training Squad which was to be formed at the Lancashire depot of the Pigs in August.

Everybody in England had heard of the famous regiment which, although only formed after the war, had a reputation for toughness and stern traditions which had caught the popular fancy. It was an airborne body which had already proved its worth in Korea and at Suez, and was generally considered to be something between the United States Marines and the Brigade of Guards. It regarded itself as the crack regiment of the British Army, and the British public which was constantly allowed to watch it at drill, at training and relaxing in canteens on its television screens (for there was none of the undemocratic aloofness about the Pigs which made other, longer established regiments so unpopular) adopted it as its own special baby. The newspapers nicknamed this splendid body of men 'The Terror from the Sky', or 'The Flying Fighters' or, when a story of human interest was needed, 'The Para-Boys'.

The only place to which the attention of the British public was seldom directed was the regimental depot at Dunks, in Lancashire. It was here that the Boys from Home were moulded, both mentally and physically, into the standard British Pig, the very mention of whose name was said to make distant sheikhs and rebellious tribesmen in savage areas of the Empire drop their weapons and chew khat with a renewed vigour.

Occasional rumours emerged from Dunks of atrocities,

mutinies, reprisals, suicides, but most people believed that they were the inventions of Left-Wing politicians, and those who did not usually winked at each other and said 'What the eye does not see', in a knowing sort of way. In fact the rumours were absurdly exaggerated, but it was undoubtedly true that the metamorphosis from modern schoolboy to fully trained Pig was not always painless or easy. For this reason the other ranks of the Pigs were mostly recruited from the criminal and the stupid, who often made, paradoxically enough, the most splendid N.C.O.s.

When O'Connor heard his fate he was astounded. His parents seemed to have no respect for his intellect at all, let alone for his artistic temperament. He had seen films on the television of the Pigs playing water polo together, and the thought that he might have to splash around shouting and throwing balls was more repugnant to him even than the occasional wild tales he heard of the brutality which occurred to people like himself, who were by nature egregious and sensitive. To these he could give no credence, but he had only a very shadowy idea indeed of what would be expected of him. They would have to make him an officer, of course, but he had heard that the officers in the Pigs were of the new type, whose commissions were earned by some kind of competitive examination, in which intellect played only a very small part, and he feared that he would not find his brother officers at all congenial.

His father, who was a newspaper editor and not really a bluff military character at all, but who liked to play the part of one from time to time, said:

'The Army is going to make a lot of difference to you, William, and I don't mind telling you I think it will improve you out of all recognition. You will meet a lot of first-rate chaps, and you'll be on your own with them, so you can sink or swim by your own efforts. My advice to you is don't try to kick against the prick; it won't work anywhere, but least of all in the Army. You will get two hundred a year from me until you get your commission, and then you can expect another six hundred. If you need more, don't be frightened to ask for it. Well, good-bye and good luck, I shall not see you until your first forty-eighter, when I expect there'll be quite a difference already.'

O'Connor felt sick with fright as he received his sinister little envelope telling him to report at the Guardroom of the Special Airborne Commando Regiment depot at Dunks, in Lancashire, not later than eleven hundred hours on Tuesday, August the twenty-first. He wrote an almost nihilistic poem about it in free verse entitled 'Oblivion and After' and posted it derisively to Brother Augustine, but received no acknowledgement.

7

At Bidcome, Lady Foxglove's courage in the face of her undeserved affliction won her praise from every side. She went her way as before, doing good wherever she could, always ready with guidance and advice, looking incredibly lovely in black lace, and with the sweetest, saddest smile whenever anybody mentioned her husband. Sir Derek's death had come as a shock to his many friends and colleagues all over the world, and at his funeral the entire medical world had assembled to see his beautiful widow, stricken by sorrow, but with a brave smile for all, follow the husband she had loved to his last resting-place.

The official biography was going to be written by a young man who had offered himself for the job, explaining that he had formerly been an assistant to Sir Derek at the Royal Bermondsey Hospital but had lately given up his career in medicine to pursue a literary one. He seemed a civil enough young man, and had known Brother Thomas Plunkett when he was a patient. Lady Foxglove had been very much interested, although of course not surprised to hear that Brother Thomas had been a most difficult patient, and had not made things any easier for his medical advisers by complaining about conditions at the Royal Bermondsey and skylarking off to some other hospital in Paddington, and then complaining about conditions there and expecting to be greeted back into the Bermondsey like a conquering hero.

'Poor Mr Dooney,' said Lady Foxglove sympathetically. 'Of course at that age the old men do get a little difficult, but I really think Brother Thomas *was* a little spoiled, and if people had not let him have his own way so much, he would not have been so disagreeable in his last days.'

He was really a most sensible young man, decided Lady Foxglove as she sat on the lawn at Bidcombe sipping a little aperitif of Lourdes water and orange juice (she felt she needed a little something these days to keep her going). There were things he told her which he assured her he would never be able to tell anyone else. He was a monument of professional reticence, and it was quite obvious that his life of Sir Derek would be most suitable in every way.

Mr Dooney was staying at Bidcombe in the room which had been Sir Derek's, so that he could go through Sir Derek's papers and consult with Lady Foxglove on broad matters of policy, although she had told him that she really had complete confidence in his tact and good taste. He worked quite hard, for now that he was a married man he had his living to earn, and with his wife (whom he still thought of as Herring, or in moments of stress, That Perishing Kipper) expecting a baby, it was obvious that the couple would be in need of the money quite soon.

Sir Derek's papers were arranged into little piles of Personal Surgical (Thoracic), Surgical (Early), Career (Surgical), Career (Military) and finally Juvenilia.

It was in this pile, among letters from his parents to

Cleeve, his school reports, a fading Certificate of Education in French, Latin and Elementary Mathematics, a photograph of the Junior Colts hockey team in which Foxglove, D. was for some reason conspicuous by his absence, and a geography notebook which was decorated by the most comical drawings, that Mr Dooney put a strange piece of paper he found at the very bottom of Sir Derek's old school trunk in which these documents had been stored. It was written in pencil, and the middle passages were undecipherable, but it was headed quite clearly:

TO DEREK FOXGLOVE, THE ONLIE BEGETTER OF
THESE INSUING LINES ALL HAPPINESSE
AND THAT ETERNITIE PROMISED
BY HIS EVER LOVING FRIEND, THE AUTHOR,
MICHAEL STOAT. Written this day in St Bartholomew's Library, at Cleeve.

It appeared to be some sort of poem, and it ended quite legibly, but, to Mr Dooney, incomprehensibly:

> O blushing flower, within thy velvet Glove
> Thou holds me faster than the Reynard's tooth,
> In silken chains of solitary love,
> 'Though such confinement's sweet enough, forsooth.
> Forgive my boldness, weed on which I dote,
> And in thy sweet forgiveness smile on Stoat.

Later that evening he showed it to Lady Foxglove, who seemed a little perturbed, and said:

'It's probably some childish nonsense, and it certainly is not worth preserving. I think you had better give it to me and I will put it in the waste paper basket.'

To herself she thought, 'Sweet Heavens, to think that I lived with him for so many years and never realized he was like that. What a narrow escape I've had! I must remember to pray especially hard for him tonight and I must see Brother Aloysius about getting some services held for him. One must always hope that he repented in time.'

The scrap of paper explained to her completely everything that had been troubling her mind about Martin's earlier friendship with young Henry Stoat. She had always heard that these things were hereditary, and she thanked the Lord piously for having granted her the perspicacity to prevent history repeating itself in her son's case.

But Mr Dooney was not quite sure that the little scrap of paper was as insignificant as Lady Foxglove thought.

'After all,' he said, 'a true portrait must show the warts and all, mustn't it, or it would hardly be Art.'

'I really must insist that you give me that horrid little piece of paper,' said Lady Foxglove. 'It would really be quite inappropriate to include that sort of rubbish in a serious study of my husband. I almost begin to wonder if you are the best man for the job if you are going to start worrying about trivialities of that sort.'

'No, Lady Foxglove,' said Mr Dooney, 'I would not be doing my duty if I were simply to hand this over to you for destruction. It might be very important, one can never tell.'

'Your duty to whom?' asked Lady Foxglove nastily.

'To the memory of your late husband, and to my calling,' said Mr Dooney stiffly. 'I have put in a lot of work on your husband's papers already, and I could not think of abandoning the book now without adequate remuneration.'

'How much?'

'Two hundred and fifty pounds.'

'That's absurd.'

'Is the memory and the reputation of your husband worth less?'

'So you're trying to blackmail me?'

'Not at all. But I could not think of destroying this important document, which would mean distorting the whole picture of your husband, for a smaller sum. One has one's pride, you know.'

Mr Dooney had not the slightest idea of what the poem

was about; he supposed that to the initiated it implied Another Woman, or something of the sort although he thought he knew the facts of life, and there did not seem anything remotely improper about it to him; although there was always something suggestive about love. Still, he knew when he was on to a good thing.

'I'll ring up the police,' said Lady Foxglove, and then she paused; was it not against the law what she supposed Derek to have done? She clutched her alabaster brow and prayed: 'Sweet Heavens, what have I done to deserve this? Show me where, in my short puny life devoted to the welfare of others, I have trangressed Thy Divine Law, and let me make amends; but do not, I beg, torture one thus, let the memory of my husband, sinful though it was, remain pure in the eyes of the world. Amen.'

She wrote out a cheque for £200, and said: 'Take it or leave it.' Mr Dooney took it, and with a dramatic flourish burnt the offending scrap of paper with his cigarette lighter there and then, and ground the ashes into emerald green of the Manor House lawn.

Lady Foxglove watched him, very much relieved. As she went into the house to telephone her bank to stop the cheque, she was not to know that Mr Dooney, with his usual incompetence, had in fact burnt a page of Sir Derek's geography notes in which he succinctly illustrated the rock strata of the Pennines in a series of neat sketches.

The bank was most disagreeable and unhelpful, and said that they could not take the responsibility of refusing payment on a valid cheque without written authority, and did she realize it was an offence for which she would be answerable in court, so eventually she had had to give in. Two hundred pounds was an enormous amount of money to her at that moment, as Sir Derek's will had been most unsatisfactory. He was not a poor man, and in order to avoid double death duties he had left his capital in trust for his son, with Lady Foxglove to enjoy the interest on it until Martin's twenty-first birthday when he would take possession of both Bidcombe, their London property and the capital, with an injunction binding him to support his mother. She wondered if she could get the executors to recognize it as the payment of one of Sir Derek's debts, but she rather doubted it.

Mr Dooney lost no time in cashing the cheque which Providence had thrust upon him, and told his wife that he had received an advance payment of one hundred pounds from the publishers, of which he very decently intended to allow her seventy-five pounds. Herring gazed admiringly at her husband and said:

'Oh, Ron, I am glad you are doing so well.'

When Martin returned from his last term at Cleeve he noticed something listless about his mother which had never been there before. She took none of her usual relish in visiting the sick and comforting the dying, and two illnesses occurred in the village unheeded. Normally the news that old Mrs Hathaway had upset a kettle of boiling water over her feet would have sent her scurrying down with prayer books, bottles of milk and pots of the celebrated Bidcombe gooseberry jam which traditionally decorated every respectable sick-room for miles around.

Although Martin returned from Cleeve covered with every honour which that august establishment could confer, his academic career had not secured him enough certificates to go to a University, which proved, as Brother Aloysius was not slow to point out, if proof were needed, the unsatisfactoriness of the examination system. After the valedictory oration had been read at school assembly by the senior scholar, the Abbot had presented Martin with the medal of St Alexander and an illuminated address. The Prefect of Studies made a brief speech in Latin in which he civilly described Martin as a *most illustrious candle,* and the Prefect of Discipline had called for three cheers; it was with these still ringing in his ears that Martin returned to face a melancholy home and an uncertain future.

He did not welcome the idea of spending the next few years until his twenty-first birthday at Bidcombe with his mother, who had really become very strange since his father's death. Often when they were alone together in the evenings she would grip his hand and stare into his eyes and generally become embarrassing, saying things like:

'Martin, you are very very precious to me, you know. You are all I have left, and if I thought that anything might happen to you, anything serious I mean, I really think I would have nothing left to live for.'

He missed the authority and importance he had enjoyed at Cleeve, and eventually persuaded his mother to let him join the Army on a three year short-service commission. He did not choose his father's regiment, which he had always thought of as somehow effete, but put himself down for the Airborne Commandos, a rather more dashing unit whose exploits he read about daily in his newspapers. His mother resigned herself bravely to the sacrifice of her son in the cause of her country, for it never occurred to her to doubt that Martin would be killed, and reduced the staff at Bidcombe to meet her own simple needs. Eventually the papers arrived telling him to report at the Guardroom of the Special Airborne Commando Regiment depot at Dunks in Lancashire, not later than eleven hundred hours on Tuesday, August the twenty-first. He regarded the small buff envelope as his liberation, and wrote a rather touching little poem about it in the style of Rupert Brooke which he sent to Brother Aloysius, who preserved it tenderly until the end of his days.

On the platform at Euston he was surprised to meet O'Connor with an enormous suitcase. It was a bit embarrassing for Martin, because before he had been made Head of the School he and O'Connor had been quite friendly, but it had been his duty to warn O'Connor on several occasions, and eventually to ignore him altogether as he rose and O'Connor fell in public esteem. He was not quite sure whether to stand on his former dignity or not, but O'Connor resolved the problem by saying:

'Oh, hullo, Foxglove. What on earth are you doing here; I thought the only trains from here went to Lancashire of all places.'

'Oh, hullo, O'Connor,' said Foxglove. 'I am going to Dunks actually, to join the Army.'

'So am I,' said O'Connor without enthusiasm. 'I expect we'll be in the same squad or whatever they call it.'

'I doubt it, actually,' said Foxglove. 'I'm joining the Pigs you know.' It was inconceivable that the Pigs should have accepted anybody as disreputable as O'Connor.

'So am I,' said O'Connor, 'why don't you have a drink?'

'Well perhaps I will have a drop of Coca-Cola,' said Martin. His mother had insidiously made him sign a pledge before his confirmation when he was too young to know better, and although he had broken it frequently in his irresponsible days before his monitorship, he felt that before O'Connor at least he could keep a front of rectitude.

O'Connor had obviously already had quite a few drinks, and Martin thought that it would be a bad start to his military career if he arrived with his fellow Alexandrian dead drunk on his shoulder, but there seemed nothing he could do about it.

There were several other white-faced young men on the platform, all with large suitcases, and without a word being spoken they all assembled in the same carriage, in mutual recognition of the inevitability of their lot. In the carriage O'Connor entertained them with some rather amusing Irish songs, and a lengthy harangue on the poetry of Yeats, but they seemed to have very little to say for themselves.

At the station they were told that it was three-quarters of a mile to the barracks, and O'Connor and Foxglove seized the only available taxi and felt too embarrassed to offer any of the other young men a lift, so they had to walk. In the taxi O'Connor for the first time felt complete confidence in his powers to cope with the Army, and felt vaguely protective of the stiff form of Foxglove who was obviously scared out of his wits.

'Don't you worry, Foxy,' he said in a sudden immoderate burst of affection, 'I'll look after you.'

'Perhaps now that we have left Cleeve you could call me Martin,' said Foxglove formally. 'What would you like me to call you?'

'Anything you like, old fellow. I'm not sensitive.'

When they arrived at the gates, O'Connor said:

'This is the place, taxi-driver. Could you go through the gates and wait while I make inquiries?'

He approached the sergeant of the guard and said: 'Good morning. I'm Mr O'Connor just arrived, and I wonder if there's anyone in charge here for me to report to?'

The Sergeant saluted and stamped his feet and said: 'Officers Mess is the large yellow building across the square, Sir. Shall I detail a man to look after your luggage?'

'Very civil of you if you would, sergeant, although I don't think I want the Officers' Mess just yet; I'm a new recruit, you see, for the Junior Leaders' Training Squad.'

O'Connor did not quite catch what the sergeant said.

Later that evening they were assembled in the squad hut for their platoon commander's address. He was an unprepossessing little man of about twenty-two, but he seemed quite friendly.

'I've just got a few words to say to you laddies tonight

before you go to bed. I want you to look upon me as your friend from now on; I may have to take steps, just as a father has to punish his kiddies occasionally. I bet all you laddies knows what it feels like to be bent over your Dad's knee for six of the best but you know it does you good. I see one of you has lost his name already, O'Connor?'

'Sir.'

'Quick work, O'Connor. Impersonating an officer, I see. Well, it looks as if you and me are going to see quite a lot of each other in the near future, and remember this that although I don't like it, I can be quite tough too. All right? Some people always seem to forget it. Now I want you crowd to work together as a team, see. Imagine you're one big family and I'm your Dad and between us we're going to be the best family in town, O.K.? It's up to you to see that none of you lag behind. O'Connor's for battalion orders tomorrow morning, the rest of you parade for interviews at eight-thirty. That's all.'

'Squad' shrieked Sergeant Bottle, their platoon sergeant, to whom they had just been introduced. Everybody sat up straight except O'Connor who had been picking his teeth before the explosion and nearly bitten his finger off with fright.

They were all fitted with uniforms, and O'Connor watched Foxglove sourly as he preened himself in front of the looking-glass in his new yellow beret, the hallmark of the Pigs throughout the world, although he had to admit that the uniform became him strangely. Somehow O'Connor never quite looked like a soldier. The clothes knew as soon as he touched them, that it was a poet who was attempting to hide himself behind them, and in their resentment they bulged and creased and the buttons flew off and O'Connor always sewed them on the wrong way round, and boot polish spread itself in gradually increasing patches all over his battle dress and face and finger-nails as he worked through the night in a frenzied attempt to get himself tidy enough for battalion orders in the morning.

The squad had been put under the care of Trained Pig O'Flannel who had befriended O'Connor in his simple Irish way. He was a man of enormous authority, and nobody realized at that time how much his friendship would mean. At eleven o'clock he approached to where O'Connor was still working on his boots in a halo of light while the rest of the squad slept, and said:

'How much do you bet me I can't get those boots spotless in twenty minutes?'

'Five shillings,' said O'Connor.

'And I bet you ten, which makes it fifteen,' said O'Flannel, and on that basis O'Connor no longer worried about his kit.

At battalion orders next morning Sergeant Bottle shouted: 'Prisoner shun by the left quick march left right left right left right mark time halt left turn salute stand still.'

O'Connor's previous experience of drill had all been at Cleeve on Corps days which he usually managed to escape, but he managed to make his movements roughly correspond to the intentions of Sergeant Bottle. The door through which he marched displayed, on a background of yellow and pink stripes:

Lieut-Col. Pyke, Officer Commanding 3rd Special Airborne Commando Regiment (The Pigs) Regimental Depot.

The sergeant of guard who had been so abusive the afternoon before was there already.

Colonel Pyke frowned slightly at the prisoner, and said: 'O'Connor you are charged with impersonating an officer on your first day in the Army. That is a pretty serious charge here, you know. Well, Sergeant Tarre?'

Sergeant Tarre began in a low sing-song reciting what he had obviously rehearsed all morning. 'At 1015 hours on Tuesday, August the twenty-first I was drawing up the guard reports when accused entered and announced himself as 2/Lt O'Connor, newly posted to this depot, and demanded access to the Officers' Mess. On being challenged he admitted that he was a new recruit. I placed him on orders, Sir.'

'Well, O'Connor?'

'Nothing to say, Sir,' said O'Connor, as he had been instructed.

'Did he give any explanation of his behaviour to you, Sergeant Tarre?'

'I believe accused may have been slightly intoxicated, Sir,' said Sergeant Tarre magnanimously.

'Oh, I see,' said Colonel Pyke. 'Well, since you were drunk I shall treat you leniently this time, O'Connor, but don't think you'll be able to get off so lightly another time. Eight days C.B.'

'Prisoner shun, salute up two three down left turn quick march left right left right left right double off and join the rest of the squad outside the platoon office.'

It took O'Connor some time to get used to the new standards of the Pigs, but when he did he found them slightly more congenial than those of Cleeve. To be drunk was a virtue; constantly to be in trouble on major charges of punching an N.C.O., making faces at an officer, intentionally destroying a rifle was also a sign of character and originality, and in the Pigs such activity marked one out for speedy promotion. Constantly to be in trouble on minor charges of dirty boots, unshaven flesh, badly creased trousers was thought ignominious, and it was from such people that the soldier servants were recruited; in the Pigs that was the final punishment. On the whole, O'Connor found he had done something clever and good in impersonating an officer on his first day.

On Sunday morning he had to report for fatigue while the rest of the squad attended church parade, and he was given the job of reporting to Cook-Sergeant Waters at the Commandant's quarters for duties in the pantry. He was given a basin of warm water and a nail-brush and told to scrub the floor. He found a carton of sugar-lumps to eat in one of the cupboards, and a two-year old copy of *The Times* lining one of the drawers, and as there was no one to supervise him he lit a cigarette and settled down to reading *The Times*. Someone came into the pantry suddenly and O'Connor in his panic started scrubbing the sugar-lump he was eating with a terrible concentration, but the person had not seen him and walked instead to the safe and started picking up silver match-holders and sugar-tongs and teaspoons and stuffing them into his pocket guiltily. Eventually O'Connor said:

'Rigid, what on earth are you doing here?' and Pyke gave a little cry of fright and dropped a porridge bowl he had been trying to fit into his waistcoat.

'My God, O'Connor, you've no right to do that suddenly. What are you doing here anyway? I live here, thank you very much.'

'I was scrubbing the floor, if you must know.'

'Why on earth were you doing that?'

'Why shouldn't I, if I want to?'

'All right, go ahead. I don't mind. But don't come jumping out on me yelling like a maniac every few minutes, that's all I ask. I didn't invite you here. I don't go barging into your house uninvited and start scrubbing the floors, do I? Why should you do it to me, that's all I want to know?'

'Oh, for Christ's sake, Rigid, I was only trying to do you a favour. I wasn't to know you would choose this moment to burgle the safe, was I?'

'You could have guessed if you'd used your pea-brain for once,' said Pyke, who refused to be mollified. 'It is the only moment of the week when everybody else is at church. And who said I was burgling the safe, anyway?' He added as an afterthought, 'This is my house. I've got a perfect right to be here and to do what I like without having you poking your nose around.'

They parted on bad terms. When O'Connor told Foxglove that Colonel Pyke was the father of their old friend Rigid, Foxglove said he knew and had just received an invitation from Mrs Pyke to go to tea with them that afternoon.

'Why didn't you tell me that before ?' demanded O'Connor.

'I didn't know you'd be interested,' said Foxglove austerely.

Later that evening a sergeant of Military Police arrived at the Junior Leaders' hut and said that there had been a burglary at the Commandant's quarters and that he had instructions to search Junior Pig O'Connor's kit. Trained Pig O'Flannel stared at O'Connor in undisguised admiration as his neatly folded kit was spread over the floor of the hut and there was no sign of the missing sugar-tongs nor the teaspoons. Everybody knew perfectly well that he was responsible for the theft, but as they had no proof he was allowed to get away with it, and the incident won him great respect from everybody. If he had been discovered with the goods still in his possession he would have been regarded with the greatest contempt, and it would have been felt that he had let down the good name of the regiment, but he had come through the whole matter with great honour.

But while O'Connor advanced in favour and public esteem, Foxglove seemed not to be making the progress one would have expected. The Pigs were always slightly suspicious of his good looks, which were too striking for anything the Army could do to hide them. With his hair grotesquely cropped, and clothed in absurd denims, even with a gas mask, he retained a sort of poise and grace which made a fully trained Pig feel slightly embarrassed to be seen looking at him. The whole matter had been summed up at his platoon officer's interview when he had been asked if he had a girl-friend, and in the abrupt manner of the Pigs, if so whether he had even screwed her. O'Connor had answered 'Yes' without hesitation to both questions, but Foxglove inadvisedly told the truth and said 'No'. The platoon officer, with the wisdom of four years' army experience, had astutely put on his Highly Confidential Report the words: *Query Queer*. There the matter rested.

Eventually the time came round for the squad to go before the Selection Board which was to decide who was suitable to be made an officer. The standards of the Board were slightly gentler than those of the Pigs, but equally strange. O'Connor felt quite at home during the discussion groups and lecturettes and interviews, but the intelligence tests puzzled him.

'Question one,' he read. 'If it takes two men one hour to sing three-quarters of a song, how many men will be needed to sing two songs in two hours?' Obviously, he realized, there was a trick somewhere, but he was too bewildered to bother with it. What sort of song could they possibly be singing which would take so long? He left that question. The next one was shorter: 141839 ** Continue this sequence. The next one was rather disconcerting, too. How many toes have you got? Obviously they meant him to put eight, because the big toes counted as thumbs. Suddenly he began to have terrible doubts which could not be resolved until he had taken his shoes and socks off to see. He had been right all along. He saw everybody else scribbling away, and once again applied his great intellect to the problems on the piece of paper:

Lizard, Hedgehog, Pillow, Motor-bicycle, Lake. Which is the odd man out? Lizard obviously.

He did rather better on the essay question. He wrote a rather neat comparison between Jean-Paul Sartre and the earlier Ezra Pound under the title, 'HOBBIES', and an amusing exposure of Milton under the title, 'My Favourite

Authors'; in 'The Uses of the United Nations' he appealed for a return to more Christian standards, and dismissed modern materialistic trends as self-destroying of their very nature. He even used the word *Isness* to illustrate a point, which showed how the Army had changed him.

Foxglove gave his lecturette on a holiday on safari in Kenya. O'Connor gave his on 'Some Trends in Modern Poetry', in which he rather daringly dismissed the neo-realists as introverted escapists, a point which he was glad to see the captain who was listening to the lecturettes took down.

It was in the discussion groups which he really excelled. The subjects chosen were always controversial and usually embarrassing. 'Should the Queen be Deposed?' 'Is Homosexuality Desirable?' The only topic which was banned was 'Capital Punishment'. O'Connor showed great initiative and always took the side which was least expected.

Foxglove said: 'No, I don't think the Queen should be deposed. I think she does a jolly useful job which most people would not do half so well.'

O'Connor discoursed on the anomaly of a monarch inside a progressive democracy, illustrating his arguments with quotations from Hobbes, Jefferson, Muggeridge and Beloff, and ended by saying that for the monarchy's own good it should be abolished.

Foxglove said: 'I think homosexuals should be put in prison,' but O'Connor refuted all his arguments quite conclusively.

The decision of the Board was announced on little slips of paper handed to each candidate on which was typed the legend: You have been recommended for Officer Training/You have not been recommended for Officer Training. Whichever message was not applicable was crossed out. O'Connor was slightly amused to see that in his case there had been some stupid clerical error and they had crossed out the wrong one, and although he was irritated by Foxglove's loud expressions of jubilation it was with a forgiving heart that he strode over to the President of the Board's office to explain the mistake.

The President, a colonel in the Service Corps, looked up as O'Connor came in, and said: 'You want to know why we failed you, I suppose? I am afraid that I can say no more than that in the opinion of the Board you did not show the qualities which we consider desirable for an officer in the modern army. We have recommended you for a Corporals' Cadre with a view to completing your service as a clerk. If I were you,' he added kindly, 'I should apply for a transfer to the Pay Corps or the Educational boys.'

For O'Connor it was a Moment of Truth. Not so for Foxglove, who obviously had shown the qualities which were considered desirable for an officer in the modern army. It never occurred to O'Connor, even in the depths of despair to which he sank, that it was anything but the modern army's defective standards which was responsible for his downfall, just as it never occurred to Foxglove that it was anything but his own charm which had won him the day. He almost felt sorry for O'Connor who looked so wretched that normally Martin would have found a kind word to cheer him up, but he remembered that before long he might find himself in the position of being O'Connor's platoon officer, and if he allowed him too much familiarity now it would be very awkward having to take his name for dirty boots later on. Martin had learned his lesson at Cleeve; and in any case, one could see it coming to O'Connor a mile off, and he had only himself to blame. He would have to suggest to O'Connor before long that it would be better if he stopped calling him by his christian name, which was going to be difficult.

But O'Connor's spirits were constitutionally buoyant, and after a few drinks in the station buffet the whole thing seemed quite simple; he would get his father to buy him out. On the way back to Dunks in the train he entertained the party with a few haunting, nostalgic Irish ballads, but for some reason Foxglove and the other successful candidates chose to sit in another compartment, and the other failures just sat moping in silence, so after a time even O'Connor began to feel depressed. When the train eventually reached Dunks his melancholy was as deep as it had been in the first few moments after he had heard the news of his failure. He supposed that he would have to go on his knees before his father and kiss his feet, and a new resolution formed in his mind.

That night when the rest of the squad was asleep O'Connor quietly dressed, putting socks over his boots, and gently shook Foxglove awake. The whole thing was rather reminiscent of the midnight feasts at prep school. Martin awoke with a start and pulled the hand off his mouth. 'What is it?' he called loudly, and O'Connor said:

'Keep quiet, it's me, O'Connor.'

'Do we wear skeleton order today, trained Pig?' asked Martin, who was only partially awake.

'Shut up, you fool, it's only one o'clock,' hissed O'Connor urgently into his ear. 'I'm clearing out of here, do you understand?'

'What do you want?' said Foxglove, as his senses began to clear. 'Why do you have to tell me that? I'm not going to help you. If I were you I'd go back to sleep.'

'Listen,' whispered O'Connor, 'will you tell them I've gone to the north of Ireland? I'm relying on you, Martin, or I really will be in trouble if I'm caught.'

'Where are you going?' asked Martin, now wide awake.

'I'm going to join Stoat in London. Will you write to me when the fuss has died down? Here's the address.'

'Now look here, O'Connor, you can't bring me in on this. Go away. I want to go to sleep.'

'All right,' said O'Connor savagely. 'Just forget about the whole thing, will you? I should have known you'd be too scared to lift a finger. When I think how I've covered up for you in my time; but you're too important now to remember that. Just forget you've ever met me, will you?'

After he had gone Martin thought about what he had said, and decided that his accusations were quite unfair. It was not that he was frightened to help him, but one had to have some sense of responsibility as one got older, a fact which O'Connor seemed unable to realize. And just because he had messed up his life, it was most unreasonable to expect Foxglove to do the same.

O'Connor crept out of the hut with his kit-bag over his shoulder, and quietly made his way through the lines to the coal yard, where there was some sacking which could be thrown over the barbed-wire perimeter fence, and some empty wooden crates which the experienced Pig used as stepping-stones.

On the way he passed one of the guards who was stamping up and down blowing on his fingers.

'Halt, who goes there?' he said, waving the pick handle threateningly.

'Shut up, you fool, or you'll have the whole camp awake,' said O'Connor savagely.

'Sorry,' mumbled the guard. 'You haven't got a woody on you, I don't suppose?'

'No, I haven't, so go back to sleep, will you? I've got some work to do.'

'All right,' said the guard, 'keep your hair on. I didn't suppose you would have a fag if I asked for one. Your sort never does. Hope you get pinched.'

'If I do I'll know the reason why, with you yelling your head off all over the place. Here, give me a leg up over this wire. I don't want to get torn to pieces just for your sake!'

121

'Oh, all right,' grumbled the guard, and with a few grunts and a curse O'Connor was free.

8

When O'Connor arrived at the Elephant and Castle address the door was opened a crack by a formidable woman who said:

'What do you want? There's nobody in and we're all busy.'

'I want to see Kenneth Stoat. I know he lives here because he told me so. Tell him O'Connor's come.'

'Never heard of no such person. I'd go away if I was you or the police will have you for causing a crowd.'

A foreign-looking youth appeared and said: 'What do you want? There's nobody here called Stoat I'm afraid, old boy. You must have got the wrong address.'

Eventually Kenneth appeared and said: 'Oh, hullo, O'Connor; what do you want to see me about?'

O'Connor told him the story, and at the end Joseba said: 'Well, I'm afraid we can't have you here. They don't take in foreigners, you see, and they usually think the Irish are even worse. Sorry and all that but there it is.'

But the fat woman said. 'You shut up, Joe. You're always shooting your big mouth off.'

When Farratoga saw the contents of O'Connor's kit-bag he became slightly more amenable.

'Gaiters, two pairs, guaranteed genuine ex-army, three and six the pair; boots, ex-Canadian Army Officers', twelve and six. Drawers cellular, as worn by Senior Army Officers, ninepence,' he intoned happily, spreading the neatly folded contents all over the floor.

Next morning O'Connor stood beside Stoat behind the barrow in Petticoat Lane, and sadly watched the boots on which he had lavished so many hours of devoted attention sold for sixteen shillings. On the barrow was a curious assortment of objects, from bunches of keys to silver sugar-tongs, matchbox covers and teaspoons. 'Where did you get them from?' he asked, noticing the crest of the Pigs on the back, but Stoat just winked knowingly and said, 'Ask no questions, old boy.' In fact Stoat had no more idea of the origin of any of the goods than O'Connor, but he was rather enjoying his new position of preceptor in the arts of salesmanship.

A boy of about twelve approached and asked about the bunch of keys.

'Well, I don't rightly know whether I should sell you those,' said Stoat, staring earnestly at the child, who blushed. 'It is a set of skeleton keys, you see. Made to open practically every lock in Europe, and quite a few in America. Of course, if you gave me your word of honour not to use them for criminal purposes I might consider letting you have them for a couple of quid, but we have to be very careful in our trade. They'd be worth a fortune in the wrong hands.'

'But I've only got ten shillings,' said the boy unhappily.

'Well, we might stretch a point,' Stoat began to say, but the boy said excitedly, 'Will you hold on to them for me if I run and get some more money?'

'All right,' said Stoat condescendingly, 'but you'll have to be quick, mind, as there are hundreds of people who would give their eyes for a bargain like this.'

The boy dashed off home to the kitchen where in a large white china elephant his mother kept the holiday money where it would be safe from burglars, grabbed a handful of pound notes and ran back, with sweat streaming down his face, to Petticoat Lane.

'Is it still all right?' he asked, and Stoat said: 'Yes, but we had quite a business keeping the other buyers off.'

After the boy had gone, O'Connor said: 'What a lot of

123

money children seem to be given nowadays,' and they both agreed that it had not been like that when they had been younger.

At Dunks Foxglove awoke with an uneasy conscience. As soon as O'Connor's absence was noticed the squad were assembled, and Sergeant Bottle said:

'It looks like Lord bloody O'Connor has gone absent. All the best Pigs go A.W.O.L. some time or other, and I only hope for his sake he hasn't destroyed or disposed of any of his kit, or they'll call it desertion. Now I've got to ask you crowd if any of you know anything about it, not that you'd be likely to tell me if you did.'

Foxglove felt that it was one of the cross-roads of his career. If he ignored his sense of duty now he would never be able to regain the self-respect which was essential for an officer who was going to get anywhere. On the other hand it did seem a little mean on O'Connor, but if he let his silly schoolboy prejudices stand in the way of his career he might as well have stayed at Cleeve.

'I think I know where he's gone, sergeant,' said Foxglove.

'Blimey, whose side are you on?' asked Sergeant Bottle incredulously. 'If you know you just shut up about it, see? It's none of your business where he's gone. I was only asking. I didn't expect any of you to be fool enough to answer.'

It was an uphill path, thought Foxglove, that of righteousness and duty. But he was not going to be discouraged by the slackness of any N.C.O. When he was an officer he would have to remember that Bottle was not a man to be relied on.

'I think it would be kinder for O'Connor in the long run,' he said magisterially. 'He's bound to get caught sooner or later, and I think the sooner he's brought to realize that he's making a fool of himself the better.'

124

'Cor listen to him,' said Sergeant Bottle. 'Well, if you're determined to drop your mate in the shit I suppose I can't stop you. Better go along and tell Mr M'Larkey in the platoon office. What's he done, pinched your girl-friend or something?'

In the platoon office, Mr M'Larkey looked up from the copy of *Blighty* he was reading on his desk, and said: 'Come in, Foxglove. What's your problem, then, laddy? Sit down and have a cigarette and tell me all about it. Just forget for a moment that I'm your superior officer, and try to speak to me as you would to your own Dad.'

'He's dead,' said Foxglove.

'That's why I feel I'm here to look after you,' continued Mr M'Larkey unperturbed. 'I've got a responsibility to you all; it isn't all just beer and ices being an officer, you know. I know how you must feel about your Dad. We all have our disappointments in life. I don't mind telling you that I wanted to get into the R.A.F. as a kid, that was the only thing in the world I wanted, and when the results came through and they told me that there were too many applications I felt fit to cry. You wouldn't think to look at me now, that I would have felt fit to cry, would you? You soon get over these things, you see. That's what I found out.' After continuing for some time in this philosophical vein, he eventually asked what was Foxglove's especial problem.

'It's about O'Connor, sir,' said Foxglove. 'I believe I know where he's gone.'

'Oh, really,' said Mr M'Larkey. 'Who's O'Connor? Oh, you mean Junior Pig O'Connor, in the squad. Well what about him?'

'He went absent last night, sir, and I believe I know where he's gone to.'

'First I heard about it,' said Mr M'Larkey with disarming frankness, 'but then I haven't had time to inspect the roll-call return yet. One gets so pushed for work in this job that there just isn't time for everything, and some of the less important things have to be left till later. Let me see, O'Connor. Yes, you're quite right, laddy. Full marks to you, he's marked absent on the morning roll. That's the way you'll come on in the Army; be observant, make a quick assessment from known facts, report briefly and quickly. Three golden rules an officer must never forget. Where do you think he's gone?'

Foxglove gave the address in Elephant and Castle, and Mr M'Larkey said:

'All right. You did very well in coming to see me about it, Foxglove. It shows you're coming on. But I warn you here and now, that if this is a ruse to put us off the scent you're going to be in serious trouble. We already had quite a few clues, and I had quite a shrewd idea where he was, and this information had better be accurate or I wouldn't like to be in your shoes.'

'It is what he told me,' said Foxglove, and felt that inner glow of satisfaction which only an unpleasant duty well done can supply.

When Sergeant Bottle and Sergeant Tarre arrived at the Elephant and Castle they were met by an angry fat woman who barred the door and said:

'O'Connor? Never heard of him. I'm afraid you must have got the wrong address. We don't take in foreigners here, let alone the Irish, and that's rules.'

'All right, all right,' said Sergeant Bottle. 'We just supposed he might have come here.'

'What do you want to see him for, anyway?' demanded the fat woman, 'he hasn't done nothing wrong has he?'

'Oh, so you know him?' said Sergeant Tarre shrewdly.

'Never heard of him in my life,' said the fat woman stoutly, 'and if I have any more lip from you, my man, I'll have the police here quicker than you can say knife, for molesting an honest woman. That's me,' she added in explanation.

'Then you won't mind if we wait here a minute or two and see if you're telling the truth.'

'Causing a crowd?' said the fat woman defiantly.

'Come off it, Reg,' said Sergeant Bottle, 'she's said she's never heard of him, hasn't she? All right, we'll go back and say there was no trace of him here, and drop that young Foxglove in it for a change.'

'You're a fly sucker, Bill,' said Sergeant Tarre admiringly.

'Using language,' shouted the fat woman as the jeep drove off bearing the two sergeants to the nearest public house where they could refresh themselves after their labours.

In Petticoat Lane business was slacking off for the luncheon hour, and Kenneth collected all their wares into O'Connor's kit-bag, and the two wandered off to the pub where they usually had sandwiches and a glass of beer. O'Connor went to wash his hands and Stoat went into the public bar to order. Two sergeants were sitting in his normal corner surrounded by about twelve pint beer glasses, some full, some empty. They were drinking at an immense speed, without speaking. If he had been a soldier he would have recognized the traditional Pig method of drinking, but as he was not he just watched them curiously, amazed that the human body could contain such quantities of liquid. But it was not to be quite so miraculous as he supposed, because after a short time one of them stood up a little uncertainly and said:

'Won't be a minute, Reg,' and staggered off to the gentlemen's lavatory.

O'Connor, coming out, was amazed to see Sergeant Bottle coming in.

'Blimey,' said Sergeant Bottle, 'if it isn't his bloody lordship.' But he had more important things to attend to at that moment, and he just said:

''Op it quick, before I see you.'

O'Connor needed no second bidding.

Later that afternoon Farratoga approached them with a small bundle, and said: 'How's business today, Kenny boy?' and Stoat answered, 'Not half all right, Joe.' O'Connor could scarcely believe his ears; he supposed that in time he would pick up the argot, but it would not be easy.

'Did you keep the keys of your people's flat in Wimbledon, I was wondering, Kenny?'

In fact Stoat had preserved that one link with his past, the only thing which he had not sold. The keys had no sentimental value for him, but they had become somehow associated with his personal integrity, and it was a point of honour with him not to sell them.

'I might have and I might not have. What did you want them for?' Farratoga gave a wolfish grin: 'Ask no questions,' he said.

'Well, I won't give them to you if you're going to sell them.'

'Oh, that's all right; I don't want to sell them. I'll bring them back to you first thing tomorrow morning,' said Farratoga with a wink. Stoat felt uncomfortable, but he did not see how he could refuse his greatest friend such a simple request and handed them over.

Later on, after he and O'Connor had packed up the stall for the day, they decided to have a little celebration in honour of O'Connor's escape from the Army and the good business which had been transacted that day.

'Goodness,' O'Connor said, 'I'll be able to teach them a thing or two at the village jumble sales and church fêtes when I get home.'

He ordered twelve glasses of beer and spread them around

him, in the best Pig manner. Kenneth stared wide-eyed as glass after glass disappeared in the most disconcerting way. Somewhere half-way between the fifth and sixth O'Connor said: 'Shan't be a minute, Ken. Don't go and scoff the lot while I'm away,' and rolled off to the gentlemen's lavatory. Stoat could scarcely believe his eyes, he supposed that in time he would pick up the habit, but it would not be easy. Was this the O'Connor who used to be so worried about the problems of Art and Social Consciousness, who had lain awake at night pondering the difficulties which confronted Genius in the Modern World? He was not quite sure which O'Connor he preferred.

Back at Dunks Sergeant Bottle reported the failure of his mission to Mr M'Larkey, adding confidentially, 'It is my opinion, sir, that it was a false trail intentionally laid by Junior Pig Foxglove to put us off the scent.'

'I suspected so from the very beginning,' said Mr M'Larkey triumphantly. 'Put Foxglove on battalion orders. Conduct to the prejudice, I think.'

'No gross insubordination and deceiving an officer?' asked Sergeant Bottle hopefully.

'No, we don't want to be too hard. After all, it is what any of us might do to help a mate in trouble.'

Sergeant Bottle, who knew the truth, held his peace. But it was very bitter for him having to watch in silence the enormous popularity which Foxglove gained when it became known that he had laid a false trail.

Indeed from that moment Foxglove never looked back. Trained Pig O'Flannel worshipped him, with the dumb unerring devotion which he had formerly reserved for O'Connor. News of his daring sacrifice on his friend's behalf spread through the camp, and wise old heads in the Sergeants' Mess nodded over their beer glasses and said: 'We could do with a few more young officers like Foxglove,' and in the Officers' Mess it was patronizingly admitted that Foxglove seemed a very forthcoming young Pig.

O'Connor became rather morose as the evening progressed. 'It's no good, Kenny, it's all a pretence. There's no room in the world nowadays for poetry, it is a drab moribund shadow which we inherit, and we have no more substance than the poorest hallucination of a blind man. Oh, I know what you are going to say. "Oh, but O'Connor," you will say' – for some reason O'Connor had relapsed into his celebrated imitation of Trained Pig O'Flannel – '"are you not being a trifle gloomy?" No, no, I say to you,' he shouted in a fine biblical manner, striking the table so that his twelve glasses of beer danced and tinkled like seaside harlequins, 'it is only at such moments as this that one sees the truth, and I can tell you that it is all a sham. Remember my words, Kenneth. To you I am O'Connor the good fellow, to others O'Connor the beast. There is no more reality in a character than there is in a charade. I am what I am, not what others would like me to be, and I only know myself by what I find myself to be.'

'If you can't keep quieter, you two, you can get out of here,' said the publican, polishing glasses behind the bar.

'There, did you hear that?' shouted O'Connor triumphantly. 'The good English approach when they are confronted by something they don't understand. Beware it bites; they are suspicious of intelligence in any form, and genius is an original sin, like bastardy, something to be hidden under pain of ridicule and hatred; know this, you half-baked cretin,' he yelled at the barman, 'that I am O'Connor, and proud of it. Yes, well may you turn away in terror, I am O'Connor, the scourge of the middle-classes, O'Connor the anarchist, O'Connor the champion of all that's wrong.'

'And I am Stoat,' began Kenneth in a half-hearted sort of way, but O'Connor said:

'I think the swine is telephoning for the police; let's get out of here.'

After they had run a short way, O'Connor said he was not feeling very well and sat down. After a time he began to sing with an ironical twist the song 'There is a Tavern in the Town' in his fine baritone voice. A man came up and asked officiously: 'Has there been an accident?' and Kenneth answered: 'No, thank you. I think my friend may not be feeling very well, that's all,' and the man said: 'Right-ho. I see.'

Kenneth said: 'Don't you think we should be going home now, William?' but O'Connor replied:

'No, you can go home if you want, I want to be alone for a while, to be myself. I think I have a very good idea for a poem. Can you think of anything to rhyme with "Oblivion"?'

'Pavilion?' suggested Stoat, but his mind was not really on the problem.

'Oh, what the hell,' said O'Connor ungratefully. 'Rhymes are out of date anyway. We have shed those shackles back black Genius free, to see, soar roar or route the reason. Not bad?'

'Jolly good,' said Stoat warmly. 'I say, William, if you really don't mind me leaving you, it *is* getting a bit chilly here and I haven't done the accounts yet.'

'Oh, the profit and the loss. Go, Kenneth; I would be alone.' O'Connor could be very gracious when he felt like it, and Kenneth, after all, was his friend. But when he was alone, he rather wished he had made him stay, as it was somehow not quite such fun reciting poetry to oneself.

After a time he felt slightly sick, and watched in a detached sort of way the confusion caused on the pavement by his efforts. He whistled half-heartedly at a woman who passed on some nocturnal errand, and reflected that this was a much better way of spending the time than polishing his boots at Dunks. He was disturbed from his reflections by an ominous cough, and two enormous boots at eye-level, which trod indelicately in his little puddle, which was just beginning to assume the shape of a map of Ireland. Towering above him was a twelve-foot high policeman, and O'Connor felt that he had seen enough and went to sleep.

Farratoga took cover behind some bushes in the garden of the Wimbledon block of flats, and opened the small leather bag which he always carried on these occasions. Earlier in the day he had mixed powdered burnt cork with face cream in a boot-polish tin, and this he now applied to his face, hands and teeth. His crêpe-soled shoes made no noise on the concrete parterre as he walked carefully to the main door and let himself in with a key which he had covered in thick vaseline grease. The light was on in the Stoats' drawing-room, and Farratoga cursed his luck as he heard two voices, both male, above the clink of glasses and the movement of a chair. The first voice was easily recognized as Dr Stoat's – the second had a nasal whine which in addition to a strange accent not recognisable as any local dialect, made it rather difficult to understand.

'So you're writing Derek's biography, are you?' said Dr Stoat. 'Well I don't know that I'll be able to help you much. I was considerably older than him at Cleeve, and, in the course of things, didn't see much of him. During the war I was on the dental side, but we used to meet occasionally in the mess, and then, of course, we were colleagues for a short time at the Royal Bermondsey, but I can't give you any gen at all on his private life. No juicy scandals, I'm afraid; you'd better ask his widow for anything of that sort.'

'It was the early period at Cleeve that I was especially interested in,' said Mr Dooney.

'Well, he was quite a popular little fellow; he was my fag for a short time as a matter of fact. Did his duty quite conscientiously, although, of course, it took a bit of time to teach him to get my Corps boots up to standard. I can't say he showed any great promise of surgical genius then, although there was some business about a frog in the Hilary dormitory; I never quite discovered the details of that little affair.'

Mr Dooney felt it was time to stop beating about the bush. 'Here is a copy of a poem which I found among his papers,' he said, and handed a typewritten slip of paper to the dentist. Dr Stoat was not a complete fool, and he realized immediately what was intended but he said:

'To Derek Foxglove, the onlie begetter ... well I'll be blowed, so he kept it, after all these years, did he? Vain little blighter he was, I always knew it; I had quite forgotten about the whole thing. Rather neat, I think, the business about 'Silken chains of solitary love', odd thing is I was never a great one for poetry, and this is just about my only effort; not too bad for a beginner, is it? I wouldn't mind paying a bit for the original copy of the piece, if you've got it.'

'How much?' said Mr Dooney.

'Ten pounds,' said Dr Stoat.

'Now be reasonable,' said Mr Dooney, and Farratoga who was listening stifled a yawn and settled down behind the high chest of drawers until the two should reach a settlement and go to bed.

O'Connor woke up feeling immensely well and pleased with himself in a small clean cell, with shiny walls which were painted blue up to the level of his shoulder and cream above. In the corner was a box-like bed from which the mattress and blankets had been removed when O'Connor was introduced. It was a warm, friendly little room with a most satisfying echo, and soon O'Connor was singing away at the top of his voice; he felt that he had never sung so well before in his life, and the corridor outside his cell rang with his good cheer. After a time the small iron door made a noise, and a glass aperture was revealed through which a single baleful eye regarded him wordlessly. Eventually the door made another noise and a sergeant came in and said :

'Now you just shut up or you'll be in worse trouble than you are already, see? Your Dad's coming to collect you with a stick.'

O'Connor said, 'I haven't got a father; he was bitten by a mad dog in Naples and died in appalling agony soon afterwards.'

'Clever little beggar, aren't you? The inspector will be coming round soon, so look out, young man, or he'll be after you.'

After he had gone, O'Connor noticed a bell on the wall, and rang it to see what would happen. The eye reappeared, and disappeared again with a most melodious twang. O'Connor found that his braces were missing, and he put his big toe against the bell and kept it pressed there, with his other foot over the peep-hole. There was a puzzled silence while the sergeant inspected O'Connor's big toe with all the caution which twenty years in the Force had taught him. Eventually the door reopened, and an angry head appeared and said : 'Look, if you want to get into serious trouble you're going the right way about it. You treat us all right and we'll treat you all right.'

'What is the time?' asked O'Connor.

'You'll find out in due course,' said the sergeant and slammed the door.

When the inspector came round he said, 'How do you do?' rather formally. 'I am Inspector Marsh.'

'I am O'Connor,' said O'Connor, 'and could you tell me when I will be allowed to go home?'

'That rather depends on you, Mr O'Connor,' said the inspector severely; 'have they given you your cup of tea?'

'We thought it inadvisable, sir, under the circumstances,'

said the sergeant, whom O'Connor immediately identified as an enemy.

'Where do you live, Mr O'Connor?' asked the inspector. O'Connor gave his Elephant and Castle address, and the inspector turned to the sergeant and told him to check on that.

'Your parents' address?'

'I haven't got any.'

'Your legal guardian?'

O'Connor gave the name of the fat woman at the Elephant and Castle.

'Your employer and trade?'

'Unemployed.'

'What do you do for money?'

'I forget.'

'Come now, Mr O'Connor, we'll find out in time.'

'Honestly, I've quite forgotten.'

After a time the sergeant came back looking very pleased with himself indeed, and said: 'I have been in telephonic communication with the address given by the prisoner, sir, and they assure me that they know no one of the name of O'Connor, and that in any case they do not take in lodgers from overseas, and especially not the Irish.'

'But I promise you I live there,' said O'Connor desperately. 'Will you let me speak to the woman on the telephone?'

'Oh no,' said the sergeant who knew all the tricks, 'you might use methods.'

'Now then,' said the inspector brusquely, 'suppose you let us have the truth. You have been quite enough trouble to us already.'

'His braces, sir, which I removed from him on his apprehension, were of a military pattern, and bore an Army identification number. Shall I ascertain from the War Office the name of the bearer thereof?'

'Yes, go on,' said the inspector, who rather disliked the sergeant.

This was a complicating factor. When he had first joined the Army O'Connor had been made to stamp all his new equipment with his number, but owing to a miscalculation of the mechanism he had reproduced his number back to front, so that it would not have been easy to identify him from that; but unfortunately he had lost his own braces within the first few days, and had had to borrow Foxglove's, reckoning as the event had proved, that no trousers could ever think of abandoning Martin's chaste thighs to the vulgar gaze. Foxglove's number was, of course, reproduced with the precision and clarity of a headline announcement in *The Times*.

'The prisoner,' said the sergeant importantly when he returned, 'is 23417566 Private Soldier Foxglove, M. who joined the Special Airborne Commando Regiment on Tuesday, August the twenty-first, 1959, on a three-year short-service commission contract, and was posted for basic training at the Regimental Depot at Dunks.'

'Thank you, sergeant,' said the inspector. 'So you're in the Royal Airbornes are you?' That obviously explained a lot but O'Connor felt that he might have quite a bit more to explain before he was through. 'Where is your leave pass?' asked the inspector.

'I'm afraid I've lost it,' said O'Connor.

'A likely story,' said the inspector spitefully. 'Get in touch with Dunks, will you, sergeant, and find out if Pig Foxglove is meant to be on leave at the moment.'

'What is the telephone number of the Piggery, *Mister* Foxglove?'

'I don't know.'

'Helpful, aren't you? We'll find it out.'

Mr M'Larkey was the orderly officer that night, and

according to the almost immemorial custom of the Pigs had rather let himself go on the beer and ice-cream.

'Hullo, yes, we have a recruit called Foxglove. Quite a forthcoming young Pig, in many ways. No, he's not meant to be on leave at the moment. Oh, you've got him locked up, have you? I didn't even know he had gone absent, but then one can't study the roll books the whole time, can one?'

'On being apprehended,' said the sergeant sternly, 'the prisoner originally gave his name as O'Connor.'

'Oh, you mean you've caught O'Connor? Good show: full marks to you, it shows the police are on their toes these days. Glad you weren't taken in by his calling himself Foxglove. There's really no similarity at all, you know, even I wouldn't be taken in by that one. They always get pulled up sooner or later when they go A.W.O.L., and usually it's for getting drunk. I'll send round a jeep to pick him up.'

'Giving false names,' said the police sergeant disgustedly, when he rejoined O'Connor and the inspector. 'Expected us to believe you were called Foxglove, did you, of all fancy ideas? I wasn't taken in by that one. Well, it will all come out in evidence, Mister O'Connor, and I wouldn't like to be in your shoes, not for all the Pigs in Christendom. You can keep the lot, I say.'

'That will do, Sergeant Blackbushe,' said the inspector.

Back in Wimbledon, Mr Dooney was finding Dr Stoat a more difficult customer than Lady Foxglove had been. He put his finger between his shirt collar and his neck, and tried to loosen the pressure which was making it sticky with sweat, and making him feel that he was not master of the situation.

'You can have fifteen pounds by cheque, or ten in cash, the minute the original is in my hands. You won't get a penny more, and so you can publish and be dammed.'

'Now look, Dr Stoat, you're a family man too and you

know what it is like; I hate to have to seem mercenary or anything . . .'

'Publish and be damned,' said Dr Stoat dramatically. Unconsciously he had been preparing all his life for just such an interview as this when his past behaviour should be exposed to the judgement of his present standards, and the more Mr Dooney whined and threatened the more inflexible became his attitude.

Finally Mr Dooney left with eight pounds in cash, leaving behind a signed promise never to publish the poem, nor any part of it, nor to mention the name of Dr Stoat in any context, nor to refer to him nor the poem in any way. He signed his name with a fine flourish over a twopenny stamp, which both parties believed to add to the statement some of the massive authority of the law. But he retained the original fragment which had been composed so many years ago on a warm, balmy afternoon in St Bartholomew's Library at Cleeve.

After the last light was out, and he had heard Dr Stoat shut the door of his bedroom, Farratoga stood up from behind his hiding-place and groaned. It was already two o'clock, and he had been crouching in a misery of cramp for an hour.

Soon his little leather bag began to fill with objects: A glass paper-weight which Mrs Stoat's aunt had given her as a souvenir from Florence; a cigarette box of tortoise-shell, and a small bowl of papier mâché which had been made by Kenneth's grandmother, and which held paper clips and postage stamps and some powdery *pot-pourri* and two cigarette ends and a broken tablet of aspirin. Dr Stoat's reading spectacles, Mrs Stoat's work-basket, a soapstone figure of a fish and a nail-file from the chimney-piece; a pot of glue, which leaked, and an agate and silver paper-knife; all the small domestic symbols of a civilized culture were being shoved hastily into the swollen belly of Farratoga's bag when

138

a noise made him spin round, quivering and with a sickly feeling of terror in the pit of his stomach.

Dr Stoat emerged from his bedroom jauntily swinging a red plastic sponge-bag, and with his toothbrush held vertically in front of him like a lictor's rod.

Farratoga panicked at that moment. Instead of crouching down and holding his breath, in which case it would have been most unlikely that Dr Stoat would have seen him, he ran back, clutched the handle of the nearest door, and bolted inside like a rabbit, shutting it quietly behind him. Dr Stoat did not see the movement, or was too preoccupied to notice it, and went on his way to the bathroom for his daily treat of a good scrubbing all over of his teeth.

Mrs Stoat lay alone in her bedroom with the night-light burning dimly in its saucer in the far corner of the room. It was really very little comfort to her unsettled nerves, because in the faint glow from the burning wick familiar objects began to take unfamiliar shapes, and the Devil stalked through the room wherever her eyes could not follow him. Since the terrible scene when Kenneth had left the house she had taken to brooding, and in her nightmares Farratoga appeared as the Devil himself, the walking personification of evil who had snatched her son away into his horrible clasp.

It was most unfortunate, then, that the room into which Farratoga had burst should have been Mrs Stoat's bedroom. With his face blackened and his eyes rolling in terror he was a sight to terrify the most hardy, but for Mrs Stoat it was too much. With a terrible scream she threw off her bedside lamp, and lay sobbing and twitching on her bed, clutching at bed-clothes and pillows to try and put anything between her and the apparition.

Farratoga was nearly as frightened as she by the havoc which he had caused, but some grain of common sense or instinctive reaction inside his paralysed brain told him to flee. Without a word he dashed from the room, taking his bulging brown suitcase with him, down the stairs, and out into the cold night air of Wimbledon.

When Dr Stoat reached his wife she could give no coherent account of what had happened, but continued to sob and scream alternately, shouting at him to go away and not come near her, and clutching a pillow to her chest as if to protect herself from something which was threatening her.

Dr Stoat telephoned to the hospital.

Part Three

9

It was about the time that Kenneth's mother finally went mad and had to be taken away that Martin lost his Faith. He did so in the most public way he could by writing to his mother and Brother Aloysius simultaneously, and reporting himself a convinced atheist on Church Parade, although this step merely ensured that he spent Sunday mornings swilling out the squad lavatories in the company of two Muslims and Christian Scientists. It was not the despair of a tortured soul, nor an intellect in the agony of terrible doubts which led to his rejection of everything he had accepted before with the same naïve charm with which he accepted presents and flattery and admiration. He did it, of course, to spite his mother.

Lady Foxglove showed the greatest fortitude in the face of this, the greatest disaster of her life. During a career entirely devoted to the disasters of others she had learned the best comportment to be assumed, the best attitudes to take, and even the best make-up to wear for such eventualities. She took considerable pains over the long letter she sent to her son, because she realized that it was one of the most important letters of her life, and would be preserved for ever in the family archives. Out of fairness to her hagiographer, and because she doubted Martin's common sense in his present mood, she made a second copy and placed it in the family archives:

My Darling Boy,

All my thoughts and prayers are with you during this terrible period of your life; I have prayed and prayed in the past that I might be able to share my fortitude with you, even if it made me weaker to the lures of the Devil, if it would have made you stronger. If the good Lord would take some of the goodness he has in his bounty bestowed on one and give it to you nobody would be happier than I.

I am sensible, believe me, that your present age is not an easy one, and that the Devil works hardest to corrupt the young. Perhaps I am to blame for not having provided that Christian family background which is the true rock on which all faith is based. I know that my work has often taken me far from home when I feel that I should have been at your side, but, God knows, I have done my best.

Try to pray, dear boy. Perhaps God will yet return.

Your loving,

MOTHER.

Normally she signed herself 'Lots of love, Mummy' but she felt that something more dignified was needed on this occasion. Having sealed the letter delicately with the tip of her pretty pink tongue she prepared to compose another of a rather different nature:

Dear Mr Dooney,

I am reluctant to believe that you are entirely hard, that there is no trace left in your heart of kindness nor of grace. Can He who made me, have made you also, and yet so different? Is there nothing you hold sacred to which I can appeal? I know that my husband's crime stinks in the nostrils of Man and God alike, but I simply cannot, believe me, *cannot possibly* afford more than five pounds ten a week. If I had six I would gladly give them to you to purge my husband's wickedness and preserve his name, but from now on you will only receive five pounds ten shillings. That is final.

The Manor House,   Yours faithfully,
Bidcombe.   JULIA FOXGLOVE.

The motor car was ordered for eleven o'clock which was to take her to the train for a Summit Conference with Brother Aloysius at Cleeve, where they would plan the campaign for the redemption of Martin's soul. Before leaving she furtively hid a large bottle of Lourdes water in her suitcase; she would not like everybody to know it, but truth to tell she had been having recourse to the Lourdes water rather more frequently of late.

Brother Aloysius met her at Cleeve station, and tactfully mentioned nothing of the business which had brought her there during the short journey to the Abbey. Instead he entertained her with stories of his new book, about the courtship of St Paul's pet Pekinese, called Chooty, and St Peter's pet pug-dog, called Fifi, and their eventual marriage, and about the puppies with which they were blessed. Brother Aloysius had been a little uncertain at first as to whether some of the love scenes would get past the monastic censor, but it had been all right, and now sales of the book were easily topping those of Brother Augustine's new work; *Essays in Comparative Existence: An Enquiry.*

Lady Foxglove smiled sadly, sweetly, yearningly, understandingly at his attempts to keep her mind off her great tragedy, and Brother Aloysius felt that never had he seen her look so lovely, so languishing, so alone; not even at her husband's funeral, he believed, had she looked quite so perfect.

When they were settled cosily in the Hospitarium and Brother Aloysius had gorged himself on the coffee and little sweet biscuits which were the Bursar's contribution to the entertainment of all guests, she said:

'If only I knew someone in whom he had confidence, who could go and talk to him privately. I feel that it needs someone of his own age whom he likes and whom he'll listen to.'

'We could send Frank Pratt-Bingham,' said Brother Aloysius. 'He is a very sensible boy, and takes a most intelligent interest in his religion and I know he was very attached to Martin at school.'

'Yes, I've met him, but I'm afraid the two of them must

145

have had a quarrel or something, because he never mentions him nowadays, which I always think such a pity. He was a most suitable young friend, and perhaps if they were still friends Martin wouldn't have gone the way he has. Who else was there, apart from that terrible Stoat who would not do at all, who was a friend of his at Cleeve?'

This was a difficult question because in fact Martin had no close friends after his divorce from Stoat. The Head of the School was not encouraged, for obvious reasons, to have any intimate friends outside the immediate circle of head monitors, and Martin had taken the responsibility of his position quite seriously and had remained rather more aloof even than was customary.

'He kept mentioning in his letters an old Alexandrian called O'Connor. Do you know anything about him?'

Brother Aloysius thought he knew quite a lot about O'Connor, more, in fact than he was prepared to tell Lady Foxglove. He frowned and murmured:

'I am not sure that O'Connor is quite the sort of person we need.'

'Why not?' asked Lady Foxglove, a trifle impatiently.

'Well, of course, I've got nothing against him personally, but I'm just not sure that he fills the ticket, if you see what I mean.'

'I don't think I do,' said Lady Foxglove. 'O'Connor happens to be in the military prison at Cirencester, so I can get hold of him quite easily. I remember Martin telling me he tried to desert from the Army. A most enterprising young man, he sounds. Of course, there would be no need for Martin to continue his friendship after they've had a little talk, but he sounds just the sort of person whose arguments would appeal to Martin at the moment.'

'Yes, I'm sure O'Connor's quite enterprising,' said Brother Aloysius doubtfully.

'Then we shall regard that as settled,' said Lady Foxglove.

'Now we must discuss what I shall say to this O'Connor when I meet him.'

In his cell in 'B' Block of Kitchener Barracks, Cirencester, O'Connor watched the sun creep slowly up the wall until it should reach the damp stain just below the ceiling which would mean that it was time for his brown, sugarless cup of tea and his two slices of bread and margarine. He felt no bitterness at all at his lot, and the cup of tea was in its way every bit as keen a pleasure as all the beer and ices ever consumed in the Officers' Mess of the Pigs. His court martial had been eminently fair, and his sentence of a hundred and twenty days not excessive in the light of the gravity of his offence. At first the Pigs had tried to treat it as a case of absence without leave, and Trained Pig O'Flannel had produced a load of what he called his buckshee kit to replace what had been sold. O'Flannel's secret store had been built up from thefts covering many years of Junior Leaders' Squads, and O'Connor was interested to see his original pair of braces, with his number printed back to front, reappear for the occasion. But everyone agreed that it had been a dirty trick to give his name as Foxglove, after Martin had done so much to help him, and eventually Colonel Pyke decided that as every piece of equipment produced bore a different number, it would have to be treated as a case of desertion.

Mr M'Larkey had offered to be his defending officer, but he and the President of the court martial, who was an elderly colonel in the Royal Horse Artillery, had somehow not hit it off. Mr M'Larkey pointed out that it was worry over family affairs which had driven O'Connor to do this thing, which he now regretted very much, that, although generally speaking a fairly reliable Pig, he was of extremely low Intelligence Quota, as the tests he had taken at the Officer Selection Board showed, and had been in some considerable mental stress at the time. The prosecuting officer, who as a very nasty young captain with an embryo moustache, pointed out that O'Connor had been at pains to leave a false trail behind him, that the speed with which he had disposed of his kit clearly indicated that he had no intention of returning, that he had given a false name to the police and obstructed them in every way, and that he was clearly a most disagreeable person who had better be locked away for some time.

All new prisoners at the Kitchener were given a spell of solitary confinement to begin with, in order to break them in to camp routine. O'Connor always rather preferred his spells of solitary, which became quite frequent after a time. It was a great strain always having to talk in an assumed Irish accent and remember that one was a jolly boy from the bogs. If ever he spoke in his normal voice he was either accused of impersonating an officer, or reviled savagely by everyone present. For one reason and another the inmates of Kitchener Barracks tended not to share the Englishman's traditional respect for his betters.

All prisoners were allowed two visitors a year, and were allowed to receive and send four letters a year. O'Connor seldom wrote or received more in any case, and so he did not feel unduly worried by the ban. He had arranged for his mother to visit him half-way through his sentence, which, as he was only serving a hundred and twenty days was to be his only visit. She was to bring five hundred cigarettes, five pounds in coppers, a pack of cards, a set of poker dice and a bottle of whisky. Strictly speaking visitors were not allowed to bring presents, but by long-standing custom the police corporal turned a blind eye to these transactions in exchange for a small percentage after the visitor had gone. The five hundred cigarettes represented untold wealth, and as soon as the hoard arrived O'Connor would be able to hire fellow prisoners to do all the less savoury occupations of prison life for him; it was not that he minded slopping out; it seemed just as harmless a way of spending the time as any other, but there was an indefinable prestige to be gained by joining the Olympian few who watched the others slopping away while they smoked and discussed art, religion, politics and the other subjects that crop up when superior people get together.

With the bottle of whisky O'Connor hoped to bribe the physical training instructor, a fiendish man made of india-rubber and with a malice so all-embracing as to be scarcely sane. It was the P.T. that O'Connor minded most of all the indignities and tortures which he suffered. The prisoners were paraded, clad only in absurd green cellular drawers, and made to jump up and down, do press-ups, run under each other's legs, turn somersaults, run round the block and do more press-ups. If Corporal Queen took a dislike to any prisoner, or thought he detected a hint of dumb insolence in his manner of turning somersaults, he would call him out and made him do press-ups for the entire forty minutes of the class. Needless to say O'Connor's somersaults were an open affront to the authority, personality and virility of Corporal Queen.

There was no doubt that Prisoner O'Connor's existence would be far happier after his mother's visit, and he began to wish that he had asked her to come earlier, but as he only had one letter left of his ration he waited impatiently for the day which would make him the richest man in camp.

Two days before his mother's visit was due, O'Connor was engaged in his weekly session of recreational training (basket ball) with a happy sort of before-Christmas feeling, when the corporal of the guard arrived and shouted:

'O'Connor, fall out and report properly dressed to the guardroom. Move.' And O'Connor ran off to get changed. He was a little puzzled that his mother should have decided to come early, but delighted nevertheless, and it as with a sense of eager anticipation that O'Connor presented himself at the guardroom in ten minutes' time.

'She says she's your mother. Do you want to see her?'

'Yes,' said O'Connor.

'Not half some Jane either. I don't know where ugly great mugs like you get such mothers. How much did she cost?'

This rather puzzled O'Connor, too, because while his mother was undoubtedly the kindest and the best of women, she could never have been described as a beauty, and certainly lacked that something which made corporals of Military Police look wistful and jangle coins in their pockets. But he was far too excited by the prospect of the wealth in store for him to pay much attention, and soon he was being marched into the visitors' room, with the police corporal panting slightly behind him.

Lady Foxglove stood up and said 'How do you do?' and then she turned to the corporal with the most charming of smiles and said: 'Now I must let you into a little secret, I am not really his mother at all, but I felt that I simply *had* to see him because I had so many things to talk to him about. You're not angry with me, are you?'

No, the police corporal was not angry with her. He gave an encouraging wink and stuck his tongue out of the corner of his mouth and jerked his head backwards and said: 'That's all right, lady. I understand. I won't look.' And he shoved his hands deep into his pockets and studied a print of 'Scotland for Ever' in the far corner of the room whistling nonchalantly.

He said: 'You've got quarter of an hour.'

Before O'Connor had time to recover from the shock, Lady Foxglove was whispering urgently to him:

'It's about Martin; I can't tell you how worried we all are and I know you'll do what you can do to help. Martin was always such a great friend of yours; he used to write me letter after letter about you, and he admired you so much that I know you won't mind my visiting you like this, when you hear what is happening. We are all afraid that he is beginning to lose his Faith. I saw Brother Aloysius about it at Cleeve and he agreed that you are the only person who could help, because you're so much closer to him than any of us nowadays. We want you to write a letter to him; I know you'll find it rather difficult, so we prepared one for you, although, of course, you won't have to follow it too closely if you don't want. Something friendly and informal, we thought, is what is needed. Here it is,' she said, and thrust the paper into O'Connor's hands.

My Dear Old Chap,

I don't know if there's anything in it, but I've been hearing that you are having difficulties these days with your personal affairs. I hope you won't mind my interfering, but after all we used to get on quite well together in the old days and I know what it is like to have difficulties. Honestly, if I were you, old fellow, I'd try to keep your eyes on the ball and make for the touchline quick; or if you'd like it another way, don't leave your wicket in the middle of an over. Do you remember when I got into that spot of trouble at Cleeve? Well, that's all over and done with now, of course, but I learned a thing or two in the course of it, I can tell you. And the most important thing is you can't hit boundaries all the time from a neglected wicket. I would chew on it, old chap.

> Yours till the cows come home,
> WILLIAM (O'CONNOR)

'But I'm only allowed to write one more letter while I'm in here,' O'Connor said eventually.

'But it's such a small thing to ask, surely,' said Lady Foxglove pleadingly. 'And I've brought you a little pot of gooseberry jam. I don't know whether you'll like it, but many people have found it a *great* comfort in times of distress. Now – I must go or that poor corporal will get into trouble.

Good-bye, William, it is so good of you to do this for Martin.'

As Lady Foxglove left the barracks, she took out her little book of good works and put a tiny little tick against the heading *Visit the Imprisoned*. It was quite an excitement for her as it was the first time she had had an opportunity to perform that particular good deed.

After she had gone, the corporal said to William: 'Well I hope it was sweet, because that's the only visitor you'll be allowed unless you care to stay here for another six months. Well, what did she leave?'

As the full extent of the disaster became apparent, William nearly wept. 'One bloody jar of bloody gooseberry bloody jam,' he said bitterly.

'Oh yes?' said the corporal. 'Expect me to buy that one, do you? Come on, turn out your pockets.'

After he had searched O'Connor thoroughly and painfully, he said: 'All right, O'Connor. Commandant's parade tomorrow morning. You should know by now that visitors are not allowed to bring presents of any description. Also using language to a member of the staff. You've had this coming to you a long time. Thought you could make a fool of me, did you? Well, we'll see who's the fool tomorrow morning. Prisoner shun; fall out and report to Queen now. Move.'

O'Connor moved. Corporal Queen seemed to be in an especially vindictive mood that afternoon, as if some sixth sense had told him that his bottle of whisky was lost. That evening William copied out Lady Foxglove's letter word for word and sent it to Martin at his Officer Cadet Training School. With it he sent his last link with the outside world.

10

When O'Connor did not turn up at the Elephant and Castle, Stoat was not worried. William had passed on, and Kenneth knew that his robust constitution was more than fit for anything the world could do to it. Like ships that pass in the night, thought Kenneth, as he laid out his barrow the next morning in Petticoat Lane. Farratoga was later than usual in arriving with his bundle of wares, and when he did there was something immensely shifty about him. He dropped his leather bag on the table and merely said : 'Well, old boy, I'll be seeing you this evening. Here are your keys back, by the way.'

The keys were covered in some greasy substance, and Farratoga's hands were still black from his adventures of the night before. Farratoga left before Kenneth opened the bag, but when he did the mystery was to some extent explained. A glass paper-weight which came first seemed vaguely familiar, but the tortoise-shell cigarette box was immediately recognized. As each homely little object came to light Kenneth felt a great wave of nostalgia. His father's reading spectacles, the nail-file with which he had often listlessly attempted to clean his black fingernails, Mrs Stoat's workbasket, with its uncompleted sleeveless pullover which had been started for him as a boy of six and which had never caught up with him, all these well-loved symbols of the security and warmth of his home made him long to go back there. He was terribly bored, with Farratoga, bored with the uncertainty of his mealtimes and the squalor of his lodgings, and suddenly, without making any decision, he repacked the little brown bag and walked with it in his hand to the bus stop.

When he arrived at the flat it was empty, but to all appearances just as he left it. He went into the drawing-room and carefully began to rearrange the objects which Farratoga had stolen. The soapstone fish and the nail-file went back on the chimney-piece, the papier mâché bowl back on the writing desk. Then Kenneth sat down and began to read the newspaper. At twelve o'clock Mrs Twiddle, the daily woman, arrived, and said in her usual hostile way:

'Oh, Mr Kenneth's decided to come back, has he? I suppose he'll be shouting for his lunch soon. Well, he should have told us he was going to condescend to return, because now he'll have to make do on sausages.'

Kenneth said: 'That's all right. Do you know where my mother has gone?'

'Can't say I do, dear. She was in here yesterday, but she hasn't been very well lately, you know what her nerves are, and she may have gone away for a while. Best thing in the world for her, if she has. She was always moping away in her bedroom ever since you left. You have no idea what a lot of trouble you've caused, my boy.' Mrs Twiddle blew her nose self-pityingly. While she was examining what had arrived, Kenneth said:

'Has anything happened while I've been away, any burglaries or anything?'

'No, not that I've heard of. Of course nobody tells me anything anyway in this place. I only see the doctor when he comes in in the evenings and Mrs Stoat hasn't had much to say for herself these last days. It's a change having somebody to talk to. Well, I must be getting on with my work, or nothing will ever get done.'

With a dexterous flick of her duster, Mrs Twiddle knocked the soapstone fish off the chimney-piece, to break into small pieces in the grate. With a merry wink at Kenneth she collected the fragments in a dustpan and put them into the waste paper basket. Kenneth felt that it was good to be home again, although he felt a certain apprehension at the thought of the meeting with his father later that evening. He was not a bit frightened of a row, but he rather shirked the emotional issues of the Prodigal Son business. His mother, of course, would be even more embarrassing in her demonstrations of delight; she would almost certainly cry, reflected Kenneth with a dismal satisfaction. But he felt he could handle her, while he was rather wary of having to act the penitent, humble, loving son to his father.

When Dr Stoat returned that evening he was feeling depressed and tired. For the first time in his life he had allowed domestic worries to interfere with his work, and he had had a row with his Registrar in front of a terrified patient, and had been proved wrong; later he had bungled a complicated extraction, and would have to wait for X-ray reports before he knew whether a jaw was broken. Earlier that morning he had been unable to find anything in its usual place; he had mislaid his reading spectacles and everything seemed to be going wrong. At the hospital they said it would be better if he did not visit his wife for some time, as she had been recommended for a new type of shock treatment which necessitated a comatose condition for most of the time.

When he saw Kenneth, he said: 'Oh, hullo, Kenneth, so you're back.'

Kenneth said: 'Yes, I'm back.' He put out his hand to be shaken in what he hoped was a meek, affectionate sort of way, and Dr Stoat shook it in what he hoped was a bluff, understanding manner. It was very moving.

When Dr Stoat told him of his mother's illness, Kenneth said: 'Oh dear.' The whole thing passed off quite well, but when Kenneth was alone in his bedroom he missed his sword and his collection of birds' eggs and his partially stuffed frog. The room seemed to have lost its welcome without them. For the first time since he left Cleeve he said his night prayers, kneeling beside his bed with his thumb firmly in his mouth, staring at the Titian print on the wall. Later on he even cleaned his teeth. As he lay in bed he resolved to write a book.

It was about a week after Lady Foxglove's visit that O'Connor tried to commit suicide. It was a dismal failure, like anything he ever attempted. He had been told that the patent mixture which was generally employed in the Army to clean brass and polish windows, was highly poisonous if drunk in any quantity. He found two tins of it lying in the gymnasium and consumed them both greedily. Corporal Queen surprised him just as he was finishing the second, and put him on orders at once for Conduct to the Prejudice of Good Order and Military Discipline. But when he was marched to the guardroom and the nature of his offence became known he was transferred to the camp hospital and Corporal Queen received a severe reprimand for leaving dangerous substances lying unattended in a public place.

After they had taken the stomach pump away O'Connor lay completely exhausted on the floor, without even the energy to groan. He had a sore throat and a foul taste in his mouth, and if he moved any part of his body he felt a pricking of goose-pimples all over him, and a terrible feeling of nausea. For the first time he was alone in a friendless world. The medical officer had not disguised his contempt as he watched O'Connor retching and vomiting on the floor, and even the orderlies had not wasted any sympathy, as they cleaned him up afterwards with an impersonal savagery. He remained in the hospital afterwards to be kept under observation.

It was never known how Major O'Connor discovered the truth of his son's condition. There was a small group of Left Wing Members of Parliament who had espoused the demolition of Kitchener Barracks as one of their many causes. It shared their attention with compulsory contraception, the supremacy of the black races, the abolition of hydrogen bombs, the curtailment of the Monarchy and the Disestablishment of the Church of England, but somehow a few of these busy people gained admittance to the prison, and were shown over the new gymnasium, the site for the new playing fields, the hospital and a new and ingenious engine recently installed in the kitchens for the rapid washing of plates. They seemed quite impressed, but in discussions with the Commandant afterwards they kept returning to the subject of Prisoner O'Connor, although they had not been shown him nor told about him. It was very seldom that any news leaked out of those high walls, but the Commandant had reason to be grateful that it was only O'Connor's case which had attracted their attention.

Two days later O'Connor was moved to a civilian mental hospital and formally discharged from the Army. After a week there he was moved to Sister Cardew's Home for the Mentally Infirm, a less austere establishment outside Brighton. He was visited daily by his mother and father and Miss Wrote, his former nurse, who lived in Brighton. The newspapers which had followed his movements with interest, charitably left him there, and within two days in the pleasant homely atmosphere of Sister Cardew's, O'Connor had recovered from the various remedies which had been applied to him in the State lunatic asylum, and was soon entertaining the other patients with his amusing Irish ballads and impromptu verses:

> Miss Long
> Can do no wrong
> Mr Spate
> Can do no rate;
> She'll have to wait
> For Mr Spate,

And she can't wait long,
I'm sorry to state.

Mr Spate was a dear old man who had retired to the home some thirty years before, when there was discussion of a serious charge being brought against him, and had lived there contentedly ever since. Miss Long was a slightly less senior resident, having been placed there twenty years before by her relatives to whom her incontinence had become too grave an embarrassment to be overlooked. Her tenderness for Mr Spate was a byword, and he responded with a charming gallantry, and overlooked her unfortunate ailment with all the tact of an earlier generation.

O'Connor was soon the favourite of everybody, and he settled into his new environment with all the readiness of a cuckoo moving into another bird's nest. He had to stay there until such time as the matter of his prison sentence was arranged. It was normal for military prisoners, on being discharged from the Army, to complete their sentence in a civilian prison, but O'Connor felt, understandably, that it might cramp his poetic temperament to be shut up again, and prepared to purge his crime in the greater comfort of his new home.

Sister Cardew was a sweet old lady and by a coincidence an intimate friend of Fanny Wrote, William's old nurse. She made sure in an unobstrusive way, that her patients, or her guests, as she liked to call them, were of the right sort, and that their eccentricities were not too marked to spoil the happy family atmosphere which existed in her charming old rectory with its flowering magnolia trees and lupin beds. She enjoyed the company of the slightly mad far more than that of the sane rest of the world, and had an altogether delightful way of rolling her eyes at the other guests whenever one of them was being particularly strange. She did not allow the very old nor the very depressed, and something as young, gay and mad as O'Connor caught her fancy immediately.

158

'You should not tease poor Miss Long so, William,' she said encouragingly to him after one of his lewder rhymes about Miss Long's infirmity, 'after all it is not her fault, and you should try to be more sympathetic.'

'Yes, Sister,' said William obediently, while he tried to think of a good rhyme for 'tease'.

Mrs Cod-Finger was William's staunch ally in his solitary campaign against Miss Long. She was probably the most disagreeable of the patients, and a rival of Miss Long's for the hand of the eminently eligible Mr Spate. She would always pick a quarrel with Miss Long on some matter of fact, and they would argue about it for immense lengths of time with incredible bitterness, both appealing to Mr Spate for support.

During the first week of O'Connor's stay the issue was whether the lupins in the large bed in front of the rhododendron bushes had changed colour since the year before.

'No, Miss Long, I am afraid that I cannot possibly agree with you. I distinctly remember remarking a year ago upon the unhealthy pallor of the pink. Of course, as we get older we all tend to confuse little things, but I confess you startle me when you declare that the flowers are constantly changing colour like sea anemones. Don't you agree, Mr Spate?'

'Or chameleons,' murmured Mr Spate, 'but let us be thankful that our garden, at least, is full of flowers, Mrs Cod-Finger.'

'They was yellow,' said Miss Long, getting excited, 'or gold I should say. It was lovely watching them wave to us out of our bedroom window. I've got a photo to prove it, Mrs Cod-Finger, and even you can't laugh off that one. More like fairies they was than these silly pink things. I told Sister Cardew it was an insult to our taste, having these stupid pink frumps bouncing up and down like fat pantomime tarts. Look, here's the photo.'

It was a fading brown photograph of two young persons

in bathing dress on Brighton beach. When it was shown to O'Connor he said doubtfully:

'They look more like pink flowers than yellow ones to me.'

And Sister Cardew rolled her eyes merrily and said: 'Well, I don't know I'm sure. What does Mr Spate think?'

Mr Spate said: 'What a delightful photograph. Dear me, how this does bring back the past,' and producing an enormous silk pocket handkerchief he started to clean his gold-rimmed reading spectacles with a nostalgic air.

Mrs Cod-Finger just said 'Bah!' and looked meaningly at Mr Spate, who continued to stare mournfully at his spectacles. But when the photograph was returned to Miss Long, she said 'There, you see' with such a triumphant air that it could not be allowed to go unchallenged, and Mrs Cod returned to the offensive with:

'Seeing as it's only in black and white, Miss Long, I don't know how you expect us to tell whether they were yellow or pink.'

'They was yellow,' said Miss Long.

When Stoat read of his friend's adventures in the daily newspapers he wrote him a long letter, addressed to Sister Cardew's Home:

Dear William,

I am very glad to hear that you are all right. We were a bit worried when you didn't turn up at the Elephant and Castle, and it is quite a relief to hear that you haven't come to any harm. After you left I managed to sell the odd gaiter which we couldn't find the pair of, so I owe you 1/9d. What is your bin like? My mother has gone mad, and if you're not careful we may send her to join you. I am thinking of writing a book, and I wondered if you would care to join me in it. I am not sure what it would be about, but perhaps you have some ideas. I haven't seen or heard of Farratoga for the last three months; I think he's just vanished into thin air, and as far as I'm concerned that's a good thing, as I was beginning to get a bit bored with the whole set-up. Crummy, I thought.

I read in the papers that Lady Foxglove visited you in prison. Isn't that typical of her? I wouldn't mind going to prison if I thought she would come and visit me. I think she is the sweetest, kindest and most beautiful person in the world, though for Heaven's sake don't tell Martin I said so. What did she say? Was she looking absolutely lovely? Goodness I felt jealous when I read about it. Do write and tell me what it's like inside a bin.

THIS LETTER is FROM

KENNETH STOAT

Stoat always had difficulty in finding the proper end for a letter, and so he usually employed some facetious phrase like: 'Yours, Ken the Killer' or 'Believe me to be, Sir, Kenneth the Inkredible'. In later life he was always very much embarrassed when he was confronted with these manifestations of youthful exuberance.

O'Connor always enjoyed reading his letters, which were many and various. Like everybody whose name has ever appeared in the newspapers he was bombarded with curious messages, some adulatory, some vilely abusive, some meaningless. One of the first to arrive had been an envelope with the Bidcombe postmark which enclosed a five-shilling postal order and the message 'From a well-wisher', in Lady Foxglove's characteristically sloping hand. Another five-shilling postal order came from an old age pensioner in Ealing, who said that he knew what it felt like, and that he had no objection to O'Connor giving his name to the newspapers. O'Connor didn't.

In the same post as Kenneth's letter was an envelope posted in Shoreditch which contained a piece of lavatory paper on which was written in lipstick the enigmatical legend: 'Ha! Ha!' William put it on Miss Long's plate at the breakfast table, and she accused Mrs Cod-Finger, whom she had always known to be slightly mad, and Sister Cardew rolled her eyes and removed the document to her private museum, where it remained between the dressing-gown cord which old Miss Trumpet had mistaken for a snake, and the teapot which Major Ribbon used to fill with bread and jam and meat bones in the belief that he was feeding his dog.

At breakfast next morning Mrs Cod found on her plate a piece of lavatory paper with the message, *You are a nasty old tart* and the correspondence continued for some weeks.

He received a letter from Foxglove which amused him as much as any of the wilder ones from unknown people had done. Martin had obviously been rather puzzled by O'Connor's letter but had a very imperfect sense of the ridiculous, and had plainly been rather touched that so hardened a sinner as William should show such tender solicitousness for his moral welfare. He wrote:

My Dear William,

I am sensible that your letter was written in good faith, and that you were motivated by an anxious desire for my welfare, but you must realize that there are some problems in life which one must face alone, and although is it a great comfort to me to know that in the hour of my doubt I have the encouragement and good will of so faithful a friend as yourself, I must beg you to disregard my troubles and leave me to struggle alone. I was especially flattered to see that even in the hour of your greatest distress you had time to comfort, as you thought, a friend in need. Perhaps through your suffering you have learned something of what you missed at Cleeve. Perhaps you have now grasped that with age comes responsibility and care. I would like to think it were so, and that if you were to join the Army now you would succeed where formerly you failed.

I saw that Cleeve beat St Gerald's 5–3 on their ground. Jolly good show!

I shall be on commissioning leave in a week's time, and may spend some of it in Brighton, when I shall be able to visit you, if visitors are allowed. But one hopes that by then you will be much better and out of hospital!

Yours, etc.,

MARTIN (FOXGLOVE).

Later that evening O'Connor received one of Mrs Cod-Finger's notes. A great deal of Mrs Cod's communication with the rest of the world was done through written orders and memoranda:

Memorandum Cod-Finger to Cardew
Duties expected by Mrs Cod-Finger of her Medical Adviser.
1. Constant Attendance and Advice on Medical Matters.
2. Proper Respect and Deportment at such Interviews.
3. Sobriety in Dress and Behaviour.
4. Remedial Treatment, when considered Desirable by Both Parties.

The plum which fell into O'Connor's lap that evening was of another order. It was not headed, and the writing was, for some reason, disguised.

Something Must be Done about Miss Long. Can you meet me in Private behind the Long Shrubbery after Dark? We must work together. This time she has Gone too Far.

GLORIA COD (-*Finger*)

O'Connor forwarded the epistle to Foxglove, without explanation. Martin did not acknowledge it, but he worried rather for his friend's health.

To Stoat, William sent a longer letter, describing in detail the delights of his new home, and enclosing a précis of the plots of four novels which occurred to him. He suggested that Stoat should come up to Brighton and stay with Miss Wrote, who he felt sure would be delighted to have him, and that they should settle down to writing the book without delay.

Kenneth was more than willing to leave Wimbledon, and Dr Stoat agreed that it would be the best thing in the world for him to go and write a book with William. He also arranged to have Mrs Stoat removed from the Royal Bermondsey where the new treatment seemed to be making very little progress, into the care of Sister Cardew, who after a few discreet inquiries, said she would be pleased to have her.

Mrs Stoat was an immediate success at the home, and delighted everybody by firmly identifying Mr Spate as the Devil soon after her arrival.

Madness, under Sister Cardew's direction, was not a depressing illness needing treatment, but an eccentric game, an endless charade, and her patients or guests were encouraged to indulge their whims to the full. They soon developed new peculiarities, and enjoyed seeing how much they could get away with. After a time Mrs Stoat joined the Long camp against Mrs Cod-Finger, and gave several instances in her own experience of lupins changing from yellow to pink without warning, and advanced the theory that the metamorphosis was plainly attributable to the anger of the Lord, who, as she pointed out, was not always prepared to observe iniquity in the way that other people seemed to be.

When Kenneth visited his mother she seemed slightly resentful of the intrusion of the bad old world into her present happy circle.

'Good morning, Kenneth,' she said formally, and Kenneth said equally formally 'Good morning, Ma', and since there seemed little else to talk about, Mrs Stoat entertained him with the account of the lupins, and Kenneth listened wide-eyed. Afterwards he joined William in the garden, who was writing a sonnet to Miss Long in which he mentioned her many excellences, it is true, but dwelt upon her vices too.

Kenneth produced an enormous wad of foolscap and placed it importantly on the table, and they both settled down to a serious discussion of their book, but after a short time grew bored of it and started playing *Consequences*. When that had palled, they revived the ancient Cleeve game of *Liars*. Kenneth said to Mr Spate: 'Did you see the dead cow in the rectory field?'

'No, this is most distressing. What had happened to it?'

'Why, haven't you heard? It had died.'

'Oh, I see.'

'Some people say it was run over in the dark.'

'That seems a fairly likely explanation.'

'But it would not account for the mortal look of terror in the cow's face, would it?'

'I suppose not, if it had such a look,' said Mr Spate doubtfully.

'They say Miss Long was out of doors until quite late last night,' said William with cheerful inconsequence.

'Be careful what you say,' said Kenneth. 'Remember that in England nobody is ever guilty until found so by a court of law.'

'Oh dear,' said Mr Spate. 'What are you two talking about?'

'Ask Miss Long,' said William significantly.

'No, you'd better not,' said Kenneth, 'you don't want to get in the way of any possible police investigation.'

'No I think it would be much better if you tried to forget the whole thing. We shall all know the truth of this terrible matter before long, I suppose.'

'Of course she is not responsible for her actions, poor lady, but it does seem rather a brutal way of setting about things.'

'Well, so long as she confines herself to cows we can't complain.'

Mr Spate looked concerned, but held his peace. Stoat and O'Connor were highly pleased with the success of their lies, and thought that in Mr Spate they had found the perfect target for their activities. But they underestimated Mr Spate's intelligence, and in fact he joined in the game with gusto, and eventually beat them at it.

As Martin's commissioning leave approached he felt increasingly depressed at the prospect of spending the three weeks at Bidcombe with his mother. Originally he had invited four fellow cadets to stay with him for some of the time, in the hope that they would act as a buffer between himself and his mother's efforts to bring him round to the Faith, but Lady Foxglove had written to say that with the present reduced establishment at Bidcombe it would not be fair to the servants to start entertaining on such a large scale, and that in any case Brother Aloysius would be staying in the house during his leave, and it would be most improper to inflict an army of rowdy soldiers on him, especially as he was writing a book at that moment, and even if Martin had no respect for the artistic temperament she, Lady Foxglove, had. Quite old-fashioned she was, and to Martin, reading between the lines, it was obvious that he was going to have to face a pretty concentrated and intensive barrage of Goodness from the moment he crossed the threshold until he returned to the Army.

O'Connor's answer to his letter offering to go and visit him at Sister Cardew's had really not been very satisfactory, but he thought that if he went to stay the three weeks in Brighton it would give him as good an excuse as any for not returning to Bidcombe.

When Lady Foxglove received his letter announcing his intention, she wrote:

My Sweet Boy,

Of course I understand your reluctance to come to Bidcombe in the light of what has passed but for your own good you should try to have strength, and not be afraid to face me after what has occurred. There are many things which I must discuss urgently with you, and I feel that I would not be doing my duty if I did not *absolutely insist* that you come to Bidcombe at once, where we shall discuss in a calm and sober way whatever differences or difficulties have arisen. Brother Aloysius may well succeed where I have failed, for I know that you respect him more than myself.

She did not sign the letter, since she was uncertain of the best way of doing so. At the same time she wrote to Mr Dooney:

My Dear Young Man,

I enclose a money order for £5 10s. to cover the week ending July 30th. I hope it gives you satisfaction, and that you derive every ounce of enjoyment from it since it will be purchased at the price of your own soul. As for any suggestion that you should come to Bidcombe to see me, I should advise you to forget it at once. Never again in my lifetime do I want to see you. Enjoy your little spree, because there is an awful lot of time in Eternity to redeem it.

I am your Obedient Servant,

JULIA FOXGLOVE.

As she read the two letters through, it seemed to her that in both cases she had expressed her meaning clearly and unmistakably, and it was with a little glow of satisfaction that she put them into their envelopes and daintily licked them shut. But it was unfortunate from the point of view of the realization of her intentions that in her charming muddle-headed way she placed the letter intended for Martin in the envelope addressed to Mr Dooney, and the money order and note for Mr Dooney was conveyed unerringly and speedily to Martin.

11

When Martin arrived at Sister Cardew's to visit William he caused a minor sensation. Mr Spate danced round him, showing off terribly, and every time Martin looked at him he bowed and minced and gambolled and pulled comic faces and was most over-excited, playing now the music-hall lunatic, now the Devil, now the melancholy circus clown with a wealth of expression and histrionic gesture which Martin found most endearing. Sister Cardew thought him the most bonny boy, but Miss Long, who was a little bit jealous of Mr Spate's attention, said that he was too pretty by half, and she didn't say it very nicely. Eventually Mr Spate tripped over a rustic garden seat, and had to be helped indoors, where he became rather morose as the evening wore on.

Martin was a trifle nervous of meeting his friend in a lunatic asylum, but he knew nobody in Brighton, and since receiving his mother's strange letter he had begun to take an interest in Sister Cardew's Home which had nothing to do with his concern for O'Connor's welfare.

There could be no doubt that he *was* looking too pretty by half in his smart yellow beret and elegantly waisted Lieutenant's uniform, and as he approached O'Connor with all the poise and self-assurance of a ballerina, William determined to use his lunatic's licence to the full.

'Hullo, Tart,' he said, baring his teeth. 'So you've come to join us, have you? I didn't suppose you'd be long after. You running from the police, too? Well, you'll find it quite comfortable here once you're settled in, and the other guests are far more agreeable than anything you would have met in the Pigs. I must introduce you to my girl-friend, Gloria Cod-Finger. What one might call a stunning brunette, although I don't suppose that sort of thing is much in your line; but there are plenty of opportunities for romance, and there's always Mr Spate for you.'

'Poor William,' said Martin understandingly. 'It is a pity to see you in such a bad way. Hullo, Stoat, are you visiting too? Can you tell me whether or not it is expensive in this home? It seems most agreeable and comfortable.'

'Fifteen guineas a week with full board. Tarts usually charged double.'

'I see. Well, I hope you get better soon, William, and then you might like to come and stay at Bidcombe for a time to convalesce. Good-bye, Stoat. I am staying in Brighton for three weeks at the Palatial, so we might get in touch and make some sort of plans.'

'Yes, we might,' said Kenneth, thinking wistfully of the invitation to Bidcombe.

When Mr Dooney received Lady Foxglove's letter he was puzzled but gratified by her sudden *volte-face*. He kissed his wife tenderly on the forehead, patted his baby cautiously on the stomach, and said: 'I must go away for a few nights, Herring. Don't bother to forward any letters.'

'Ron,' said Herring in a hurt tone which she adopted whenever he forgot himself and addressed her by her surname.

'Virginia, I mean, then,' said Mr Dooney, and avoiding the baby's evil eye he took his raincoat and his bright woollen scarf down from the pegs above the cot, and walked out of the two-room flat which contained the sum of his aspirations, passions and desires. It was no good pretending, even to himself, that young Tarquin Dooney, his son, was a great beauty; but then he would hardly have known or cared if he had been, since to his hard masculine eyes nearly all babies looked the same; but what was slightly more disturbing was that Tarquin did not remotely resemble any other baby he had ever seen. He had been born with a full head of teeth, which was rare enough, and an uncommonly powerful jaw, as Mr Dooney had discovered on his first attempt to fondle the child under the midwife's austere gaze. He had very nearly lost his left index-finger, and if he had not dropped the creature at once, he almost certainly would have. One of the child's eyes was of a watery blue, and this one was always fixed motionless on his stomach. The other was a large almond brown, and followed one about the room with an intense malice which was all the more disconcerting for being unspoken. Six months after his birth he was still completely hairless except for his legs, which were covered with a rich red fuzz as they had been at the hour of his birth. Originally Mr Dooney had intended to sell the child to an adoption society of which he knew, but when he had presented his little bundle to the matron in charge she refused to accept it, saying that they would have to find a wolf or bear to adopt it as no human mother would. Herring was absolutely devoted to it, even though its foul temper and powerful jaw made it too dangerous to suckle, and she could only feed it at all with great personal daring. She crooned to it from a safe distance, and into the unwinking expressionless orb of its solitary eye made affectionate faces and endearing gestures. Sometimes she told it nursery rhymes or fairy stories, as it lay awaiting with a massive patience the hour of its greater strength. At first she told him delightful fairy stories, of princesses and woodcutters, and tinkling brooks and magic castles, but as these seemed to make little impression she adapted the art-form to suit her offspring's taste.

'Not many years ago,' she said, 'there lived in Fairyland a huge giant named Mordrarg, who was dreaded by the fairies even more than the dragons or witches who frequented those parts. This was because all he ever ate, for breakfast, luncheon or dinner, was fairies, with mermaids, of course, on Fridays. They thought this very greedy, because they were usually content with a little dew, or rosemary pollen before a dance. However, one day, after a feast of more than usually plump fairies, Mordrarg discovered to his alarm that there were no more fairies left in Fairyland. Imagine his dismay, sweet Tarquin, as he searched frantically under every buttercup leaf, and combed every beam of sunlight, without finding so much as a gossamer wing to make some soup! He had eaten them all!

'He retired to his castle, gnashing his teeth with a terrible noise, and sat brooding over his empty plate for three days. On the fourth day he arose, pulled in his belt, and strode out of the castle. He had resolved to leave Fairyland, and seek his food in the land of men.

'Now there lived among men at this time a man and his wife, called Sam and Doreen. They lived in a nice little cottage in the middle of the town called 22B. Sam was strong, and wise, and good, and his wife was as lovely as the day is long. Her hair was as golden as home-made margarine, and her complexion as fresh as a goldfish. They had been married many weeks when one day there came a thunderous knock on the front door. Mr Mordrarg had arrived, and he was feeling hungry. Sam jumped up from his delicious meal of cabbages and tea.

'"That must be the man from the Sanitary," he said to reassure his wife, and opened the door.

'"Young man, I feel hungry," shouted the giant, with a mighty stomach rumble.

'Now Sam was a sensible man, and thought it would be better to feed him, so he ran inside to the larder, where he brought out a tin of corned beef, half a pound of lard, two carrots, twelve cabbages, and a sausage. The giant ate them all in an instant, and then called out again:

'"Young man, I am still hungry." Here he beat his stomach, and the hollow boom was heard for many miles around. Sam told him timidly that there was nothing left in the house.

'"Yo ho," said Mordrarg, "you're a healthy enough young man for me."

'Now Sam was a clever fellow, and he did not want to be eaten when he was still so young. So he said:

'"Sir Giant, there may be a few cabbages left in the garden," and ran into the kitchen.

'"Now, precious," he said to his wife, "run out into the garden and pick some nice, young cabbages for my friend."

'"Willingly, my sweet," she answered, and flitted out of the room as softly as a flying ship.

'"Fie, fo," Mordrarg was saying, and was just about to say "fum" when he saw Doreen. In a single gulp, she floated down his throat like a jellied eel, and was never seen or heard of again. The hunger of the giant was appeased, and he went away to eat people in other lands, and Sam lived happily ever after.'

Herring laughed a little cracked laugh and approached closer to the baby.

'Did you like that story, my precious?' she asked fondly; 'then you shall hear another. In the reign of King Hildebrand (of Evil Memory) there lived in Bologna a torturer's daughter called Ruth . . .'

Tarquin lay motionless in his cot, and his single brown eye fixed unwinkingly on Herring as she gestured and mouthed to amuse him. Perhaps lurking somewhere behind the impassive face and inscrutable eyes there was an intelligence and an intention, but no human being could have divined it.

When Mr Dooney arrived at Bidcombe there was a Ladies' Retreat being held by Brother Aloysius. Shadowy figures glided over the lawns, their heads buried in some devotional work, or speculating on sacred matters.

'Excuse me, could you tell me where to find Lady Fox-glove?' he asked one of them, but the lady walked straight past without answering or making any acknowledgement. To another Mr Dooney said, 'Good evening', and the figure bowed and smiled, but when he asked, 'Excuse my butting in, but have you any idea where I can find Julia Fox-glove?' it went on its way wordlessly.

In the drawing-room Lady Foxglove sat with Brother Aloysius over a little glass of sherry.

'Since my husband's death,' she was saying simply, 'I have begun to realize what loneliness and suffering are. It is difficult to comprehend suffering when one has not oneself suffered, and nowadays I feel that any little help I can give, any comfort be it ever so small, to those less fortunate than I, any goodness is all that I have to live for.'

'Poor Julia,' said Brother Aloysius. 'In Derek you lost the finest and the best man in England.'

'He was so patient with my little faults,' she sighed, 'so kind, so pure.'

'He was the perfect complement to yourself,' said the monk happily, and both sighed; she sweetly deprecating, he smugly insisting. How infinitely remote seemed the true picture which she kept locked in her heart; her husband's secret vice, the vile double-life he had been living the whole time he was with her, his goodness a pretence, his affection a sham. And she a woman!

'I did try to live up to the standards he set, but it was hard, you know, hard. Sometimes even I, too, was weak.'

Brother Aloysius leant forward eagerly, and Lady Fox-glove's eyes travelled wistfully over his shoulder to the french window and garden outside as she wondered which of her minutely catalogued peccadillos they would discuss that evening.

In the garden, his nose glued to the french window, was Mr Dooney. As their eyes met he smirked and bowed. Lady Foxglove sat paralysed, the blood draining from her face.

'Oh, my God, go away. Can't you leave me alone for one minute. Haven't I been punished enough? For Christ's sake I am only a human, why must you torment me so? Are you the Devil himself?' she shouted.

'Julia!' said Brother Aloysius, but Mr Dooney opened the french windows and said: 'It's all right, padre. I am a medical man. I think she has been under considerable nervous strain recently, and the best we can do is to prescribe rest and a change of environment.'

'Keep away from me, you fiend,' she yelled, and Brother Aloysius said:

'Julia, you must try to take a hold on yourself,' and Mr Dooney said: 'Now, now, your Ladyship, this won't do, you know.'

In the two-roomed flat in Putney, Herring was preparing Tarquin's evening bottle, keeping up a flow of conversation as her busy trained fingers collected sterile rubber teats, saucepan and warm milk; when it was ready she sat beside the cot and looked at the tiny creature who owed his life to hers. She intentionally withheld the bottle for a time, because it was the only hour of the day when Tarquin's stoic calm could be ruffled, and a tiny hint of animation was allowed to cross his porphyry countenance. Today he seemed less patient than usual and bared his teeth.

'Shall I tell you another story, to give you an appetite, my precious?' said Herring spitefully, and Tarquin growled. 'Perhaps you are bored with stories. I shall sing you a song, a happy song of my girlhood, and when you're old enough we shall sing it together, and it will be like the days at the Medical School all over again. Now listen, for it is a very beautiful song, and to me very sad'; and she started to sing in a clear high voice the rhymes they were taught at the Royal Bermondsey, and used to chant together in their bedrooms:

> Every day a good nurse will
> Take her place the stools to fill
> An idle nurse will ever spoil it,
> Who won't wash her hands after the toilet
> Take great care of your fingernails
> Scrub out seats and bowls and pails,
> Use the flannel your ears beneath,
> After eating wash your teeth.

It was a charming lullaby, sung with feeling and beauty, but Tarquin rolled his eye and growled once more. Herring moved her face closer to his, and whispered: 'Oh, my little precious, how wilful you are. I always want to remember you like this, showing your strength of character so soon.' Her head was now so close to his that if he had sensation he could feel the warmth of her skin and smell the sour damp taste of her breath. 'You shall have your milk, my jewel, when I have kissed your precious forehead, when I have felt your life coursing under my lips, when I know that I have made you and you are my own son.' And her dry, warm lips touched his for a moment, and suddenly she saw in his eye something she had missed before.

There was something quite sexless and remote about the single high scream which brought all the neighbours running up to the Dooneys' flat. It was not so much a scream of pain, or fright, or even surprise, as an automatic alarm, an instinctive reaction which was all the more horrifying because it gave no hint of its message.

When Mr Dooney visited her in the hospital later that evening, they had bandaged her eyes, but they said that there was no further chance that she would ever see again. Tarquin's sharp little fingers had done more damage than the whole science of eye surgery could repair.

After Mr Spate's accident with the rustic bench he became more reserved, and seemed to regard the antics of Stoat and O'Connor with a jaundiced eye. They had upset the time-honoured routine and atmosphere of his daily life. Miss Long became sour and embittered, and her lapses more frequent. Mrs Cod became truculent and unmanageable, and had even suggested one evening that he should call her Gloria, in the hearing of everyone. Sister Cardew had been perfect, of course, and after a few coy jokes had managed to put her in her place, but the indignity was keenly felt by Mr Spate, who after twenty years elaborate courtship still called the object of his few remaining desires 'Miss Long'. His tumble in front of Martin, too, had left a mark. When Martin arrived, it seemed to Mr Spate as if for thirty years he had been walking in a garden of carefully nurtured dandelions and daisies and that suddenly in his wanderings he had come upon a delicious wild rose, newly opened from the bud. He had savoured its fragrance and admired its beauty from every angle, but when he tried to get closer he had fallen, hurting himself terribly. It would have been more poetic if he had killed himself, but then, of course, he hadn't. His leg had hurt more than he realized anything could hurt, and it was only with the greatest difficulty he restrained himself from crying.

Two weeks later as he sat knitting in Sister Cardew's study after dinner a crafty plan formed in his head, and he waited until the others had left before putting aside the enormous scarf which he had been knitting for thirty years with the vague intention that it should one day adorn a refugee from Hungary or Palestine.

'Sister Cardew,' he said cunningly. 'It is strange the difference that the arrival of young O'Connor has made to the lives of us all.'

'Yes, indeed, he is a bundle of mischief to be sure.'

'Ah, but we must remember our own childhood, my dear.

Not mischief but life. Our William has all the charm of a foal finding its legs, all the exuberance of a lamb in the meadows on a fine spring day, all the delightful inconsequence of a kitten, the endearing clumsiness of a puppy. He is the epitome of youth, the finest flower of the human state.'

'Well, I don't know if I should go as far as that,' said Sister Cardew doubtfully, 'but he seems a lively enough lad for his age.'

'Ah, his age,' sighed Mr Spate and closed his eyes, opening them again with what he hoped was a lecherous gleam. 'Of all ages the one which is to me the most delectable.'

Sister Cardew was not impressed. Although she knew and felt faintly proud of Mr Spate's past history when he was an up-and-coming young actor, she also knew his present medical history, and that he was far too old to cause any more trouble of that sort.

'I'm glad you like the little fellow,' she observed shortly, 'I confess I have a soft spot for him myself.'

Mr Spate changed his tack :

'Like him ? Why I feel as if he were my own son. At that age, of course, a father cannot lecture or punish his son. There comes a time when he has simply to watch him make mistakes, and hope that he will realize them himself in time. But it is distressing, my dear, for a fond parent, most distressing, and sometimes very difficult.'

'Why, what has the little devil been up to now?' asked Sister Cardew suspiciously. She had suspected that all this was leading up to something.

'Why, haven't you heard?' inquired Mr Spate innocently, echoing, although he did not know it, the catch phrase of the famous Cleeve game of *Liars*.

'It was immediately after dinner, and he did it quite publicly. I think it must have been something in the meal which displeased him, and I must confess I found the boiled carrots most unpalatable myself, although, of course, I would not dream of going to such extremes as young O'Connor.'

'What are you talking about, Mr Spate?'

'Dear me, if you really do know nothing about it the situation is quite alarming, because I have always been led to believe that in any quantity the metal polish which you employ so frequently, and, may I say it? efficaciously, is a most dangerous substance to imbibe. But I am sure that you have taken adequate measures.'

'If this is another of your jokes, Mr Spate,' said Sister Cardew savagely, but Mr Spate held up his hands in protest.

'Really, my dear lady, this is hardly a joking matter. I should say, although, of course, I cannot pretend to any great degree of medical experience that there was little time to lose if we are to avert a tragedy.'

After Sister Cardew had stormed out of the room, he tittered wickedly into his hand at the thought of his own naughtiness, and then resumed his knitting, taking the same infinite pains over each stitch as he had for the last thirty years.

When Sister Cardew ran, spitting with fury, up to O'Connor and asked 'Have you been drinking my Brasso?' it never occurred to him to answer anything but 'Oh yes, rather'. His *hubris* was indomitable and would never allow him to miss a single opportunity to indulge his curious sense of humour. Punishment was always out of all proportion to the crime, overwhelming and, to any normal human being, crushing, but O'Connor rode the waves of his misfortunes like a gull floating on the surface, and the storm always left him dry, unperturbed, and no wiser than before. He defied all the laws of catharsis, for his suffering had not taught him an iota of self-knowledge, but he always remained the same ebullient O'Connor, an affront to the Gods and a challenge to Destiny. Stoat was the opposite to his friend. He wallowed in his misfortunes like a waterlogged ship which for some reason never quite sank, but received buffet after buffet from the furious sea, which regarded his ugliness and impotence as an insult; perhaps he would eventually find peace when he had sunk and rested on the sea-bed beneath the storm. While Foxglove, gentle Foxglove, was the petrel, untouched by any of the havoc who flew straight and fast miles above the storm of which he was the augur.

When the ambulance arrived William began to have misgivings about his latest little joke, and drew Sister Cardew aside and confessed frankly that in fact he had not touched her Brasso. But once the great machinery of the divine mills is set in motion it is not so easily stopped, and soon William was bouncing down the drive in the ambulance with his ears singing unmusically from a thorough boxing. Sister Cardew knew perfectly well he had drunk the metal polish, and she wasn't going to be put off by any of the lies. She was sorry she had ever let him into her home now, she ought to have known that he would do something silly of the sort.

After the stomach pump had been removed, and the hospital reported that they could find no trace of metal polish, although they had found some partially digested carrots which could have caused mild food poisoning, Sister Cardew was still determined that he should never return to her home.

'He's more trouble than he's worth, that boy, and you can keep him,' she concluded, and banged down the telephone receiver defiantly. Mr Spate's lie had worked.

William was kept in hospital under observation for two days and by the time he was let out to join Kenneth at Miss Wrote's it was nearly time for Martin to rejoin his regiment.

Martin's leave had not been very enjoyable. Apart from his one visit to Sister Cardew's Home he had been living quite alone in his hotel in Brighton. He kept his resolve not to go down to Bidcombe after his mother's incomprehensible letter, and felt a certain satisfaction when he received Brother Aloysius' tactful letter explaining the nature of his mother's breakdown. Martin had only one goal in life and that was to reach the age of twenty-one, when he would revenge himself to the full for everything he supposed himself to have suffered.

William and Kenneth met him once again before he left Brighton for the Army. William lived in daily terror of the police discovering about his banishment from Sister Cardew's Home because now that he was out of its protecting shades he was liable to complete his military prison sentence in a civilian jail. He changed his name, and insisted that both Kenneth and Miss Wrote call him Arthur in private and Mr Connolly in public. He attempted to grow a moustache, which was not a great success, and dyed his hair with quite spectacular results. Every morning he and Kenneth would take up their place on the promenade by the sea, and Kenneth who had discovered rather to his surprise a talent for using chalk would draw on the pavement a large pink madonna, or sometimes a dog or a nude. O'Connor held the hat and made humorous faces and unintelligible jokes in his rich Irish brogue, and between the two of them they usually made five pounds a day. Occasionally a policeman would pass, and then William would ram the hat on his head and thrust his hands deep into his pockets and whistle nonchalantly. This was always a great success with passers-by, and usually reaped at least half a crown after the policeman had gone.

One afternoon Stoat was on his knees touching up the underlip of the madonna, while William performed his antics with the hat when he heard a familiar voice say : 'Could you tell me, please, the way to the station ?' He looked up, his spotty face covered with chalks of every conceivable hue, to see an elegant young second-lieutenant of the Pigs standing over him. 'Hullo, Martin,' he said.

Martin looked puzzled, and then said self-consciously: 'Oh, hullo, Stoat. I wondered if you knew the way to the station?'

'I think you go down to the second traffic signal and then turn left, actually.'

'Oh do you? Thanks a lot.' Then feeling that the situation called for a little more comment he said: 'I think your drawing is jolly good. Why has the madonna got a moustache?'

'Oh,' said Stoat a little sheepishly, 'that is Mr Connolly's work.'

'Oh I see,' said Martin, but he was plainly much more embarrassed than Stoat to have found his friend in this position. 'Well, I'll be seeing you,' he said finally, and made to go towards the station, but William, who had just caught sight of him, was not going to let him go so easily.

'Och and begosh,' he cried delightedly, 'if it isn't the most salubrious tart that we have here. Are you not going to spare a penny for a poor Paddy after your own heart, my pretty one? And whun oi say a penny it is more a half-crown that I'm meaning, if you follow me.'

He thrust his revolting green hat under Foxglove's nose and danced impatiently on the pavement while Martin fumbled in his pockets. After a time Martin decided that a quiet rebuke was needed.

'I am sensible, O'Connor, that in our time we have had disagreements and that perhaps you labour under the impression of an injustice but I must tell you that you do not strengthen your case by your present behaviour. One would almost be tempted to believe that you have no self-respect at all if one were to judge you by your appearance. Here is half a crown.'

'Listen to him for the tuppenny tart that he is, I ask you,' screamed O'Connor, shaking his fists in the air in simulated rage, 'calling poor old Paddy names and all. Hi'll have you know, sir, that moy name is Connolly, and proud to make your acquaintance I'm sure, such a fine young gentleman that you are.' William shook his peroxided hair and made faces.

'O'Connor, I have always known you were a great wit, and one of the most amusing intellects in the Poetry Circle, but there are times when one simply is not in the mood for your individual brand of humour. Will you please get out of my way and let me get to the station?'

'Oh, a most eloquent tart, I see. An' it please your mighty Pigship to walk over my virtuous body I shall be proud to boast that I have been trampled on by the most forgiving tart in Christendom. A tart with a heart of gooseberry jam, moy little darling. How's her ladyship these days?'

'O'Connor, you are not making a word of sense. Will you get out of my way?'

Just then a voice sounded from the back of a small crowd which always gathered to watch William's performances.

'Is he troubling you, Sir?'

Martin treated the enormous policeman to a quick smile of gratitude, the smile which illuminated his countenance like a torch and made strong men and women prepared to go to their deaths in his service.

'Well, yes, officer, he is being a little difficult.'

William rammed the hat on to his head and mumbled, 'Wull, oi'll be on my way, and the top of the morning to you', but his arm was held by a hoop of steel and further hoops were applying themselves to the scruff of his neck.

'Now then, young man, I want your name and address.'

'And what might you be wanting them for, my man?'

'You'll find out in time. Now, let's have the right name first time, shall we?'

O'Connor gave his name as Arthur Connolly and Miss Wrote's address. Martin listened with a patient smile and then said: 'I think I should tell you, officer, that his name is O'Connor and he is a deserter from my regiment who was discharged from the Army on the grounds of insanity. This is for your own good, William, that I'm telling him the truth.'

The policeman wrote down both names impartially. O'Connor suddenly felt slightly unsure of himself, and reacted, as was his wont, in a violent diatribe.

'Would you listen to his word before mine, constable? Don't you realize that he is just a tuppeny tart, and if anything is against the law that is. If you want promotion in the Force he's your man to arrest.'

'I think,' said the policeman with the same magisterial impartiality, 'that we had better adjourn further discussion to the police station, where I shall take particulars of the complaints I have received, and it will be decided what course of action, if any, will be taken.'

'If it is all the same to you, officer,' said Martin, 'I think I must go now, as I must catch a train.'

'On the contrary, Sir, I think it would be advisable to come to the station with me now where you can make a statement.'

'Oh, I have no wish to prosecute the matter, officer. It was a very small nuisance, and the matter seems to be under control now.'

'Nevertheless, Sir, it would be preferable if you would leave a statement before you left.'

'Oh, very well.'

As the curious procession moved off with Kenneth, uninvited, tailing on behind, O'Connor muttered in Foxglove's ear: 'Insidious little tart. I could break your neck for this,' and Martin answered: 'Well really, William, I thought I might let you off.' The policeman wrote down the exchange as they walked.

When they reached the station the constable said: 'Let us

get this clear. You claim that your name is Arthur Connolly and your address to be the one you have given me?'

'Yes.'

'And you claim that his name is William O'Connor, address unknown, and that he was committing a nuisance this morning when I arrived?'

'I suppose so.'

'Well, is that the nature of your claim or not?'

'Yes it is.'

'Very well, we shall now telephone the address given and discover the truth.'

When the telephone rang in Miss Wrote's quiet little house she was very excited. The machine had been installed at enormous expense before the war, and although she used it occasionally to have a chat with her friend Sister Cardew, it was very seldom indeed that it summoned her.

'Hullo,' she said timorously into its cold black ear, 'this is Miss Wrote's residence, Miss Wrote speaking.'

'This is Sea View Police Station, Constable Mole speaking,' it answered. 'We're sorry to trouble you, ma'am, but we have a youth here who gives his name as Arthur Connolly and claims to be resident in your house. Can you tell us anything about him?'

'Who? I don't think I know anyone called Connolly. Oh, you mean William. Of course I know him, very well indeed. I do hope he is not in trouble again. He has been doing so well lately, as a street artist, you know. What has he been up to?'

'Well I wouldn't like to say that he's in trouble, and I wouldn't like to say he's not, if you see what I mean, ma'am,' said Constable Mole carefully.

'I see,' said Miss Wrote meekly.

'Now what did you say he was called again?'

'Arthur Connolly. A very great friend of mine.'

Policeman Mole was craftier than he looked:

'And you wouldn't by any chance know anybody of the name of William O'Connor?'

Poor Miss Wrote got very flustered. She was determined to be loyal to William, and rather enjoyed the role of outlaw which fate had made her play, but Nature had not cast her in the right mould to sustain a deception for any length of time.

'Oh dear, William O'Connor, did you say? I'm not sure whether I know anybody of that name. Let me think. I believe I may have heard it before somewhere.'

'There seems to be some doubt whether the youth concerned is called Connolly or O'Connor.'

'Well, I'm afraid I can't help you. I expect he might be called either.'

'Well, will you come and identify the young man? You can tell us whether he's your great friend Connolly or your acquaintance O'Connor.'

'Very well,' said Miss Wrote in a worried sort of way, and put the nasty little black engine back on its cradle with distaste.

When she arrived at the station, Constable Mole turned to William and said: 'Not one squeak out of you, my man, and none of your methods, see,' and then turning to Miss Wrote said: 'Can you tell us now, ma'am, the name of the young person confronting you?'

Miss Wrote simply did not know what was expected of her. She stared at William from every angle, walked round him, examined his clothes, in an agony of indecision. Eventually, she said: 'I'm afraid I'm not quite sure.'

Martin said: 'He's O'Connor, and you know he is.' Miss Wrote brightened at once, and said, 'Oh yes, so he is to be sure.'

Stoat said, 'Shut up, you idiot. He's Connolly.'

Poor Miss Wrote was nearly in tears. She said: 'William, which are you for Heaven's sake? I mean Arthur.'

O'Connor's chivalrous heart was stirred. He said: 'It's all

right, Fanny. I'll tell them the truth. I am William O'Connor the dangerous criminal, the scourge of the police, the terror of all the tarts, O'Connor the noble champion of all that is wrong, betrayed by a fickle little tart who isn't even worth tuppence. Now you can go, Marty, you have done enough damage for today. I thought you were a friend and I can see you're a crawling perverted little snake.'

'That's right,' said Miss Wrote, very much relieved that the responsibility had been shifted from her shoulders.

With all the thoroughness for which the English police are justly renowned, Constable Mole took statements from everybody present, including Kenneth, who still insisted out of obstinacy that William was called Arthur Connolly.

Martin's statement read : I, the undersigned, Martin Foxglove, a second-lieutenant in the Special Airborne Commando Regiment, was walking to the railway station at eleven o'clock on the morning of Tuesday the seventeenth of November when I was accosted by William O'Connor, a former private soldier in my regiment, of established bad character, who attempted to extort money from me, using insulting language and in a manner likely to cause a breach of the peace. I reported him to 2337 P.C. Mole.

William's statement read : I, the undersigned, William Patrick O'Connor, poet and philosopher of no fixed address, was attending to my business on the promenade on the morning of Tuesday the seventeenth of November when I saw a youth known to me as Martin Foxglove behaving in a manner likely to cause a breach of the peace. I rebuked him, and informed him that his behaviour was answerable to the law, but he continued to behave in an improper manner. I reported him to 2337 P.C. Mole.

Kenneth's statement was more obscure : I, the undersigned, Kenneth Benjamin Stoat, an artist, of no fixed address, was attending to my business on the promenade when I observed an altercation between a youth known to me as Martin Foxglove, a soldier, of Bidcombe Manor, Cirencester, Glos, and a young gentleman of my acquaintance, Mr Arthur Connolly, a poet and philosopher of no fixed address. The argument appeared to be on some philosophical point of linguistic nicety, which was aggravated by the appearance of 2337 P.C. Mole until it became heated and illogical. I can only describe the constable's behaviour as rash and ill-considered, and his interference as officious.

Miss Wrote's statement was noncommittal : I, the undersigned, Miss Frances Gwendolen Wrote, a retired nanny and welfare worker of 7 Mulberry Walk, Brighton, declare that I have known both Mr William O'Connor, the eminent poet, and Mr Arthur Connolly, the celebrated philosopher, both of no fixed address, for over eighteen years, and believe them both to be of excellent character. I have not met Mr Foxglove before, but out of my experience of his type of person, I should recommend, in my capacity as welfare worker, that he be helped rather than punished.

After Miss Wrote had signed her statement in her clear, firm hand, they were all allowed to leave the station with an undertaking from O'Connor not to change address without notifying the police. After they had left, the massive machinery of the law began to digest and to read, to sift and to verify, and finally, most imponderable and terrifying process of them all, to reach conclusions.

When they arrived at Mulberry Walk, Kenneth said : 'I don't expect they'll do anything. Why on earth do you always have to be so rude to poor Martin ? He only wanted to be friendly, and he can be awfully kind when he wants.'

'He's a tart,' said O'Connor stoutly.

'You know as well as I do that he's not,' said Kenneth, a little hurt, 'sometimes I wonder if you're not a bit loony after all.'

This was enough to start William off on his celebrated impersonation of the Mad Hermit of the Caves, but when he had tired of it, and the performance was always rather exhausting, he sat down in Miss Wrote's armchair to watch her happily clearing up the broken jug and lamp standard which were his props for the act and said: 'He may not be a tart in the way that your evil mind thinks of tarts, but can't you see that his obvious chastity is just another play, another of his attractions? He is one of Nature's bloody darlings, and it's so impossible to dislike him with his pretty tricks and winning ways that it needs an O'Connor, an evil genius, the champion of all that is wrong, to see what a tart he is. Oh, he is the most charming, the most likeable, the most beautiful person in the world, he has all the looks of a narcissus, the wealth of a Croesus, a mother to whom the Virgin Mary can't hold up a candle, a house which makes the temple of King Solomon seem tame, but I prefer my verminous dirty old Stoaty every time.'

'You're just jealous,' said Stoat nastily, and O'Connor gave a little dance of joy: 'Bitten again. You can't stroke a Stoat. Give him a breadcrumb and he'll take a finger. What does it feel like to be a Stoat?'

'Oh, all right I suppose.'

'Good.'

After that they could neither of them think of anything to say. The trouble with fancy conversation is that it is difficult to keep up for any length of time. Soon they resumed their interminable game of poker dice.

The law decided that there was an inadequate case for a prosecution. Clearly what had in fact happened was somewhere between the two accounts. O'Connor had been shocked by something in Foxglove's manner which had disgusted him, and had abused him violently. An account of the incident was sent to the War Office, where it was appended to Foxglove's Confidential File, and followed him from unit to unit throughout his military career, to the

188

delight of the various sergeant-clerks who were the only people to read it. Through them it always circulated the Sergeants' Mess, and by degrees the humblest recruit had his miserable existence momentarily lightened by the retailing of a dirty joke at the unapproachable Mr Foxglove's expense.

In the course of its investigations the Law discovered that William O'Connor was a certified lunatic of criminal tendencies at present in an institution. When Sister Cardew assured them that O'Connor had been discharged as sane some weeks ago, the Law rubbed its head and wondered if someone had been leading it up the garden path.

As distant echoes of these investigations began to reach Major O'Connor he acted with the promptness and decision which had made him one of the most dreaded newspaper editors in Britain. After two long-distance telephone calls, it was arranged for William to complete his sentence in a Church Home for Christian delinquents, where the authorities were rather more amenable than in a civilian prison. In fact there was slightly less than a fortnight left to serve, and William left cheerfully for his new home, leaving behind a tearful Miss Wrote, who begged him to return as soon as he was out. Kenneth returned despondently to Wimbledon, his book still unwritten.

12

When news of Lady Foxglove's latest excursion in good works reached those Christian circles in which she occupied so illustrious a place, opinion was divided as to whether it was her best work so far, or whether it was conclusive proof of her approaching insanity. Many people felt that good works were all very well so far as they went, but that this time she had gone too far, and that she must have been motivated more by the desire for notoriety than Christian charity in adopting, at her age, a baby from an unknown home and giving it her name. Of course there was no doubt that the child would now have a good Christian background, but there were institutions provided for that sort of thing, and it really was too ostentatious of Julia to go round buying up babies and calling them fancy names like Tarquin. Nobody, apart from Lady Foxglove and Mr Dooney, ever knew the true details of the adoption. She had assured everybody that the child's parents were completely unknown, and that she, for one, would never inquire. None of her friends could ever have guessed the terrible scene which had occurred when Mr Dooney had thrust the revolting bundle on her, nor the sanctions he had applied in making her promise to keep it. Nobody could have seen the darkened room in a London hospital where Herring wept quietly and tearlessly all day long after her husband had told her that he had sent the child to an adoption society. She was alone in a dark world, and the only thing she had ever loved was removed from her.

The baby was installed in the old nursery wing at Bidcombe, and a very expensive nanny was hired from London to look after it. Lady Foxglove began to regret that she had ever got rid of Nanny Bill, who had been much cheaper and hadn't expected to have a maid to run and fetch for her the whole time. But Miss Primrose did not last more than a week, and when she left she said: 'I'm sorry, Lady Foxglove, but nowadays one can afford to be a little more choosey about the babies one takes on, and I am afraid that Tarquin and I will never get on really well together. I have nothing against you or the baby, it's just that I'm afraid we're incompatible.'

After Miss Primrose came Nanny Chudleigh, but she had to be sacked after a bottle of port, left over from Sir Derek's days, was found to be missing, and she had threatened to skin the cook with a carving knife if ever she dared send watery cabbages up to the nursery again. As she left she said: 'You can't sack me because I've resigned. I don't look after spastics and I don't look after hanimals and you can keep the nasty unnatural little thing.'

After Nanny Chudleigh came Nanny Biggs, and one of her first improvements was to have a gas stove installed in the nursery block, but it needed more than that to quieten the furious temper of her charge, who seemed to thrive on gas as readily as on air. After she lost a fingernail to him in a disagreement over the proper quantity of milk for a nine-month-old baby she admitted that she was beaten and left.

To begin with Tarquin was brought down to the drawing-room from time to time to be admired by the guests, but it was no good pretending he was a great success, and after a time it became too embarrassing to have to explain to everybody who came to the house that it was better not to stroke him. He always used to make the most horrible noises during his brief appearances and on one occasion, in the arms of Nanny Biggs, was violently and inexplicably sick.

At the age of a year he was still completely hairless except for his legs which grew redder and furrier every day. Every kind of lotion and remedy was applied to his head, but the only effect was to make his pate shine like a lantern. Old Mrs Cattacomb, in the village, had heard that horse manure was a certain cure for hairlessness, but when it was discovered that Tarquin was eating it the cure had to be abandoned. To Lady Foxglove he was the personification of her husband's sin, the daily reminder of her failure as a wife and her gullibility as a woman. She hated the child as she had never hated anything before and the baby seemed to sense her hatred and to cultivate it and grow in it using its aura as the spore of some deadly bacteria uses a pile of dirt as its home and its food.

Soon his public appearances became less frequent, and

after a time stopped altogether. When anybody inquired after him, Lady Foxglove would give her famous long-suffering smile, and say: 'Who? Oh, you mean poor Tarquin. Things are not easy for him, poor dear, but I felt that I simply had to give him a home. I don't know if you've ever felt a Call, I certainly never had, but when it came, I knew that this was it. With Martin grown up now, it seemed such a pity to squander all the beauty and goodness of Bidcombe on myself, so I resolved to share it, and I must say the dear little fellow gives me hardly any trouble at all.'

This was true enough. It was in Tarquin's third year that the supply of nannies gave out. After that they would not come even for two weeks at a time. Somehow word had got round among the nannies of England, primly debated over large black perambulators in Regent's Park, furtively whispered between nursery maids having a secret cigarette in the lavatories, coldly knitted into jumpers by lonely love-sick governesses in countless schoolrooms, that Bidcombe was no cop.

Tarquin ruled alone in the nursery corridor, and his servants were the draughts and the flies and an occasional mouse which were the only visitors to his kingdom. Every morning at eleven, the cook would heat up a tin of stewed prunes, pre-digested chicken and carrots and would peel an apple. Since it was not the cook's job to wait on the nursery, Lady Foxglove would carry the delicious meal up to the silent corridor, unlocking the door quietly, and leaving the tray just inside it, before retiring and ringing a bell. She always tried to shut her mind to the noises that came through the door immediately after the bell had sounded, and as she wandered down to the drawing-room she would take out her little pocket book and with a whimsical smile put a tiny little tick against *Give food to the Hungry*.

In the evening, when Tarquin's second and more elaborate collation had been prepared, Lady Foxglove would listen carefully to see if he was waiting for her on the other side of the door, and, if he was not, would leave the tray on the floor and collect the broken fragments of china which were always the only remnants of his earlier feast.

On this rich and varied diet Tarquin grew larger and stronger daily. Nobody inquired after his sanitary arrangements; there was a perfectly suitable bathroom in the nursery wing and nobody cared to speculate as to whether he used its amenities or not. It would have been absurdly affected to expect a child of three to need lavatory paper or towels, and in any case it would have embarrassed Lady Foxglove to have to ask for them.

Among Lady Foxglove's more fashionable friends he was known as The Beast of Bidcombe, and they were always most solicitous after his health when they arrived to stay. 'How is your charming baby, Julia?' they would all ask. 'We thought him *so* amusing and vivacious.'

Lady Foxglove would smile wanly and say: 'Dear Tarquin. He's so independent these days, you know. Lives a life of his own entirely, and nothing will persuade him to come and visit us in the drawing-room any longer. I must confess I am devoted to the boy, and can't think how I would manage without him. He seems to give one's life some purpose. You understand what I mean.'

Her less fashionable friends piously closed their ears to the malicious rumours which were being spread abroad, and, during their stay at Bidcombe, were careful to avoid all mention of the child, just to be on the safe side. When, at eleven o'clock every morning and at seven o'clock every evening, Lady Foxglove would leave them with a charming smile and each day a different excuse, they would carefully avoid giving each other meaningful glances, and discuss the weather with nervous animation until she returned.

Herring never really forgave her husband for his perfidy in

disposing of her only child. She became sullen and morose, and after a time Mr Dooney had her transferred to an institution by the sea, where she settled down quite happily to write five-hundred-page romances which enjoyed a large public on the other side of the Atlantic, and enabled Mr Dooney to live in tolerable comfort in an hotel in Torquay. Nobody ever behaves quite the same in private as they do in public, and Herring, when alone in her little two-roomed flat with her beloved Tarquin, had been in the habit of saying and doing things which would have surprised her girl-friends or her husband. Now that in her blindness she was perpetually alone she lost all the inhibitions which had confined the poetry in her soul, and spent the days crooning quietly to herself, or inventing extravagant stories on paper to beguile her large and growing reading public. Only she understood that her blindness was all part of a much greater plan, and that Tarquin's little fingers were the instruments of a fate like that which had overtaken Ruth, the torturer's daughter in Bologna, during the reign of King Hildebrand of Evil Memory. In the crazy jigsaw of her mind the last piece had been fitted with a deftness which only the Gods could have contrived, and she was triumphant in the knowledge of her superior, solitary perception. In short, she was mad, but happy. In the vivid patterns of her unseeing mind there was always discernible one axiom, around which the kaleidoscope of her fancy whirled and glittered. Somewhere there lurked the knowledge that she was waiting for something, that this pleasant half-existence would only last for a time, and that on some occasion in the future her erring fancy would again encounter reality and find a second truth, like the first which had been revealed to her in the moments after she had seen the look in Tarquin's eye three years ago. It was this knowledge which sustained her through the dim years while she crooned and scribbled alone in her bedroom, and the wind howled round her windows, or the sun came feebly intruding on a dark world through the old diamond-pane glass windows, and her thin white hands felt the warmth, but the eyes saw nothing.

When Martin eventually returned home after his dramatic apostasy it was to supervise the arrangements of his twenty-first birthday celebrations. His mother said: 'It is lovely to see you after so long, Martin, and most thoughtful of you to think of coming to make all the arrangements yourself, because, with so much on my shoulders at the moment, I simply can't find it in my heart to celebrate.' She gave him one of her long, loving, wistful stares, which always made him curl up his toes inside his socks with embarrassment, but out of sheer force of habit he flashed her the famous Foxglove smile which they both understood so well, and said:

'Poor Mama, you must be off your head with worry these days, with everything to plan for, and your own move coming on top of everything else.'

Lady Foxglove automatically treated him to a sweet, grateful smile, but she looked pensive, and after a moment said: 'What were you talking about when you said that my move was coming on top of everything else?'

'Well, on top of all your other worries,' said Martin innocently. 'What to do with Tarquin, how you're going to manage without a cook, how to set about closing down the chapel.'

'Martin, I was not inquiring what you meant by everything else; God knows I have enough on my mind at the moment. I wanted to know what you meant by my move.'

Further discussion was postponed by the arrival of Martin's soldier-servant (or *Jhon* as they were for some reason known in the Pigs) who said that some men had arrived who wanted to know where to erect the marquee. Pig Percy-Scroop-Beauchamp was an enormous giant of a man whose imponderable stupidity had made him unfit even for a sabre-platoon of the Pigs, but he followed Martin as obediently and devotedly as a dog. Now that Martin was a full lieutenant he was entitled to a *Jhon* by himself which was a great relief to Pig Percy who had found the division of his loyalties most exhausting.

'Tell them to put it on the south lawn facing the swimming pool,' said Martin authoritatively, rather pleased at the opportunity to show off his new authority.

'Ur,' said Pig Percy-Scroop-Beauchamp benignly, and went off to smoke a cigarette in the newly erected urinal behind the rhododendron bushes, brooding darkly on his latest mission.

Martin said : 'We must discuss all that later. I expect that you have sent out most of the invitations already ?'

'Yes, dear,' replied his mother in a worried sort of way; 'I have invited all the village, except, of course, the two Misses Umbrage, who wouldn't have come anyway.'

The Misses Umbrage were divided into Miss Umbrage, large, and Miss Umbrage, small. They were Lady Foxglove's only rivals in the field of good works in the village, and it used to amuse her to give them the occasional half-crown for their Homes for Deaf Doggies, or five shillings to their organization against Cruelty to Helpless Children, but one day they had gone too far and demanded a pint of her blood. It was really too gruesome, the whole thing, and Lady Foxglove had answered back with a demand that they should adopt two Christian leper children, and since then they had not been on speaking terms.

'I expect that you will want to invite some of your new Army friends,' she said uneasily, 'and there are always your old friends from Cleeve. We mustn't forget Frank Pratt-Bingham, must we?'

'Oh, I don't think we want him,' said Martin.

'Why not? I thought he was so nice, and you were such great friends.'

'I think he's a bit too much of a bugger, you know,' said Martin carelessly, savouring every moment of his new power.

'Oh, I see,' said Lady Foxglove meekly. Martin pressed home his advantage spitefully: 'We must ask poor old Henry Stoat. I've been meaning to do something about him for a long time.'

'Yes,' said Lady Foxglove, 'I took an especial liking to Henry Stoat. What about young William O'Connor?'

'No, I don't think we want him,' said Martin, but was disconcerted when his mother said: 'Oh, I am so glad. I felt sure that you would grow out of him, although, of course, I had to do what I could for him while he was in prison.'

'I think perhaps that we might invite him after all,' said Martin with a rashness which he was never allowed to forget. Little did he know it, but in order to spite his mother and to be partly proud he had set in motion the machinery of fate which was to end in his greatest humiliation.

A day before the great festivities were to begin, Lady Foxglove was drawing up the list of music for the Bidcombe Platinum Band, when Trained Pig Percy came into the drawing-room and shuffled his feet. Lady Foxglove crossed out 'Lilli Marlene' and substituted in her characteristic sloping hand 'Bless This House, but not too loud or there might be complaints', and looked up with a busy smile at the enormous figure who was clearing his throat importantly: 'Urs summum ze door,' he explained and beamed when Lady Foxglove said: 'You mean there's someone at the door? How kind of you to tell me. I really don't know where we should be without you, Mr Percy. You are the greatest help, and I hope Martin promotes you or something when all this is over.'

Lady Foxglove walked purposefully towards the front door followed by Pig Percy-Scroop-Beauchamp who sniffed her exotic personal scent as he walked behind her like a boar routing for truffles. Standing in the porch was a small deputation. Miss Umbrage, large, looked large and grim and purposeful; Miss Umbrage, small, looked small and sour and nasty, and between the two was an elderly man in a curious kind of uniform, something between a police inspector and a bus conductor, and he was looking embarrassed and a bit ashamed of himself, as well he might, thought Lady Foxglove, who had decided that he was a zoo attendant, who had no right to come to the front door.

'Dear Miss Umbrage,' she said sweetly, 'how lovely it is to see you again. I really thought that you must have moved from the village, I've heard so little from you. How are your deaf doggies and your helpless children?'

'Very nicely, thank you,' said Miss Umbrage, large, grimly.

'Your Ladyship,' said Miss Umbridge, small, sourly.

The person in the middle cleared his throat, and seemed about to say something, but Lady Foxglove forestalled him.

'Well, I'm afraid that I am far too busy these days to spend my entire day gossiping on the doorstep. It was exceedingly civil of you to call, but I have so much to attend to, you know, so I simply must leave you.'

'Oh no you don't,' said Miss Umbrage, small, as she began to close the door. 'It's not quite so easy as that,' added the lesser of the two. 'Go on, you tell her, inspector.'

'Acting on complaints received from our local representative, Miss Winifred Umbrage' – the smaller of the two pursed her lips – 'which reports were confirmed by our district overseer, Miss Ethel Umbrage,' – the larger one nodded her head – 'and on behalf of the National Society for the Prevention of Suffering in Helpless Children, I am empowered, under the Act of 1948, to make an inspection of

198

the premises and circumstances of living of one Tarquin Foxglove, an adopted child of this address.'

It is in such circumstances as this that Foxgloves tend to come out in their true colours. Lady Foxglove, for all her charm, her delightful muddle-headedness in business matters, had somewhere inside her a spring of the toughest steel which was all the more disconcerting because it was hidden for most of the time, and when it was suddenly revealed it came as an ugly shock to people who had never suspected its presence.

'You must be off your head if you think that I am going to let you see him at this hour. He was put to bed a long time ago and I certainly should not think of waking him up to satisfy the prurient curiosity of a couple of old maids who have probably never seen a healthy child before. He is fast asleep now in his little cot, with his clean sheets tucked down, smelling ever so faintly of his bath, with his hair brushed and his teeth clean, dreaming, perhaps, of the party tomorrow.' Even as she spoke she saw in her mind's eye the empty, damp corridor, the broken crockery, and heard the scuffling feet on the other side of the door.

'Oh yeah?' said one of the Misses Umbrage.

'I am afraid that I must insist that I be allowed to inspect the premises, and then the whole matter will be cleared up,' said the inspector obstinately.

'Well, you can't,' said Lady Foxglove, and the Misses Umbrage gasped.

'May I interview the child's nurse or nanny?' said the inspector.

'I am the Tarquin's nanny,' said Lady Foxglove proudly.

'You've never had to look after a baby in your life,' said small Miss Umbrage sourly.

'Have you?' asked Lady Foxglove.

Martin arrived when the discussion showed signs of becoming heated. Taking in the situation at a glance he showed all his officer qualities and some of his Foxglove blood by approaching the inspector and saying in his most stern voice: 'Of course you can inspect the nurseries. You have, of course, a search warrant from the Home Office?'

'Under the charter of the Society it is not necessary to have a warrant to enter a place where there is adequate reason to believe that suffering is in process.'

'You have a copy of the Charter?'

'It is not customary for officers of the Society to carry it around with them on duty. The relevant passages may be ascertained on inquiry to the Society's Headquarters.'

'You must realize that it is out of the question to recognize an authority of that kind on hearsay. We have only your word for it that the Society exists at all, and to present yourself at a person's front door in the company of two known trouble-makers of the worst possible character, and to demand entry with some cock-and-bull story about Cruelty to Children is to invite civil proceedings on a summons of malicious trespass. Trained Pig Percy will show you the quickest route off the premises, and I must warn you that he is entitled to use whatever reasonable degree of force may be necessary in the event of your obstructing him or resisting arrest.'

Although, in fact, as the Pigs had discovered to their dismay, Percy-Scroop-Beauchamp was incapable of hurting a fly, his appearance suggested that his interpretation of a reasonable degree of force might not be entirely within the meaning of the Act. He had been listening to the exchange with a terrifying frown of concentration, and on hearing his name mentioned he uttered a low 'Ur' of approval and pleasure which made little Miss Umbrage hold her whalebone umbrella in a tighter grip, and made the honest inspector blanch.

'That will not be necessary,' said large Miss Umbrage with dignity; 'by your attitude you have confirmed our worst fears. Come, Winifred, we have done what we can. Now the affair will have to be left in the hands of the police.'

'You must realize,' said the inspector, 'that your refusal to allow an independent inspection of the premises will prejudice your case at any subsequent proceedings. I shall return with a representative of the police and a written authority to make an inspection, and I warn you now that your open demonstration of ill-will in this matter may be taken by the court as a clear expression of criminal intent. Have you no feeling for little kiddies at all?' he said, changing his tone. 'How can you harden your hearts to their helpless appeal.' He was quoting from a circular from the Society, 'Don't you realize that kiddies have just as much right to respect and proper treatment as you, that their tiny innocent faces are made in your own likeness . . .'

'Oh shut up,' said Lady Foxglove, and the Misses Umbrage gasped.

After the deputation had walked stiffly to the main gate, with Percy loping beside them, the Foxgloves held a council of war.

It is recorded that when the invading armies of the Allies reached Belsen, the troops who witnessed the horrors of the camp for the first time were so affected by the sights and the smells and the testimony to human depravity that many of them were taken ill and had to be sent home on leave.

The Foxgloves were made of sterner stuff. As they advanced slowly in line abreast, down the long, damp, nursery corridor, Martin, Pig Percy and Lady Foxglove, the first people to set foot in it for over three years, they saw things which made Auschwitz seem a Butlin's Holiday Camp, Devil's Island a tropical paradise, Belsen a holiday health spa. The dauntless three never faltered. They first came across the Beast cowering in a corner of the night nursery but he scuttled sideways, like a tarantula with his over-developed hairy legs and bald pate, into the old linen cupboard, where he was cornered, wrapped in a blanket, and carried effortlessly by Trained Pig Percy-Scroop-Beauchamp to the bathroom.

Martin got a hose and started squirting the floor with a thoroughness which was bred of his experience in the Junior Leaders' Squad latrines on Sunday mornings. Lady Foxglove used a damp cloth on the walls, and Pig Percy used an enormous scrubbing brush on Tarquin. Soon Tarquin's pate was shining with its former brilliance, his nails were cut, and the problem arose as to how to clothe him. In the years of his solitude he had also grown a bristly red beard, and Martin was reluctant to let Percy loose with a razor. He had a half-formed apprehension that Percy might pull his head off or something if he were bitten too hard, because there was no doubt that, with all the good will in the world, he did not know his own strength.

Fortunately Martin had purchased an electrical shaving device against the day when the first rude hair should break the alabaster purity of his cheek, and soon he was rubbing an after-shave lotion, which presumably he had bought for the same eventuality, all over the legs and body of Tarquin, who had suddenly become more passive.

After three hours of sponging, hosing and scrubbing the nursery was almost as it had been in the old days of Nanny Bill. Martin's rocking horse was discovered in an attic and installed in the day nursery, and Tarquin placed upon it, where, to everyone's relief, he started rocking backwards and forwards with the greatest gusto. If he could be shown to the inspectors in that position there would be no need to explain his apparent inability to walk on two legs. There was still the embarrassing problem of his nudity, and also of the smell, because, despite all their efforts, it still seemed as if the rooms had been used as a charnel house in the time of some particularly revolting plague. An entire bottle of Lady Foxglove's extremely expensive Odour of Sanctity was necessary to dissipate it, and then the new smell was so strong that they wandered in a sort of anaesthetic daze.

Eventually Lady Foxglove found in a chest, lovingly folded by the dead hands of Nanny Bill, the delightful yellow velvet page's suit in which Martin had conquered all hearts at a cousin's wedding when he was six years old. With difficulty Tarquin was sewn into it, although he found the novel confinement irksome and kept scratching himself where children are taught not to scratch.

'What happens if the little beast fouls himself before they have a chance to look at him?' he asked.

'He must be given nothing to eat,' she replied simply. On the way to her bedroom, exhausted, she took out her secret notebook, and with the faintest of private smiles put a tiny tick against the exhortation: *Clothe the Naked*.

Next morning, the day of Martin's twenty-first birthday, dawned with an especial brilliance, the birds sang throatily and well, the frost lay on the virgin surface of the Manor House lawns, and the air was sweet and crisp, with the distant fragrance of pine. Bidcombe put on its Sunday suit and smiled on its new young master, so handsome, so dashing, the toast of young and old for many miles around.

Martin awoke quite early, and getting out of bed at once, as the Pigs had taught him to do, he put on a dressing-gown, and walked down to the nursery corridor looking more like an angel of the Lord than a young lieutenant in the Pigs.

Percy-Scroop-Beauchamp was sitting outside the door to the nursery wing, occupying his solitary vigil with a piece of string which he tied first round one ear, then round the next, then fastened one end to a big toe and the other end to his tongue. There is almost no end to the amount of entertainment which can be derived from a piece of string, and the various extremities of the human body provided an almost infinite number of permutations of joinable parts. When Martin arrived he untied himself, stood up, stamped his feet and saluted smartly, 'Urzun bin nothin' to 'port, sir.'

'Good – no noises, no attempts to get out?'

'Urz bin some noises,' admitted Pig Percy, and held his finger to his lips melodramatically. Through the door there came the faint creak of the rocking horse, backwards and forwards, like the pendulum of an immensely ancient clock.

'Well, I don't expect you'll have long to wait now before those sods arrive. Report any untoward activity.' Between men Martin always tried desperately hard to be a man's man, but there was something incongruous in the sound of the familiar Pig obscenities coming from such patently virgin lips.

On his way down to breakfast Martin noticed a little black Morris Minor parked in the front of the house, and when he reached the morning-room his mother was already there looking ravishingly lovely in the black full-length dress she had worn for her husband's funeral.

'Darling Martin, many, many happy returns of the day, you must let me break all the rules and give you a little kiss today, and wish you every possible good luck.'

As ruby lip momentarily touched amber brow, Martin's toes curled up inside his socks like wire springs, and two tiny spots of colour appeared for a moment on his cheeks where the olive translucent skin was so tightly stretched over his cheek-bones. The prurient horror which he felt on any contact with his mother was because he and she were like separate poles of the same loadstone, and any attempt to bring them together created a field of reaction and resentment which each, in a different way, exploited.

'Tell me, has it arrived?' she asked, well pleased with the success of her little gesture.

'Has what arrived?' asked Martin.

'Oh dear, I do hope it has. It was to be my little surprise for you on your birthday. Let's go and see,' and she led him by the hand to the porch, and showed him the little motor car.

'There,' she said proudly, 'it's all yours. Would you like to try it out now?'

It was like an American film they had both seen, in which husbands kept giving wives motor cars in this manner. Martin responded wonderfully.

'Darling Mummy, how sweet of you. But how did you possibly afford it? I don't know what to say, I am so overwhelmed.'

Lady Foxglove smiled smugly. In fact it had been rather a sacrifice, but like all sacrifices rather in the nature of an investment, and since she no longer had to pay for a nanny for Tarquin she had managed somehow.

Martin continued: 'And so *useful* too. Everybody says it is a great economy nowadays to have two motor cars, and when they deliver my new Jaguar this evening I shall be able to keep it in reserve. I don't think I really need to try it out now but perhaps after breakfast I'll take it into Cirencester and collect Brother Aloysius from the station at the same time.'

Mother and son smiled at each other poisonously. They knew each other far too well to make the effort of keeping up any pretence worthwhile when they were together, but somehow they both avoided any open sign of hostility. Martin held all the cards now, and he played them one by one with an elaborate show of hesitancy.

The first caller after breakfast was not the anti-cruelty deputation, but a young man with a villainous expression who came to inquire about the music to be played that evening.

'I'm from the Bidcombe Chromium Swingers,' he explained.

'But I thought we were having the Bidcombe Platinum Band,' said Lady Foxglove at a loss.

'That's what we used to be called,' explained the young man patiently. 'I've got a list here – we do a very nice St Louis Blues, if you like the old-fashioned, or we can have the Knees-Up if it's an elderly gathering.'

'Do you think you can play "Bless this House"?' asked Lady Foxglove timidly.

'I suppose so,' said the young man in disgust, 'but the boys won't like it much. By the way, you don't mind if we bring a few supporters, do you?'

'No, I don't think so,' said Lady Foxglove doubtfully, wondering what they were.

By the time the anti-cruelty deputation arrived the marquee was erected and the armies of men who had been wandering aimlessly about the lawn all morning had vanished behind the rhododendron bushes, which emitted clouds of cigarette smoke and occasional bursts of laughter. The Inspector of Cruelty came first, followed by an extremely embarrassed Police Constable Bloater between the two Misses Umbrage.

Lady Foxglove led them straight up to the nursery wing where the enormous form of Trained Pig Percy was dozing on a chair outside the door, with a piece of string hanging disconsolately from the side of his mouth. He woke up with a start, pulled the string from his mouth, saluted the inspector, produced a key from inside his sock and unlocked the door. A great gust of Odour of Sanctity came out of the passage as the door was opened, and small Miss Umbrage wrinkled her nose and said in her decided way: 'This place smells like a brothel.'

'How do you know?' asked Lady Foxglove rudely as she led them to the day nursery, which was as spick and span as it had been in the days of Martin's childhood.

On a rocking horse by the barred window a small figure in

yellow velvet breeches, lace cravat and cuffs and white silk stockings rocked backwards and forwards, oblivious to the passage of time and all his former pleasure, with a look of concentrated ecstasy in his single brown eye.

'Poor little chap,' said one of the Misses Umbrage automatically. The inspector produced a tape measure and started measuring the dimension of the room.

'I'm afraid that there's nothing we can complain about in the accommodation,' he said, 'it seems to conform to the specifications laid down. Perhaps there are some bruises on his body,' he added hopefully, but Tarquin's tough hide was not given to any such expression.

'Woozy doo a poor wee boy?' asked large Miss Umbrage, apparently addressing Tarquin. Tarquin quite properly refrained from comment.

'I'm afraid that Tarquin is a little shy in front of strangers,' said Lady Foxglove. 'He does not usually pay attention to people who come forcing their way into his nursery. Go on, Tarquin, say "Hullo" to the old lady.'

Miss Umbrage regarded Tarquin's indifference as a challenge to her womanliness.

'Woozy doo a little fellow?' she asked coaxingly, and as the figure in yellow velvet continued to stare fixedly at the ears of his mount, became more insistent.

'Itchy-witchy boy?' she suggested, 'who's a ging-ging then? Are you a good boy then? Who's a good boy? Say Aunt Ethel. Aunt Ethel. Goodi love your Auntie Ethel?' She pushed her face into the passage of the rocking horse, so that Tarquin would be forced either to rub faces or stop rocking. As his face approached, something she saw in his eye made her jerk her head back fast, but not fast enough to avoid a deep cut in the bridge of her nose, which bled profusely. Neither Lady Foxglove nor Martin who had just arrived on the scene made any attempt to conceal their delight, and something of their merriment communicated itself to Pig Percy, who gave a puzzled chuckle like stones being rattled in an empty bucket. Tarquin sucked his finger-nails with a happy, reminiscent air.

'Oh, the horrid, spiteful little thing,' cried Miss Umbrage, holding a handkerchief to her nose. 'I know where he learned those tricks from. I expect she trained him to do it, the fat, hypocritical bitch.'

'Now then,' said Police Constable Bloater.

'Really, Miss Umbrage,' said the inspector, 'we all have our accidents, but we must remember that he's a kiddy like any other, isn't he?' He didn't sound too sure, though.

After the deputation had left, Martin drove to Cirencester station to collect Brother Aloysius who was arriving from Cleeve for the festivities; he also intended to order himself a Jaguar motor car, or his snub to his mother would rather lose its sting.

Pig Percy ostentatiously locked the door of the nursery wing as the last Miss Umbrage left, and settled down again on his chair with his piece of string.

Lady Foxglove subsided into her armchair in the drawing-room with a refreshing glass of iced Lourdes water, and composed herself to meet Brother Aloysius. They would be able to discuss her lack of charity to the two Misses Umbrage, which would be the greatest fun for them both.

Before she could decide which aspect of her sin to discuss, a splendid figure in an orange uniform was shown into the drawing-room, who pulled at his waxed moustaches importantly and said: 'I am the conductor of the Bidcombe Platinum Band, and it has come to our notice that you propose to employ our services this evening to celebrate the twenty-first anniversary of your son's birthday.'

'That's right,' said Lady Foxglove, 'but I thought you were called the Bidcombe Chromium Swingers nowadays.'

208

'A splinter-group, ma'am,' said the giant contemptuously, 'and of no consequence or musical ability at all.'

'Oh I see,' said Lady Foxglove. 'Can you play "Bless this House"?'

'We *always* play "Bless this House" on occasions of this sort,' said the giant with dignified rebuke. 'I expect you will also be requiring "For He's a Jolly Good Fellow" and "Happy Birthday".'

'No. I don't think so,' said Lady Foxglove.

'The Platinum Band *always* plays "For He's a Jolly Good Fellow" and "Happy Birthday".'

'Well, they won't tonight. What else can you play?'

'Our repertory is long and comprehensive, ma'am, being a careful choice of all that is most memorable in the English tradition of secular and folk music, but I must stress that the band will be most upset if it is not allowed to play "For He's a Jolly Good Fellow".'

'Never mind about that. Can you play "Greensleeves"?'

'Of course. Also "The First Nowell", "Pomp and Circumstance" (variations) Elgar, "The Dam Busters' March", "Good King Wenceslaus", "Men of Harlech", "Colonel Bogey", "Away in a Manger", "The Grand Old Duke of York", "Lay down your Arms and Surrender to Mine", "Auld Lang Syne", "God Save the Queen", "'Twas on the Isle of Capri", "The British Grenadiers", and have I said "You are the Honeysuckle"?'

'No, I don't think so.'

'Then "You are the Honey Honeysuckle, I am the Bee".'

'Good,' said Lady Foxglove. 'Then let us have "Greensleeves.".'

'"Greensleeves" seems a most suitable choice, if I might be allowed to say so, Ma'am. We shall, of course, bring our supporters, as is customary. A light supper is usually provided for the members of the band and their supporters after the first two tunes. But we can leave those arrangements to your ladyship, no doubt.'

After he had gone, Lady Foxglove took a big gulp of Lourdes water and resumed her reading of *The Lives of the Saints*. There was so much to be learned from them, she had found, of help in practical daily affairs.

She rather dreaded the evening's entertainment. At Martin's christening, which was the last time the Manor House had opened its gates to the neighbourhood, old Mrs Cattacomb had got terribly drunk and started a fight with Mrs Hathaway, who had called her a witch. Not that that was likely to be repeated, of course, now that Mrs Cattacomb was nearly ninety-two and Mrs Hathaway had been dead over three years, but there were almost sure to be some incidents. She must remember to tell them not to give Mrs Cattacomb more than a pint of stout an hour, although she probably couldn't make much trouble if she tried, being half paralysed and blind.

Outside the nursery corridor Pig Percy sat listening to the gentle creak of the rocking horse, his two big toes cleverly tied together, an unlit Woodbine drooping from his lips. In his simple way he was chuffed at this new monumental skive he had discovered, and as his eyelids drooped and the god of kip overcame him, he wondered how long it would last. Life was divided for him into Work, Skive and Kip. If at any hour of the day he had no work, he would smoke a cigarette and play with his bit of string, and that was skiving, something faintly wicked and wildly enjoyable, the reward for all his labours. All work was equally unpleasant, whether it was cleaning Martin's belt or hosing out the Bidcombe nursery. Scrubbing down Tarquin had been a nasty sort of thing for a man to have to do, but he had been rewarded by this delirious, epic skive which promised to last all day.

In the baby Morris, Brother Aloysius said: 'I hope that you won't think that I'm interfering in your private affairs, Martin, but you know that I've always been a friend of the family, and now that Derek has passed away I feel that perhaps you miss a man's hand, as it were. It does seem to me that out of sympathy for your mother, if nothing else, you should at least put on a front of Christianity. I know that it is not always easy to believe, and some people find it more difficult than others, but if you could just preserve the outward appearances of a Christian, the Faith might return to you in time.'

'God knows, Sir, I have tried, I have tried,' said Martin, who rather enjoyed this kind of situation; 'the thought of the pain I must be causing my mother, of the anxiety I am causing you, is with me every hour of the day. But it is *no good*. It would be making life a sham, a mockery of Christianity, it would be to deny the integrity of real worshippers if I pretended to pray when my heart was empty of prayer. But thank you all the same.'

'It is as I feared. If there had been a man in the house to guide and comfort you when you first had doubts, this might never have happened. I have spoken to the Abbot, and fortunately he has given me permission, should Lady Foxglove ask me, to give up my monastic duties for a time and become the domestic chaplain at Bidcombe. I have always felt somehow that, after Cleeve, Bidcombe is my spiritual home, and that some day I should live there and write my books; I hear that there is much missionary work to be done in the village, if dear Julia's picture of its inhabitants is accurate, and perhaps in time Bidcombe Village would become a little shrine of Christianity in a pagan world, a tiny pocket of the cosmos where the Church of God would prevail throughout the Dark Ages that I see coming, where, undisturbed by movements and revolutions and wars . . .'

'What the bloody hell are you talking about?'

Brother Aloysius simpered delightfully: 'Perhaps I was letting my imagination run away with me. I had anticipated, of course, a certain degree of opposition from you. But for your own good, at this crucial stage of your career, I am sure that Julia will be absolutely firm with you and insist that you put up with my hateful presence for a time at any rate.'

Brother Aloysius watched Martin's face in the driving mirror. It had set into an inscrutable mask, like one of the beautifully formal idealized portraits of the Umbrian Quattrocento. No human being could guess what was going on behind those enormous, sad brown eyes set in a perfectly oval face of golden amber underneath raven black hair whose neatness was uncanny. Perhaps a small indication of the thought-processes so completely hidden from Brother Aloysius was that at that moment Martin tried to run over a cat, but it eluded him effortlessly, and watched with the contemptuous poise of a superior being as the little Morris hit the bank at the side of the road and rolled over with a noise of breaking glass and scraping metal.

Neither of the occupants was seriously hurt. Brother Aloysius as soon as he had been helped out of the wreckage of the car, was discovered to have a nasty cut above the left eye. Martin felt a little weak in the legs, and his stomach was slightly upset. Brother Aloysius felt vaguely that it was an occasion to which he should rise. He smiled bravely at the group of cottagers who had been attracted by the noise, and were gazing incuriously at the scene. 'I'm all right,' he said, 'how's the young gentleman?'

Martin was sitting on the bank, staring dumbly at the cat which stared insolently back.

'Thanks be to God,' said Brother Aloysius piously. 'Let us say a prayer of thanksgiving for our fortunate escape. In the name of the Father, which art in Heaven, and morning star, guide of the wanderer here below, visit we beseech thee O Lord that vouchsafeth not.'

'Shut up,' said Martin. 'You're not making any sense,' and it was quite true that Brother Aloysius was feeling a little dazed, and the words didn't seem to be coming quite right, but he was sure that prayer was the right thing, and he continued to mumble to himself for a bit, before being violently sick in the ditch, after which he kept quiet.

''Twas Tibbles done that,' said an awestruck voice, and Tibbles walked daintily across the road and rubbed itself against the speaker's leg.

Luncheon had to be kept waiting at Bidcombe, and when they eventually arrived neither was feeling very hungry. Brother Aloysius had an enormous cotton-wool dressing on his forehead, which was out of all proportion to the size of his wound, and Martin was still slightly paler than was his wont.

'Darling Martin, I cannot tell you how relieved I am to see you,' said Lady Foxgove with the infinite depths of insincerity which only a Foxglove ear could detect: 'I should never have forgiven myself if anything serious had happened to you. It was foolhardy of me to have allowed you out in your new car so soon, but I wasn't to know, was I, that a tragedy would occur? *Dear* Brother Aloysius, how can I ever apologize sufficiently for this breach of hospitality? I had so many things to discuss, but now they must all wait. Won't you have a little glass of sherry to settle your nerves after your *terrible* ordeal? I know Martin won't, so it is no good offering it to him.'

'No, thank you,' said Martin, 'I think I would prefer a glass of whisky.'

'Martin, you know we don't keep whisky in the house nowadays. I think the accident must have affected you in some way.'

'There's some in my father's old cupboard.'

'That was all drunk by Nanny Chudleigh.'

213

'No it wasn't, that was the port. Unless you've drunk it yourself it should still be there.'

'I gave it all to the Christian fête in Cirencester for their bottle stall.'

'I don't believe you.'

'Martin!' The gentle rebuke with which she sounded the name was a triumph of nice calculation. It conveyed to Brother Aloysius all the trials of living with a spiritual rebel; it expressed brave resignation in the face of the bite which is sharper than a serpent's tooth; it illustrated pathetically the helplessness of a mother before a wilful child. Martin went to the cupboard and took out a bottle of whisky. Lady Foxglove gave Brother Aloysius a yearning glance.

Martin had been upset, quite seriously, by the accident on the road, but it was not the shock nor the physical shaking which had affected him. What had worried and at the same time frightened him was the spectacle of the cat Tibbles quite unscathed by his machine, the agent of his accident escaping with impunity. It was as if Martin had for the first time received an insight into what it was like to be Stoat. Tibbles had usurped his prerogative; always in the past it had been Martin who was unaffected by disaster, who sat placidly licking his velvet coat while tragedies of his own causation rolled and thundered beneath him.

Stoat used to make himself wretched by his own clumsy malice, never Foxglove. It was as if he had been unseated suddenly from his horse, and the weight of the armour which had before been his protection now impeded his recovery. Perhaps Tibbles was simply one greater than Foxglove, endowed by the gods with one degree more bounty than he, but he thought it most unlikely. It was the first time that his star had been beaten by another, and he felt a kind of dread that that was to be the pattern of the future. From now on every human being he met might prove to be a Tibbles; slowly the gifts which nature had lavished on him as a child, beauty, birth and wealth would fade and Tibbles would become more frequent, until eventually he would end as Stoat, ugly, lonely and poor. His melancholy increased as the afternoon wore on, and Lady Foxglove rejoiced, thinking she had scored a major victory.

The party was due to begin at eight o'clock, and by six o'clock the village started drifting up to the marquee in order to lend its hand with the arrangements and eat the first meat pies as they arrived. Old Mrs Cattacomb was pushed between two grand-daughters to the beer bar, where she sat in her invalid chair receiving the villagers as they came past. The Chromium Swingers arrived at eight o'clock sharp, and while their supporters lounged around the entrance picking their fingernails, the musicians consumed vast quantities of sausage rolls noiselessly inside the tent. When Martin and Lady Foxglove arrived there was a gasp of admiration, as well there might be. Martin had donned the Pig's Full Dress Mess Kit for the occasion, and in its smart red monkey-jacket, narrow blue overalls with a broad red stripe, and yellow beret with its characteristic gold tassel he really did look most striking. Lady Foxglove acknowledged the gasp with a deprecating little smile, and then came forward with Brother Aloysius and clapped her hands. The Chromium Swingers continued to eat, staring intently at their plates, but everybody else turned to listen. 'Quiet, please, everybody, for Grace,' she called and Brother Aloysius assumed a suitable expression and started to recite: 'Bless us O Lord and these Thy gifts.'

'What did she say?' shouted Mrs Cattacomb to her left-hand grand-daughter. 'Hush, Gran,' she said. 'Quiet for Grace.'

'Eh?'

'She said keep your mouth shut for Grace,' hissed the grand-daughter.

'And 'o's Grace, may I ask?'

''im is, I suppose, with the skirts.'

'Go on with you, telling stories to your old grandmother. I expect it's a girl-friend of young Mr Martin's; takes after his grandfather, that young man, 'e was a great one for the girls, 'e was, if I say it myself.' She gave a revolting chuckle as if at the memory of past pleasures. In fact Martin's grandfather had been a model landlord, faithful husband and devout Christian, but for posterity he was henceforth the prototype of the wicked squire, and one of Mrs Cattacomb's grand-daughters even began to get ideas about her ancestry.

As this conversation had been conducted at the top of the voice, and Brother Aloysius' prayer had been a more seemly murmur, it was not surprising that more people heard Mrs Cattacomb than the monk, and soon wise old heads were nodding over foaming tankards of beer and saying: 'Lucky's the girl, that's what I say,' and 'A very fine young groom he'll make, I shouldn't be surprised.'

Stoat and O'Connor met on the platform, and shared a taxi to the Manor House. O'Connor said: 'Well I'll be blowed if it isn't my great friend Stoat. Where have you been these years?'

Stoat said: 'Oh, I don't know; I've been around I suppose. What have you been up to?'

'Oh well, after I left you I had to go to a sort of school for Christian Delinquents. Creepy joint it was, and they were all so gloomy you wouldn't believe it. I'd rather the pagan variety any day. Well, I got a bit bored of that after a few days and skipped it, and joined the pantomime in Tunbridge, but then there was a bit of a bust-up with a silly old tart who wore a wig, so I chucked that and joined something rather terrible called a skiffle-group where we all tried to grow beards and have Free Love, but it never really worked. Then I wanted to stand for Parliament but my father got a bit bolshie, and he was so disagreeable that I went to Morocco for a time where there was a Swedish woman called Anya or something in Marrakesh who was quite nice, but there was a bit of a fuss when they found I hadn't got a passport – I lost it, you know, in the public lavatories at London Airport and thought it was too gruesome to pick it up again. But they were so unpleasant, those stinking little wog policemen, that I decided to hop across to Aden, where I found Rigid living like a fighting cock and terribly rich all of a sudden, so I collected some money from him and came home, and now I'm a gossip columnist for the *Daily Truth,* which is a pretty crummy job but quite fun.'

'I don't believe a word of it,' said Stoat, as nasty as ever.

'Oh well, you never know,' said O'Connor wistfully. It was an accepted convention that whenever old Alexandrians got together after a length of time, they told each other lies about what they had been doing in the meantime, and it was really most unnecessary of Stoat to challenge the story, much of which apart from the African episodes, was true.

When they arrived at Bidcombe, William had no change so Kenneth paid for the taxi, and they both wandered up to the marquee.

There was a constant stream of elderly persons coming out of the marquee from the beer-table and disappearing into the bushes for a few moments before returning to the beer. From one of these William learned that young Foxglove was engaged to be married, which occasioned him no little surprise.

They were received by Lady Foxglove who said: 'Hullo, Henry, this *is* nice. I haven't seen you for years and years, and how *well* you're looking.' As she extended a limp, fragrant hand Kenneth was far too infatuated to comprehend the depths of insincerity which were all too plain to O'Connor. William curtsied and said in his insufferable way: 'I never really thanked your ladyship for her delicious gooseberry jam. Yum Yum, Yum Yum,' and he rubbed his stomach coarsely and licked his lips. Lady Foxglove pretended to smile, and said, 'I am so glad you are out of prison at last, William. I have been praying so hard for you.'

'Oh yeah?' said William, and embarrassed Kenneth so much that he walked away to get a sausage roll. When William glimpsed Martin in his smart uniform enjoying a joke in the far corner of the room with Miss Philippa Swift the daughter of the local M.F.H., he whistled, and shouted, 'Hullo, Tarty, I'm here. It's O'Connor again. Good old O'Connor.'

Martin walked over and said: 'Look here, O'Connor, if you're going to make a fool of yourself I'm going to have you turned out. I only invited you because my mother insisted, and if you start being rude to me again I'm going to be very angry.'

'You're not; you would be bloody delighted. You want me to be as rude as possible or you wouldn't say that.'

'Look here, O'Connor.'

'Boo to a goose.'

'All right, but you've been warned.'

Martin sent word to Pig Percy to leave his post by the nursery door and come down to the tent; but before the order could be put into effect a diversion was caused by the arrival of the Bidcombe Platinum Band marching very smartly in their orange uniforms, and surrounded by a solid wedge of supporters as they played "Bless this House". The Chromium Swingers, who had been guzzling quietly up to that moment, collected their instruments and assembled in a far corner with their supporters in front. One of them, a boy of about fourteen, started singing "Bless this House" into a microphone, and the others made sympathetic noises into their machines. The struggle was short, and the issue never in doubt. After the Swingers had been put to flight, the Platinum Band changed to "Greensleeves" and after a dozen bars of that they decided it was time for supper, and music was given a rest.

O'Connor asked Foxglove, 'Tell me, Tart, is it true that you're getting married?'

'If you call me that I will have you turned out.'

'You can't turn me out, I'm the Press. Who is the lucky girl?'

'There is no truth in it. I am not engaged to anyone. I have no girl-friends, it's all a lie. Does that satisfy you?'

'All right. Keep your hair on. What is your new brother like?'

'Tarquin is absolutely charming and I am very fond of him indeed.'

The great success of the evening was Pig Percy's entrance. When news reached him that he was invited to the party, he regretfully untied his big toes and put his socks on. His great skive was over, and now the grim reality of the outside world was upon him again. Still, scoff was scoff, and even a Pig had to eat occasionally. It was typical of the good man's devotion to duty that it never occurred to him for one moment that he was supposed to leave the dangerous animal on the other side of the door unattended, so he unlocked the door, tucked Tarquin under one arm, and wandered resentfully to the marquee. Tarquin was looking rather less resplendent than when he had appeared before the Cruelty tribunal. His smart yellow breeches had an enormous stain which was all too prominent as Percy carried him back to front so as to be able to give his behind a spank whenever he bit or kicked. His lace cravat was awry, and one of his white stockings had been half torn off, exposing a hairy area of leg. The position in which he was being carried produced some of the noises for which he had been celebrated as a baby. There was a hushed silence as Percy walked up to Foxglove, stamped his feet, and said 'Good evening, Sir.'

Martin said: 'What on earth have you got under your

arm?' This was an unfair question. Percy pondered with a terrible frown of concentration, before admitting he didn't rightly know.

'Well, get rid of it at once,' said Martin, who had decided to rise above the whole thing. Percy took it up to the nursery again, puzzled and slightly indignant.

After the last guest had departed, Lady Foxglove said: 'I don't know whether it was a success or not. Goodness knows, one did one's best to make it enjoyable for them all, but nothing ever seems to go right nowadays.'

'You were wonderful, Julia,' said Brother Aloysius, and the two of them settled down to a cosy chat.

Martin sat wretchedly in his bedroom, hating everybody and making plans.

Percy resumed his game with the piece of string. It was about one o'clock when the gentle creak of the rocking horse stopped and there was a loud bump. When he reported the accident to Lady Foxglove she was most distressed, and Brother Aloysius crossed himself and thought how there was always something rather moving about the death of a child. Poor Julia really was upset; she had obviously loved the child more than she had allowed herself to show.

'Now there will have to be an inquest and goodness knows what will happen,' she wailed. When Martin was summoned he showed all his officer qualities once again.

'It is clearly the duty of our domestic chaplain to bury the child. I can't see what he's here for if it isn't for that sort of thing.'

'But it's not so simple as that. You have to have a death certificate signed by two doctors and a burial order and inform the police.'

'We shall say that he has been adopted by a Higher Person, whose name we don't know.'

They all three bowed their heads reverently.

The last service ever to be conducted in the chapel at Bid-combe bore very little resemblance to the seemly little groups which used to congregate there in the past for Retreats and Sermons by Brother Aloysius. By the light of a solitary candle the time-honoured service was held over the small bundle wrapped in a blanket at the foot of the altar. Percy, impres-sed by the solemnity of the occasion, stood rigidly to attention throughout, holding the candle like a rifle at the Present, and saying "Amen" whenever he caught Martin's eye.

Martin, in order to add dignity to the proceedings, had donned a sword, although in fact it was incorrect to wear one with mess kit; Brother Aloysius had seemed doubtful about the legality of the business, and it had needed all Martin's powers of persuasion, coupled with the unspoken threat that domestic chaplains who refused to conduct burials when requested were liable to lose their jobs, before Brother Aloysius, with many mental reservations, agreed.

Lady Foxglove looked incredibly lovely in a heavy black veil, and the obvious sincerity with which she joined in the responses, and her sorrow, so pitifully written on her com-posed face, touched the heart of everybody present except Martin and Pig Percy, who was not looking.

The panegyric was short but moving: 'Tonight we bury the mortal remains of Tarquin Foxglove, who, as by his life he was an example to us all of humility, by his death has shown us the transience of human existence, a point on which we should all meditate when we commend the soul of this blameless boy to his Creator.

'As the birds in their little nests, so Tarquin in his little nursery, lived the span of his appointed days in innocence and freedom from care. When one visited him in his nur-sery one could not but be impressed by how, while seeming so far removed from the cares and guilts of an older and more responsible generation, he was yet an integral part of the house, and added to its character something of his own patience and humility, while he borrowed from it his sustenance and environment.

'While he did not live long enough to add by his worldly achievements to the lustre of his name, of his house, nor his Church, by the unquestioning fulfilment of the small part for which he was cast he has lived up to the great traditions of a noble family, who need not feel ashamed of this, the least of its progeny in the eyes of the world, but equal, or nearly equal, in the eyes of God.'

'Amen,' said Percy with feeling.

As the first cold light of morning crept through the ivy-covered windows of the chapel, turning Lady Foxglove's golden countenance to an unhealthy grey, bringing with it the sanity and common sense of the outside world, turning yesterday's enthusiasms into embarrassing memories and by a trick of perspective yesterday's anxieties into today's tasks Brother Aloysius threw a handful of rubble into the grave in the middle of the chapel, and said in conclusion, 'Because in the beginning you were dust, so to dust you shall return.'

He took off his robes, Percy blew out his candle, Martin took off his sword, Lady Foxglove her veil, and all four settled down to the task of filling up the grave, and replacing the heavy red tiles on top. Martin sealed the joints with a mixture of green soap and soot, which he had read about somewhere, and when they all returned to bed there was nothing to show that a new occupant had been added to the ranks of sleeping Foxgloves whose resting-places were commemorated on the floor of the chapel.

Before she went to sleep Lady Foxglove opened her little *aide-mémoire*, and put a large tick against the exhortation: *Bury the Dead*. It was her last good work.

In the train back to London, O'Connor travelled separately

from Stoat, and prepared his report for the *Daily Truth,* of which his father was editor. He had acquired the knack of the gossip column without much effort, and every subtle art and every ingenious guile known to that exacting trade was used by him in his account of the evening. He ended it triumphantly :

'Commenting on rumours which were going around, Mr (Marty) Foxglove said : "No, as a matter of fact, old boy, I have no interest in girls at all, but I am extremely fond of my foster-brother.' Tarquin Foxglove, who was adopted by the family three years ago, put in a brief appearance towards the end of the evening, dressed in a yellow velvet jacket and breeches, white silk stockings and lace cuffs. He had no comment to make to the *Daily Truth.*' After sucking his Biro for a time, William headed the paragraph "Brotherly Love", and sent it, on arrival to the newspaper offices. That was for him the end of the Foxglove Saga. He never saw Martin again, nor Bidcombe, nor Lady Foxglove, and never knew the effect which his article had on Martin's career, nor the worried discussion in the Officers' Messes of the Pigs throughout the world. After a time he gave up his Gossip Column and made his name writing rather amusing articles, mostly about himself in the left-wing weeklies. He stood for election as a Radical Conversative in a Labour stronghold at the age of twenty-nine, and was decisively beaten. At the age of thirty-four he stood as Independent Labour candidate in a Tory stronghold and lost his deposit. He did not court the company of his fellow Old Alexandrians, and Cleeve did not give prominence to its connection with one of its less illustrious illuminati. At a much greater age he was invited to give a lecture to a philosophical society called the Pentagonal Ectoplasm, a new and very select group of five most distinguished intellects in each of the five schools at Cleeve which flourished under the vague auspices of Brother Augustine, although he was too old to influence it much. His talk, entitled "Oblivion – and After" was a great success, and the cause of much trouble later on. It was also the occasion of his last meeting with Stoat, by then called Brother Simon, who seemed rather less anxious than he to revive old memories and tender associations.

Stoat joined the monastery soon after Martin's twenty-first birthday celebrations. He had not enjoyed the party, and had come away disappointed and rather hurt; he had only seen Martin for a few minutes when they had casually discussed the latest cricket scores from Cleeve, in which neither of them was faintly interested, as if that was all they had in common. He preserved the memory of Lady Foxglove as an ideal to which he always clung throughout the times of his doubts and discontents in the novitiate, and the picture of her as she had appeared at her last public appearance, beautiful, composed and radiantly holy was an inspiration to him throughout his entire life. He joined the Community at Cleeve because there seemed nothing else much to do. He had started writing several books which were spiteful about everything he loved, but fortunately never finished one. His father was completely engrossed in his dentistry, and his mother was immovably settled into the happy circle at Sister Cardew's Home. So Kenneth devoted his life to prayer and meditation, hoping one day to achieve a measure of self-improvement which would make it all worthwhile. To the other monks he was a byword for malice and savagery, and it seemed to many of them as if old Brother Theobald had been reincarnate in the ill-favoured form of Brother Simon Stoat.

But the final episodes of the Foxglove Saga had not yet been enacted. On the day after Tarquin's funeral, Lady Foxglove made a miscalculation of the balance of power inside Bidcombe, and feeling the support of Brother Aloysius to justify it, indulged in a nervous breakdown. To Martin, who had no time to sympathize with his mother's self-pity, her ill-considered attempt to attract attention was an ideal opportunity, and she was whisked off, protesting violently, to Sister Cardew's Home with a promptness which many people found indecent. Brother Aloysius returned to Cleeve a few days later.

On the publication of O'Connor's article in the *Daily Truth* it was made obvious to Martin that his only honourable course was to resign his commission in the Pigs, and taking Percy-Scroop-Beauchamp with him he settled down to a life of melancholy ease at Bidcombe. The passing of the years did not make him any more amiable, and as his looks began to fade and he felt that he was getting poorer and duller every year, he settled into a daily routine which could not disguise that it was designed purely to kill the time between breakfast and bed in the evenings. Mr Percy, as he was now known, spent all the time in which he was not working, on a chair outside the old chapel, which was closed and used as a store-room. For him the days passed swiftly and happily, and his piece of string never lost its fascination and he secretly reckoned himself one of the luckiest people alive, for whom in life there was no worry, no sorrow, no remorse, no apprehension, no doubts, no illusions, no responsibilities, for whom heaven had been found on earth in the form of one gigantic skive. He despised Martin for his anxiety and his vanity and his melancholia, and knew, in his heart of hearts, that he had found the way of truth and the light, and that his little bit of string was the key which opened every door on earth.

Lady Foxglove did not settle so readily in her new home as Mrs Stoat had done, but, as Sister Cardew wrote to Martin soon after her arrival, they were often a little restless for the first year or two. Mrs Cod-Finger, who had tended to regard herself as the social queen of the home very much resented her title, and Miss Long became obsessed with the idea that she was trying to seduce Mr Spate. Poor Mr Spate was too old now to do more than bow whenever she passed, and his knitting was getting slower and his brain less keen. There would soon come a moment when Sister Cardew would have to send him packing, because she could not stand the very old, and they spoiled the atmosphere of her home. The only new arrival since O'Connor's time lived in the room next to Lady Foxglove's, and every morning she serenaded herself as she washed, singing, as a delightful *aubade,* the songs of her youth. After a time Lady Foxglove was able to distinguish the words as they drifted, clear, high and beautiful every morning through the narrow partition of her bedroom; the tune was faintly reminiscent of "Bless this House" and carried the breath of spring and the happiness of a new-flown bird through that melancholy home:

> Every day a good nurse will
> Take her place the stools to fill ...
> Take great care of your fingernails
> Scrub out seats and bowls and pails
> Use the flannel your ears beneath
> After eating wash your teeth.

Every afternoon she would hear Herring tap-tapping down the garden path to the summer house where she wrote her novels, and if she wasn't careful she would be cornered by the horrid blind woman and told disgusting stories which she, for one, often found difficulty in believing. Poor Lady Foxglove, what she had to suffer! One day Herring said to her:

'Shall I tell you a story, dearie?' and before Lady Foxglove had time to reply, Herring began:

'When I was a little girl, well, not much younger than I am now, but different, you know, so that you wouldn't recognize me now if you'd known me in those days, I met a young man called Ron, who was strong and wise and good, and as handsome as the day is long. We had not been married many months when a little baby boy was born to us, and we called him Tarquin, and he was fierce as any tiger and braver than the great lions in the forest. The happiness we knew in those days, in our charming little house in the middle of the town called 4B was more perfect even than that enjoyed by Ruth, the torturer's daughter, when she lived with her husband Groin on the island of Bliss before the catastrophe, but it could not last. In the cold evenings of the winter months I would watch my Tarquin growing like a precious flower, but while he grew I remained the same. For he was young and strong and destined to be a great leader of men, I think, but I was old and foolish, and so he punished me, and went away to live with a princess in a foreign land. Don't you think that is a lovely story, my pretty?'

'Yes, indeed,' sighed Lady Foxglove, edging away from the crazy woman who pursued her remorselessly, thrusting her horrible mutilated face into Lady Foxglove's.

'And I, the blind old crone that you see, lived happily ever after, and my precious Tarquin went away to punish people in other lands, and each year as I write my books in the morning, and sing my little songs through the evenings, I know that he is growing stronger every day, and richer and perhaps more beautiful, and that one day he will have the world at his feet, and I shall know that Tarquin has come into his own.'

Lady Foxglove thought of the bedraggled little bundle which had been ceremoniously lowered into the hole in the chapel floor, and said: 'Yes, to be sure, Tarquin has come into his own.'

That evening Lady Foxglove wrote a desperate letter to Martin, and another to Brother Aloysius: 'I know that I have not always been as kind nor understanding as I should, that on occasions I have allowed spite and malice to affect my judgements, but I beg you, do not allow me to be punished as I am being at the moment. There is a mad woman here who would kill me if she knew who I was, and I go in mortal terror hourly lest she discover the secret of our activities in the chapel at Bidcombe before I was sent away. I have been sinful in my time, let me be the first to admit it, but I cannot believe that I have done anything to justify this. If you have a spark of goodness left move me to Bedlam, anywhere where I will be free of this terrible woman.'

When Sister Cardew read this letter that evening she gave a delighted chuckle, and put it in her private museum beside the bottle of Brasso that O'Connor never drank. It was her duty to read all the letters which her guests wrote, although, to spare their feelings she never told them, to prevent anything which might distress relatives, and it was amazing what she found in them sometimes.

Herring seemed to have an instinct for seeking out Lady Foxglove, and as the weeks passed and no reply came to her letter, and Herring's persecution increased, Lady Foxglove grew desperate. Letter after letter followed the first into Sister Cardew's private museum, until she seriously considered starting a separate album to house them. After a time they became quite frantic. Lady Foxglove could not step outside her bedroom but Herring would be waiting for her, with her slender white stick and her cloying endearments, and her endless fund of terrible stories. In November Lady Foxglove wrote:

Martin,

I think she has guessed about Tarquin's death. What else can account for her behaviour to me? Do you want to stand by and watch me butchered? Your mother's blood will be on your hands. Murderer!'

Sister Cardew had a good laugh over that one. She toyed

with the idea of getting it framed, but then forgot about it.

One day Herring said, in a confidential whisper: 'Shall I tell you what he done to me, my son Tarquin. It was with his tiny thumbs, such dear little thumbs, they were, not much bigger than the velvet green caterpillars you see on a gooseberry bush in July, but strong, mind, and sharp as a heron's beak. . . .'

'I don't want to hear,' said Lady Foxglove desperately, trying to edge her way past Herring to her own bedroom.

'But you must listen, dearie, because this story has a moral, from which we can all learn something, even yourself.'

But Lady Foxglove gave a push, and Herring fell with a clatter on to the wooden boards of the corridor, and while she was groping helplessly for her stick Lady Foxglove ran past her and locked herself into her bedroom.

After this episode Lady Foxglove stayed in her room, and gradually fell into a decline. Sister Cardew wrote to Martin that in her opinion his mother was no longer responding to treatment, and that she was not profiting by her stay in the home.

Every morning, when she heard the dreaded anthem sung joyfully in the next bedroom, Lady Foxglove covered her head with her pillow and tried to meditate on holy things, on the love of St Paul's Pekinese called Chooty, for his wife Fifi, and their puppies, but the devil intruded on her thoughts, and in her imaginings she saw Chooty eating up his puppies and Fifi rolling her hips sensuously on a red velvet cushion as she watched, and then Chooty with the blood of his young still dripping from his mouth, would struggle lecherously with his wife on the cushion, and from their hideous lust fresh monsters would be born to feed Chooty's insatiable greed.

Use the flannel your ears beneath
After eating wash your teeth.

Sister Cardew's letter came as a great relief to Martin, who was finding the twenty-five guineas a week she charged quite an onerous burden on the Bidcombe finances. He had under-estimated the death duties payable, and in order to keep the house going and pay income tax and provide an occasional treat for himself – a television set, a new motor car or a holiday in Switzerland – he was spending capital fast. He wrote a letter to Mother Alice O'Callaghan, in Paddington.

Dear Mother Alice,

I know that you will be as disturbed as I to hear that my mother, who always counted you as one of her closest friends, is extremely ill in a nursing home near Brighton, and desperately needs the superior facilities and more suitable atmosphere of St Bridget's Home, and I wonder if, as the greatest personal favour, you could not find a room for her in your home.

I know that your normal charge is six pounds a week, but in the light of the intimacy of your friendship and the devotion she has always shown to you, would it be unreasonable to ask that she only pay five guineas? As you know, she is a lady of simple tastes, and would not expect to have a fuss made of her in any way. I doubt if she would need sheets, if they are a great inconvenience to you. She has always the greatest horror of inconveniencing people unduly.

It was an ugly, unloved, lonely and poor Martin Foxglove who signed his name so sincerely at the end of the letter, and when Mother Alice's reply came, to say that she would love to have her ladyship but could not possibly think of charging less than five pounds ten, it was the first glimmer of happiness to relieve his melancholy in some years.

When Lady Foxglove was installed in her tiny box-like bedroom, with a solitary crucifix above her head as the only ornament, she smiled contentedly and said :

'This is so much nicer. If you knew what I had been

through you would realize what a relief it is to be back in a good Christian atmosphere. Here I feel I can expand and bloom, while in the other place I was stifled, frustrated. When the soul is separated from spiritual nourishment the body, too, tends to languish. Don't you agree?'

The still figure at the end of her bed made a very slight obeisance, and continued to finger its beads.

'Or perhaps you have never really been inside a pagan temple. If so, you do not know how lucky you are. They seem to have lost sight of goodness entirely in the world today, to have no respect for sanctity at all. Is that what you've found?'

This time Sister Alfreda made no acknowledgement, but concentrated hard on avoiding distraction, as her fingers moved over the beads and her lips fluttered noiselessly.

'Perhaps you don't agree. You may have been luckier than I and have found people who although not especially good in themselves, were prepared to recognize goodness in others. That in itself is a virtue, and who knows but when it comes to the Final Judgement, God might in His infinite mercy, take into account that they were properly respectful of other people's virtues?'

Sister Alfreda did not seem to know. She continued to pray, and the beads clicked through her fingers with the regularity of an electric clock.

Every week Martin sent her a pound note as pocket money, and at Christmas a jar of gooseberry jam. Every week ten shillings was sent to Mr Dooney in his hotel in Torquay, and ten shillings went to Mother Alice for "extras". "Extras" was her Lourdes water, and every evening Mother Alice refilled the bottle from the tap in the pantry. With her invaluable nursing experience she knew that the efficacy of Lourdes water was largely psychological, and besides, it would have been the sin of simony to sell Lady Foxglove the real stuff.

After a time she gave up the effort to engage Sister Alfreda's attention, and lay still, or bounced up and down on her mattress and listened to the squeaks. She tried to think of every word she knew beginning with B: Beautiful, Blue, Bonny, Baby, Bastard, Buggery (Get behind me Satan), Basket-work, Bill, Bitch. It was no good. The stains on the ceiling assumed strange shapes, and she invented stories round them, but after a while she would be sweating with terror at the force of her own imagination, and all the time Sister Alfreda sat and wordlessly awaited the Hour.

She died soon after Christmas, as she had lived, in the odour of sanctity, and everybody agreed that it would be difficult to imagine a more perfectly Christian death.

Bologna, June 1959

More about Penguins

If you have enjoyed reading this book you may wish to know that *Penguin Book News* appears every month. It is an attractive illustrated magazine containing a complete list of books published by Penguins and still in print, together with details of the month's new books. A specimen copy will be sent free on request.

Penguin Book News is obtainable from most bookshops; but you may prefer to become a regular subscriber at 3s for twelve issues. Just write to Dept EP, Penguin Books Ltd, Harmondsworth, Middlesex, enclosing a cheque or postal order, and you will be put on the mailing list.

Some other books published by Penguins are described on the following pages.

Note: *Penguin Book News* is not available in the U.S.A., Canada or Australia.

Evelyn Waugh

This *enfant terrible* of English letters in the 1930s became a best-seller with the publication in 1928 of his first novel, *Decline and Fall*. Many of the characters in this masterpiece of derision reappear in the subsequent novels, which, culminating in *Put Out More Flags*, present a satirical and entertaining picture of English leisured society between the wars.

The following are in Penguins:

BLACK MISCHIEF

BRIDESHEAD REVISITED

DECLINE AND FALL

HELENA

THE LOVED ONE

MEN AT ARMS

OFFICERS AND GENTLEMEN

THE ORDEAL OF GILBERT PINFOLD AND OTHER STORIES

PUT OUT MORE FLAGS

SCOOP

UNCONDITIONAL SURRENDER

VILE BODIES

A HANDFUL OF DUST

Not for sale in the U.S.A.

Le Grand Meaulnes

Alain-Fournier

Le Grand Meaulnes (The Lost Domain) is one of the greatest French novels of the century – the only novel of a brilliant young man who was killed in action in 1914 at the age of twenty-seven.

It is a masterly exploration of the twilight world between boyhood and manhood, with its mixture of idealism, realism, and sheer caprice. But that is not its only magic – there is a magic of setting, of narrative, of the abject beauty of the heroine, of the inexplicable elusiveness of the 'lost domain' itself . . .

Not for sale in the U.S.A. or Canada

The Glass-Blowers

Daphne du Maurier

The great du Maurier tradition
The warm, human saga of a family of craftsmen in
eighteenth-century France – with the violence and terror
of the Revolution as clamouring background to its tragic
climax.

'Three cheers for a novelist who can write convincingly
of human relationships and the horrors of civil war without
sick-making accounts of sex and savagery'
                                         – Sunday Telegraph

also available by Daphne du Maurier in Penguins:

THE BIRDS AND OTHER STORIES

FRENCHMAN'S CREEK

HUNGRY HILL

JAMAICA INN

THE KING'S GENERAL

THE LOVING SPIRIT

MARY ANNE

MY COUSIN RACHEL

THE PARASITES

REBECCA

THE SCAPEGOAT

I'LL NEVER BE YOUNG AGAIN

Not for sale in the U.S.A.

The Venus of Konpara

John Masters

When the building of a dam threatens a 3000-year-old secret.

Man-eating tigers, forest fires, poison arrows block the path of four men and two women as they blindly grapple with the ancient evil shut in the Caves of Konpara. One of their number, the beautiful Rukmini, is said to be the reincarnation of the golden goddess of love.

To guard the secret of India's past, she must be sacrificed . . .

The Venus of Konpara is another Indian adventure by the superb story teller who gave us *Nightrunners of Bengal, Bhowani Junction, The Lotus and the Wind, Coromandel!*

also available in Penguins:

BHOWANI JUNCTION

COROMANDEL

THE DECEIVERS

FANDANGO ROCK

FAR, FAR THE MOUNTAIN PEAK

THE LOTUS AND THE WIND

NIGHTRUNNERS OF BENGAL

Not for sale in the U.S.A. or Canada

Inside Mr Enderby

Anthony Burgess

Engaged in the one sure refuge from the ever-predatory female, Mr Enderby locks himself compulsively away in the smallest room, and there closeted he once again scribbles away at his poetry in isolated security and release.

On his marriage to a glamorous, wordly-wise widow who carries him off to Rome on their wedding-trip, he is soon convinced that the *dolce vita* is not so much a living but more a way of death.

Not for sale in the U.S.A.

An End to Running

Lynne Reid Banks

A second dazzling novel from the author of *The L-shaped Room* – written with the same maturity, honesty and realism.

An End to Running is the story of a spiritual bankrupt – a man who runs from one situation to another in a desperate attempt to live up to the standards he sets himself. But his 'new life' on an Israeli Kibbutz with his devoted mistress is no easier than the phoney literary life he left behind in London.

Inspiring, or depressing?

An End to Running will certainly not leave you unmoved.

also available in Penguins:
THE L-SHAPED ROOM

Not for sale in the U.S.A.